FALLING FOR GRACE

FALLING FOR GRACE

Trust at the End of the World

ROBERT FARRELL SMITH

Deseret Book Company
Salt Lake City, Utah

Library of Congress Cataloging-in-Publication Data
  Smith, Robert F., 1970–
    Falling for Grace : Trust at the end of the world / Robert Farrell
  Smith.
      p.   cm.—(Trust Williams trilogy ; bk. 2)
    ISBN 1-57345-585-7
    I. Title.   II. Series: Smith, Robert F., 1970–   Trust Williams
  trilogy ; bk. 2.
  PS3569.M53794F35   1999
  813'.54—dc21   99-40611
                                         CIP

Printed in the United States of America

10 9 8 7 6 5 4 3 2 1   72082 - 6554

One smile and I was captive.
Two words and three children later,
I'm still in awe.
Krista.

Since the dawn of time man has predicted and prepared for that one giant event that would end it all. Not just a simple flood, mind you, or a bothersome plague, but an occurrence so catastrophic, so powerful, that all pestilence and adversity would have to bow before it. For almost as long the time and place of such an advent has remained unknown and hidden—even the angels above were said not to know. That was then, this was now, and Noah Taylor claimed he knew. According to him the end would come on December seventeenth at exactly 3:15 P.M.

Hell's bells and heaven's whispers, misery was on the horizon. There were fewer than thirty-eight days left of life as we knew it.

1

LIFE AND LIMB

NOVEMBER 9TH

I could hear Pete Kennedy breathing to the tune of "She'll Be Coming 'Round the Mountain" through his nose. My blue eyes gazed over at Leo Tip and President Heck as they crouched down together behind a fallen tree. President Heck was decked out in a safety-orange jumpsuit his wife Patty had made him, and Leo was wearing a pair of fake antlers he had constructed himself. I was baffled as to why we weren't currently surrounded by a horde of does who had been tricked into thinking Leo was some hot buck. Leo adjusted his antlers and picked up his rifle.

Pete suddenly stopped breathing. I looked up at him. He had on a small knit cap and a big faded flannel shirt. He looked like a grown-up gang member who didn't know how to properly wash and care for his colors. I watched his jaw drop and eyes grow big. Then quietly and with muted enthusiasm he pointed toward a huge buck that was wandering into our sights. It was the biggest animal I had ever seen. It walked slowly, radiating such confidence and self-esteem that even I began to feel inferior to it. The deer came to a stop in front of a tall thin tree and posed as if auditioning for a special-edition belt buckle. We had seen a couple bucks earlier in the day, but it would take the two of them to equal a single side of this one.

Leo, having the best shot and position, lifted his gun and pointed toward our huge prey. In the far distance a bird sang. President Heck nudged Leo, giving him both encouragement and the go-ahead. I watched Leo's hand twitch as he began to squeeze the trigger. Once again I just couldn't stand for this.

"Haaaawwwchhhewwww!" I forced out a fabricated sneeze.

The giant buck flinched and bounded away as Leo jerked and misfired. President Heck leaped from his spot and began shooting in hopes of hitting the dashing deer. Pete shot off his rifle a few times and then pulled a pistol from his holster and continued blasting. Leo, not one to pass up an opportunity to waste bullets, kept shooting as well. I covered my ears and watched in amazement. The buck was long gone—he had jumped away unscathed—but these three continued firing. Birds took flight from every tree. Small animals came out of hiding all around us and scampered away from all the noise. Not a single shot hit anything with feathers or fur. Nope, they just kept firing at the spot the deer had once occupied.

The tall thin tree that had been behind the buck was now being blown away by my trigger-happy companions. I assume that they would have eventually stopped shooting on their own, but that theory would never be tested due to the fact that the maimed tree was beginning to fall toward us. It cracked and screamed as it tore its wounded torso from its trunk. Leo and Pete stopped shooting so as to better be able to holler. President Heck kept firing in a panic at the thin pine as it came directly toward him. With a loud thud the tree hit President Heck on the head, knocking him to the ground.

It took a couple seconds for Pete's screaming and the echoes of gunshots to drift off and leave us in silence. President Heck lay there next to the fallen tree, his orange attire making the dark earth beneath him look black. We huddled over him, gazing down, until he opened his eyes.

"President Heck!" Pete said with concern.

"What?" He moaned.

"You okay?" Leo asked.

"I'm fine," he said, sitting up. A huge goose egg was growing on the top of his head and making his hair look as if it were doing the wave.

Leo gazed at the fallen tree.

"Is it dead?" he asked somberly.

Pete knocked Leo on the shoulder. "Don't be dumb," Pete said. "Trees don't die, they just . . ."

Pete paused, realizing that he had never really contemplated the mystery of where trees go. He scratched his head and remained silent.

"Darn it Trust," Leo said to me, suddenly remembering that this was all my fault. "That's the third buck you've scared off today. The antlers on that one would have looked amazing over my fireplace."

3

"Wouldn't they," Pete agreed. "You coulda put them right above that picture of you and CleeDee at the fair."

"I've always liked that picture," Leo reflected.

"Me too," Pete agreed. "Those electric lights make CleeDee look fancy. I . . ."

"You know," I interrupted, "maybe I'll head back to the meadow. I've probably had enough hunting for one day. Besides, Grace and I still need to go to Virgil's Find."

Leo and Pete just stared at me.

"I'll head back with you," President Heck said. "This knot on my head might need some tending."

I helped him up from the ground. Leo took his antlers off and straightened out the left one. He put them back on.

"Come on, Leo," Pete commanded, "let's go do some real hunting."

Pete and Leo walked off to find something to shoot at. President Heck and I turned toward the direction of town and started downhill.

"I guess hunting ain't your cup of stew," he said almost kindly.

"I guess not," I replied as we walked.

"I remember when I was just a kid," he reminisced. "I used to be all squeamish and cowardly about death, like you. Then my father took me out and made me smack our family pig over the head with a shovel. I felt real bad at first, but the bacon seemed to cheer me up. That's how life works, you give in to change and it feeds you."

"Actually, I have no problem with—"

"I'm glad you understand," he interrupted, not hearing

me out. Then he began whistling to himself as he turned to walk downhill.

President Heck was a number of things to me. At the moment he was my branch president, my girlfriend's father, and my friend. He was closing in on fifty. His brown hair had finally surrendered, letting the gray invade in full force. He was actually quite distinguished-looking when he wasn't speaking (or wearing orange coveralls, for that matter). But his best asset by far was his oldest daughter, Grace. I had served my mission with these people and fallen in deep like with Grace. My mission had come to an end this last summer, but it only took me a few months to realize that I needed to come back to Thelma's Way—to find out if Grace and I had a future.

It was still too soon to tell. There was no doubt that Grace and I loved each other, but there were piles of issues and feelings and problems we needed to work through. I was staying at the boardinghouse while we sorted things out. In a way it was as if we had just met. Sure, I had served almost two years practically in her backyard, but we had never dated, or even really been alone together.

We had a long way to go.

I had hoped I could just come back, sweep Grace off her feet, and then the two of us could be one. It was still a possibility, but I could see now that it wouldn't be "for sure" without real effort.

My parents were livid that I had returned for Grace. In their view, I was jeopardizing my potentially affluent future for the sake of some unpolished Tennesseean. I had come back to Tennessee without telling them, and they now felt as if I had trampled on their plans of living vicariously through me. We weren't speaking, for the time being. Of course, for the time being, I was thousands of miles away from them, trying to keep up with a whistling orange.

My sense of direction was pathetic. I had lived and worked in this area for almost two years, and I still couldn't find my way around. My parents should have named me "Lost," or "Confused"—it would have been so much more fitting than "Trust."

President Heck stopped.

"You know, Trust," he said, "I don't think you belong here."

"What?" I asked, surprised.

"I was just looking up at those turtle-shaped clouds and I got the strongest feeling that you need to be back at home with your folks."

"That's silly," I smiled, somewhat taken aback.

"I know," he stated. "Turtle-shaped clouds. But if you look at that one right there you can see the . . ."

"No, not the clouds," I clarified. "Going back to *Southdale* is silly."

"I don't think so," he sniffed.

"What about Grace?"

"Well, the wife and I have been talking."

"And?" I asked.

"And I think maybe we could send Grace out your way to get some college in. She's always been wanting to further her education."

"Grace in Southdale?"

The idea was absurd.

"Sure," President Heck said. "It might be good for her to get away."

I had honestly never thought of such a thing. Taking Grace from Tennessee was like taking the water from the beach, or the marshmallows from my favorite cold cereal. I couldn't imagine the Volunteer State drawing a single voluntary tourist without the lure of Grace Heck at its core. Sure, I was a little exaggerated in my thinking, but it still didn't seem right. Plus, as discombobulated as the idea of removing Grace was, it seemed even less plausible trying to fit her into Southdale. My hometown would eat her alive. I could see my parents now.

"Mom, Dad, this is Grace."

"Trust, I told you never to bring a girl from Thelma's Way into our house."

"Why don't you just put her outside, Son, so we can eat."

Grace had lived her whole life in Thelma's Way. She had spent her lifetime simmering slowly. I couldn't drag her into the seething, boiling ways of Southdale. There wasn't a single thing in my hometown that she would relate to. Even the gospel was faster there. My ward back home had just posted its own web page with announcements and pictures of the latest ward activity. Grace had grown up in a ward that thought the Internet was the extra stitching on the backsides of winter long johns.

She just wouldn't mesh.

"Do you think Grace would want to go to Southdale?" I asked.

"Sure," President Heck said. "Patty and I have put aside some money. We might be able to help her out a little."

"Grace in Southdale," I said softly.

"You don't really think Grace would be happy living her whole life here forever, do you?" he asked. "She's always tinkered with the idea of seeing the world outside. She could just try it for a while," he said, beginning to walk again.

"I honestly hadn't thought about it," I confessed.

"It might be good for the two of you to spend some time in your part of the country," he went on. "I know there must be a lot more things for people to do there than here. She could meet your folks, go to school."

"You think Grace would go for it?"

"Can't really see what you'd be tearing her away from."

"Well, what about her family, for starters?"

"Grace is ready for more," he winked. "It's time for her to start looking into a new family, if you know what I . . ."

President Heck tried to elbow me in a friendly manner, but he missed and lost his balance, falling to his knees on the ground. I didn't even have time to catch him. His head knocked against an old tree trunk. I tried really hard not to laugh. President Heck rubbed the new knot on his head.

"I used to like trees," he laughed, embarrassed, trying to stand himself up.

"Are you going to be okay?" I smiled, grabbing his elbow and lifting.

"I'll be fine," he fussed. "Toby will wrap my head when I get back."

Toby Carver was the unofficial doctor of Thelma's Way.

By unofficial I mean he owned an Ace bandage and tried to cure everyone in town by wrapping up their ailments. Sister Watson was wearing his bandage at the moment. She had procured a really deep splinter a couple days back while stacking wood. Her fear of tweezers prevented her from having the sliver removed. She was hoping that by keeping the finger wrapped the splinter would just disappear. I'm sure Toby would ask for the bandage back, claiming that head injuries receive first priority.

We walked on in silence, with me thinking about Grace and Southdale. After a while the meadow came into view.

"I'd have a hard time leaving," I said, almost to myself.

"Things are easier if you just don't think about them," President Heck replied.

I could see the boardinghouse off in the distance. A speck of red moved across the porch as smoke twisted up and out of the chimney.

"Do you want to talk to her?" President Heck asked. "Or would you like me to?"

"I'll do it," I replied. "I'll do it today."

2

READY, SET, GO

◇

NOVEMBER 11TH

The next day I called my parents from the boarding-house and told them that I had partially seen the light and was coming home. They said they were partially happy, but wanted to know what the catch was. I told them the catch, in every sense of the word, was Grace, and that she was coming home with me. Surprisingly, my parents were okay with this. I think they saw the opportunity of picking her apart on their turf as somewhat of a blessing.

"Mom, I'm not bringing her home so that you and Dad can make her feel uncomfortable and unwanted in person."

"We'll see," Mom replied sweetly.

"You'll see what?" I asked, bothered.

"Trust, why don't you talk to your father."

I could hear Mom hand the phone to my father. He cleared his throat.

"Son?" he questioned, as if there was a possibility that

10

I had morphed into someone else while my parents were making the phone handoff.

"It's me, Dad," I said.

"Son, we feel . . . well, we're encouraged by your change of heart. But we can't pretend that we are delighted about your feelings for this person."

"Grace is her name," I helped.

"Son, I just don't want to see you thumbing your nose at all the opportunities that lie ahead of you."

"Thanks, Dad," I said, hoping to end the conversation.

"Son, this is an important time in your life. Our community won't let you drift forever. People expect more from a Williams child."

"I'll try not to let you down, Dad," I rolled my eyes. "I promise to only drift a little."

"Good to hear, my boy, good to hear. Now here's your mother."

I could hear my father whisper, "We're reaching him," to my mom as he handed her the phone.

"He always did respect your opinion," she whispered back as she took the phone from him.

"Trust? Are you there?"

I couldn't imagine what my parents thought happened to people waiting on the phone over here.

"I'm still here, Mom."

We talked for a few moments more, making arrangements and trying hard not to say things that might get someone upset. Sybil Porter tapped me on the shoulder and informed me that she needed to use the phone to place an order for makeup. Sybil had been working really hard on getting in touch with her femininity. She had spent her life under the many shadows of her older and manlier brothers. Recently she had moved in with Sister Watson, and Sister Watson was trying to turn her into the lady folks figured Sybil really wanted to be.

Sybil tapped me a little harder.

"I'd better go, Mom. But if someone could pick us up from the air . . ."

Sybil pushed me and "Grrrrred." I turned to look at her. She glared at me for a moment and then frowned as if she were remembering how to act.

"Sorry," she scowled. "It's just that if I call in the next fifteen minutes I save twenty percent on all eye and lip liner."

"Mom, we've got an emergency here," I said into the phone. "Grace and I will see you tomorrow. Bye."

I hung up the phone and moved aside so Sybil could use it. I walked out of the boardinghouse and down the porch. Grace was outside watching some of the local kids play on the rotting pioneer wagons in the meadow.

She had her long red hair tied behind her neck. A couple thick strands hung in front of her face as she looked on. I watched her push them back behind her ear. She was more beautiful to me than a thousand wordy poets could ever describe, her presence a previously undiscovered chemical compound—one that supplied huge amounts of oxygen to my brain. I hoped that I was doing the right thing by taking her away from Thelma's Way.

Grace noticed me and smiled as I approached.

We were going to Southdale.

3

OPEN HARMS

NOVEMBER 12TH

As our plane descended, I held Grace's hand and watched Southdale grow big around us. Each foot we lowered left my insides feeling even more knotted. Like taffy in the hands of a nervous pessimist, I was being twisted and pulled. Bringing Grace back home was a big deal.

From out of the plane window Southdale appeared brown and unspectacular. I could see the Dintmore Hills, and the Southdale River. The hills rippled across the landscape, flattening out a few miles away from the city and making the earth appear as if it were having a cellulite problem. The now shallow Southdale River slowly pushed through the middle of town, dividing the city. A recent drought had thinned the river out something terrible. From high above, it looked no wider than a road, but covered bridges spanned its water in stripes, and the new Wedge Freeway cut across it downtown, wide and topless. Southdale itself seemed to bleed even more in every direction than it had just a few months ago—homes and neighborhoods where once there was nothing. New malls and shopping centers were rising from the ground like blocky weeds.

Southdale was supposedly named for Dale Wedge, a Scottish immigrant who helped settle what was then called Weaver's Claim. According to legend, Dale had taken two bullets in the head while arguing with a cousin over water rights. Both bullets got lodged between his right ear and brain. Amazingly, they seemed to cause nothing but a few days of pain. Well, with little discomfort, and fantastic bragging rights, Dale decided to leave the bullets in his head. They didn't seem to affect him mentally. (Of course, he was no cerebral wizard in the first place.) After the shooting, people noticed that Dale seemed to lean south just a bit. Some reasoned that it was due to the extra two ounces of silver embedded behind his ear. Others figured it was the magnetic pull of the earth on the metal. Of course, it could just have been that Dale's right leg was shorter than his left. Whatever the reason, Dale leaned, and in doing so earned himself the nickname, "South Dale," or so the story goes. Shortly after his mysterious death, the town voted to change its name from Weaver's Claim to Southdale. Sure, there were still some who insisted the town got its name from the fact that it was one of the southernmost towns in the state. But those folks were labeled crackpots and invited to settle farther west.

I liked Southdale—I always had. I liked the small hills that surrounded it. I liked the people and the pace. I liked the warm, mild, year-round weather. It was an almost perfect American city. Crime was low, wages were up, and a national magazine had just ranked it seventh in its "Great Places to Raise a Family" poll. I had to agree. True there were moments I had begun to wish that it was a little smaller or more green and hilly, but that was my only real complaint. And now with the addition of Grace, my city had everything. The fact that I felt this way made me wonder why I couldn't relax.

"Are you ready for all this?" I asked Grace as our plane approached the runway.

"I hope so," she answered softly, her green eyes taking in the big city below us. "This certainly isn't Thelma's Way, is it?"

"You'll do great," I said, wanting to reassure her.

"I think you have more to lose than me."

Grace was already coming around. She had been a mystery my entire mission, staying away from town, hidden from view. She had kept her distance, and in doing so, had laid claim to my heart. Now here she was, sitting next to me, about to meet my parents. I stared at her shamelessly for a few seconds.

"What?" she asked self-consciously.

Her white skin and red hair stood out against the horribly busy fabric that was covering the seats on the plane.

"What is it, Trust?"

Her long fingers closed as she pressed a hand to her chest.

"Trust?"

Her pink lips teased me.

"What are you looking at?" She smiled.

"Nothing," I replied, wanting more than anything to make this work.

My father, Roger, picked us up from the airport. He was all smiles. He shook both of our hands and asked Grace how she spelled her name. (He had read in one of his many business books that this gesture let people know you were truly interested in them.) He treated Grace as he would a client. He tried to be clever and funny in a sterile sort of way. It seemed more pathetic than personal. We took a detour on the drive home, stopping off at a nice restaurant for a light lunch and a heavy lecture. Once Grace and I were trapped in a booth, he started talking at us.

My father was an interesting person. He was tall and fairly fit due to all the tennis he played. He had thick dark hair that he insisted wasn't dyed. But by the end of each month Dad's hair would fade, only to turn jet black a day or two later. He had become very successful in the last few years with his investment company. In the process, how-ever, he had found that he no longer needed the gospel. Oh, he didn't mind my mother taking us to church and participating, but he wanted no part of it. He had come to think that all religion was silly unless it could make you money. It was a humble outlook.

Dad wasn't really too involved with us kids anymore, either. In the last few years we had been mainly raised by our mother with Dad checking in on us mostly during Sunday dinners, and never in depth. I loved my father, but I longed for the father I remembered from my childhood.

I wanted so badly to talk to him about my mission and

what I had learned. I wanted him to tell me how much I had grown. But unless I could present it in a portfolio, with a spreadsheet showing my increased value during those two fiscal years, he just wouldn't be interested anymore.

At the restaurant, Dad went on and on about when he was a kid and all the wonderful things he did to make his parents proud. The entire conversation was peppered with innuendo showing his displeasure at Grace and me. He just couldn't see how marrying a poor girl from Tennessee could benefit my future professional life. He told us about his courtship with my mother, and how things were so rosy due to their similar backgrounds. Then he told us a story about a Canadian boy who married a Hawaiian. "Ended in a bitter divorce," he said dramatically. "Ruined both of their reputations."

I had warned Grace about my parents acting a little weird toward her. But now there was no denying it—they were hoping that Grace was a phase and not a destination.

"Actually, Dad, Grace and I are just going to date. We only want to see if there is something between us."

Dad tried to smile. The waitress dropped off our food and we all started picking at our plates.

"Grace, what does your father do?" my dad asked bluntly.

"He works in Thelma's Way."

"Doing?"

"Dad," I argued, knowing full well that he was aware of what Grace's father did and did not do.

"How about your mother?" my father asked while picking up his glass to take a drink.

"She's a seamstress," Grace answered. "And she teaches school to my brother and sister at home."

Dad spit out what he was sipping. In the Franklin planner of life, *homeschooling* was a four-letter word. He could think of nothing more repressive or achievement-stunting than isolating a child in the home.

"Homeschool?" Dad clarified.

Grace nodded and took a bite of her sandwich while trying to look unaffected by my father's arrogant attitude.

Dad didn't say another word the rest of the meal. When we were done he took us home and dropped us off, claiming he had somewhere else to be.

Our home was located on the east side of Southdale in a nice neighborhood that lay low against the river. The houses in our area were big three- and four-floored models with large double-acre yards around them. In the summer the yards were lush and green, with lawns spilling about like dark green paint. At the moment, however, the scenery was bare, brown, and colored as if God owned nothing but rust-colored crayons. The homes had all been built a few years back, giving our neighborhood more character than any other spot in Southdale. I had loved growing up here.

Mom greeted Grace on the front porch so she would be able to warn her about not wearing shoes in our home. She hugged Grace like she would a thorny cactus.

"It's so nice to meet you, dear," she tried.

"It's nice to finally meet you, Sister Williams," Grace said graciously.

"Call me Mrs. We're not in church," my mother said pettily.

My fifteen-year-old sister Margaret told Grace she would be happy to help her with her hair, and my eleven-year-old brother Abel's only words were, "She doesn't look that weird."

All things considered, I thought things were going rather well.

4

CLOSE PROXIMITY

NOVEMBER 13TH

Grace and I had thought long and hard about where would be the best place for her to stay while she was in Southdale. We both agreed that it wouldn't be right to have her under the same roof with me. Her parents had offered to pay for an apartment, but there really weren't any inexpensive ones in our part of town. So we decided to hit up my longtime neighbor, Wendy.

Wendy was a widow, in the loosest sense of the word. There had been a man she met a few years ago on the bus. Henry, she thought his name was. He had said hello to her for two straight years, only to up and disappear on her a couple of years back. The bus driver claimed Henry had retired, but in Wendy's mind, he was dead. She wore black for a month afterward, which made sense in a backward kind of way, not because she was mourning the loss of someone she had never had, but because black was slimming, and Wendy had put on a few pounds while grieving.

Wendy had lived next to our family forever. She had

inherited her home from her parents after they passed away. Her folks had also left her enough money that she would never have to worry about working. She didn't worry. Not only did she not have any employment, she also didn't bother to lift a finger around the house. Her place was a mess and her yard was the topic of many neighborhood association meetings.

Wendy was heavyset and short. She had the driest eyes I had ever seen—her eyelids squealed every time she blinked. She kept her hair short and had a long nose that hung over her top lip. Wendy wasn't a member of the Mormon Church, nor did she ever plan on being one. She claimed the doctrine was too restrictive. I couldn't imagine what she thought our beliefs would keep her from. All she ever did besides ride the bus back and forth to her book club was stare out of her front window and make calls to the other neighbors whenever something or someone looked out of place.

Well, Grace and I thought that since Wendy had the whole house to herself, maybe she wouldn't mind having a little company. And surprisingly enough, Wendy liked the idea. So Abel, Grace, and I helped Wendy clean out one of the bedrooms on her top floor.

Abel was big for an eleven-year-old. He was as tall as some of the priests in our ward, and would soon pass up those who were taller. He had the perfect little-brother personality—smart, funny, and always entertaining. He had changed from being a pain to being a peer within the two years I had been away. What impressed me most at the moment was how kind Abel was to Grace. Both he and

21

Margaret seemed to be happy for us. It was nice to have my siblings on my side.

We finished cleaning out the bedroom and then worked on the bathroom next to it. When that was done, we all stood around in Grace's room acting as if we had accomplished something impressive, and wishing there were someone around to tell us so. The bedroom was big, with a large window that looked out and across the yards and down into my window.

"You won't mind me looking down at you?" Grace asked.

"Thank goodness for curtains," I joked.

"Isn't that the truth," Wendy said with a passion, creeping us all out.

Saturday night as I lay in bed, I looked out my window toward Grace. The night air looked still and heavy. My window seemed to buckle under the weight of it. The light in Grace's room went off, causing the silhouette of Wendy's home to completely disappear.

I searched for stars but found none.

5

DEBATING THE ODDS

NOVEMBER 14TH

The moment we walked through the chapel doors the whispering began—like air leaking from obese tires, the hissing spit about. I watched Sister Fino almost throw her back out bending over the pew to blab something to Sister Johnson. Brother and Sister Treat held their hymnbooks in front of their faces to hide their gossiping lips, and Leonard Phillips actually pointed at us. I squeezed Grace's hand. This was not going to be easy for her. And part of me was struggling with it too. These people were polished, refined to the point of bland. This, after all, was the ward that had spawned my once-girlfriend Lucy. I couldn't help worrying people would look down at me because I was taken with Grace. Of course, I felt horribly guilty for even thinking such a thing.

We walked down the aisle and took a seat next to Brother Leonard Vastly. He looked at us as if to say "Why me?"

Sister Morris was pounding on the organ keys and

spreading prelude music over the whispering Saints—her large fingers struck too many notes, as usual. I could see Sister O'Shawn six benches back, telling her husband something with great animation. Then she shoved him up out of their pew and across the aisle toward Grace and me. The O'Shawns were the Thicktwig Ward irregulars. No matter how hard they tried they just didn't seem to fit in. Brother O'Shawn worked for a computer company writing math software. He was tall, and walked with a sort of "I've not yet mastered gravity" swagger. He had extremely dark hair with a perfectly round bald spot, which from any distance greater than two feet away made it look as if he were wearing a flesh-colored yarmulke. He wore a cell phone clipped to his belt even during church. I suppose he was just being prepared in case someone needed some emergency math software. Sister O'Shawn was a homemaker, but admittedly, not a very good one. Her kids always wore pajamas to church, even when our schedule shifted to the 1:30 meeting cycle. She was constantly talking about how much laundry confused her. She dreamed of Southdale getting a temple so she could work in a laundry room where she wouldn't have to worry about sorting whites from darks.

Brother O'Shawn stuck out his arm to shake my hand.

"Trust," he said sweetly. "How nice to see you here. So, this must be the girl that we've heard so much about."

Grace took Brother O'Shawn's hand and gave it a gentle shake.

"Can she understand what we're saying?" he asked me with his other hand to the side of his mouth.

"I can understand you perfectly," Grace answered for herself.

"Wonderful," Brother O'Shawn replied awkwardly. "Does everyone talk like you back home?" he asked, referring to Grace's Tennessee accent. He spoke a little too loudly and a little too slowly, as if Grace were some rare native that didn't have a clue.

"Most people do," she replied kindly.

"Well, I'm sure it will wear off eventually," he remarked, still too loud, reminding me of just how socially inept all those hours of designing software had made him. "So, are you just visiting?"

The entire congregation seemed to lean in, waiting for Grace's answer. Sister Morris decreased the volume of her prelude music.

"I'll be going to school here for a semester," Grace informed him.

"How nice," Brother O'Shawn smiled, scratching his forehead. "So where will you be staying while you are here?"

All around us, ears perked up.

"I mean, certainly you're not residing at the Williams' home."

"Certainly not," Grace smiled.

"She's staying with our neighbor Wendy," I answered.

"The nonmember?" Brother O'Shawn said, leaning closer and allowing us to see that his white shirt was tinted pink, evidence of his laundry-challenged household.

"Yes," I said.

25

"So you met Grace on your mission?" he asked, as if I were on trial.

"Yes."

"Well, the circumstances are not entirely appropriate, but we welcome you here anyway," he said, looking directly at Grace and speaking to her as if he were bestowing some great blessing. "Now, would you two classify yourselves as a 'couple?'" he asked, making quotation marks in the air, "or just 'good friends?'" again with the fingers curling like bunny ears.

"Somewhere in the middle," I answered.

"Be careful or that fence might give you splinters."

"Excuse me?" I asked.

"The heavens don't like fence-sitters. I'm speaking figuratively, of course."

"Of course," I replied.

Brother O'Shawn's cell phone rang. He snapped it open as if he had watched far too many Star Trek episodes. "Talk to me," he said. Then, "Oh, it's you, dear . . ."

I looked back at Sister O'Shawn. She was six rows back with her own cellular device clutched to her ear. I could almost hear her talking into it from where I stood. Brother O'Shawn "Okayed," and "Rogered," and then signed off, flipping his phone together like a phaser and hooking it to his belt.

"Well, I need to return to my family," he said, as if we were just begging him to stay. Then, looking at Grace and remembering to raise his voice, he added, "It's nice to meet you . . . uh . . ."

"Grace. Grace Heck."

"Oh," he said. "In our home *heck* is a sloppy word."

"I'm sorry to hear that," Grace replied.

Brother O'Shawn smiled awkwardly and stumbled off. Apparently, the congregation had eavesdropped on enough of our conversation to restimulate their own, because they all turned back to their neighbors and began whispering again. Sister Morris picked up the volume on the organ, and Bishop Leen stood up to walk toward the pulpit. I looked over at Leonard Vastly. He had scooted about as far away from us as possible. I spotted my mother and sister coming in the far chapel doors.

The whispering spiked as others noticed them too.

Mom looked as if she wanted to pull her scarf up over her head to shield herself from recognition. It was as if she were a criminal being whisked into the courthouse; as if my bringing Grace back from Tennessee had besmirched her good name.

My inactive father had worked long and hard to bring our family to a position of respect within the community. Both he and my mother had hoped my mission would turn me into a bilingual, well-polished, go-getting, ladder-climbing, shiny, young Republican. Instead I had gone native. I had come home with a slight accent and a local girlfriend.

Horror of horrors.

Dad was not happy. And if Dad was not happy, then Mom was red-ring-around-the-eyes miserable.

My mother had never felt that she lived up to the image my father's position demanded. She tried, mind you, but it was an impossible goal. So she filled the supposed

gaps by trying to raise children that Dad could feel completely smug about. Now her oldest boy, the chip off the
old block, had ruined things for her. They had been so
happy about my premission dating. Lucy Fall would have
been the ideal daughter-in-law for them—blond, tan, and
oozing with better-than-thou. Now this. Apparently,
Grace just didn't measure up.

The prelude music stopped and Bishop Leen tapped the
microphone. Nelson Leen had been the bishop for six
years. He was a short, light-skinned man with a long neck
and thinning blond hair. His skin was so fair, in fact, it was
almost translucent. From anywhere beyond the fifteenth
row of the chapel, his features started to fade. He liked to
say he was proud of the Norwegian blood coursing through
his veins, and that if you looked real hard, you could see it.

Bishop Leen owned a successful landscaping company
called "Leen's Lawns." Consequently, all of his gospel
analogies had to do with landscaping: "We must combat
the weeds of Satan," or "Let us roll down the lush lawns of
truth." He was passionate about the parable of the olive
tree in Jacob, chapter 5.

He started the meeting with a few words of welcome,
and then announced that due to ward conference the pre-
vious week and Noel Miller's mission farewell the week
before, our ward was having its fast and testimony meeting
a couple of weeks late.

Today.

My heart skipped a beat. I couldn't believe it. Why
hadn't my mother warned me? Sure, we weren't on the
best of terms, but she owed it to the ward to let me know.

You see, to say that Mormons don't condone gambling wouldn't actually be completely true in Southdale. Sure, we frowned upon slots and roulette like everyone else—visiting Vegas for the buffets and amusement parks alone. But I'd wager my last copper penny that there wasn't an active member of the Thicktwig Ward who didn't feel fast and testimony meeting was a proverbial roll of the dice.

One month we might be edified past the point of realizing that we were sitting in a pew, surrounded by people who knew altogether way too much about us. Then, the next month, it took every ounce of willpower to keep from bolting from the room to flee the droning boredom. Standard fare, I realize, but in our ward the stakes were much higher, thanks to Brother Rothburn.

There was an unwritten rule in the Thicktwig Ward: no visitors or investigators on fast Sunday. If someone unknown to Brother Rothburn showed up, he always took it upon himself to stand. He always bore powerful testimony of Joseph Smith, but after that his thoughts would start to wander—and I mean wander, like a picnic napkin on a windy day.

I had just broken that unwritten rule by bringing Grace.

Pleading ignorance would get me nowhere. Had I known that today would be fast and testimony meeting, Grace and I would have attended another ward in town. But it was too late for that. I considered taking off my coat and throwing it over Grace's head but figured she wouldn't go for that. I looked around for Brother Rothburn and spotted him on the third row. He was sitting at the end of the pew, near the aisle, next to the Cummings family. Poor Sister Cummings was aware of the problem. She was taking evasive action. She appeared to be asking him questions about the tie he was wearing to keep him from looking around.

Everyone sitting anywhere between where Brother Rothburn was and where Grace and I were suddenly sat up taller, hoping to block his view if he were to start scanning the congregation. I put my arm around Grace and tried to push her down.

"Trust," she protested, "what are you doing?"

"Believe me, it's for the best . . ."

We sang the opening songs and sat nervously through the ward business. I felt some peace during the sacrament when I could pray and all heads were bowed, but before I knew it, Bishop Leen was back at the pulpit inviting one and all to share the microphone.

Sister Johnson was the first member up. Once again she had drawn her eyebrows in a little thick. She no longer had real ones thanks to an accident at a ward picnic about five years ago. You see, Sister Johnson wore extremely thick glasses. Her vision without them was as poor as a bat's in bright daylight. Well, at the picnic she fell asleep in her lawn chair. About ten minutes into her nap, her large lenses caught the sun and magnified its rays, setting both her eyebrows aflame. She woke up fast enough and ran around screaming before she found a punch cooler to dunk her head into. Her life was spared, but it was too late to save her brows. Now she had to draw them in. But apparently, she had to take her glasses off to do it. They never looked anywhere near normal.

Sister Johnson told a nice story about a nephew of hers who had made some bad decisions in life. He ended up marrying a girl that couldn't cope with motherhood. She used it all as some sort of analogy for the life of the Savior, but it seemed so out of place.

Next up to the pulpit was Janet Laramie. Sister Laramie was a polished woman. She lived her life in peach-colored suits and big self-adjusting sunglasses. Her mouth constantly smacked from the thick coat of glossy lipstick that covered her thin lips. She always held her left hand up as if she were continually hailing a waiter or a staff person of some kind. Sister Laramie owned two small poodles, Minty and Shoo-nu, and was often out of town attending dog shows. She had blond hair that was so poofy that it was perfectly round. It created a halo-like effect with the choir lights behind her. I had always liked Sister Laramie, but I began to wonder if she felt the same.

"Now, I'm not up here to make friends," she said, looking directly at me. "But I felt impressed to stand before you all and relate a story."

Grace looked over at me with concern.

"All of you here know the Williams boy, Trust."

There was a silent gasp from the congregation. Speaking my name directly could prompt Brother Rothburn to turn around and take a gander, causing him to spot Grace.

He began turning his head to look our way. A desperate Sister Cummings handed him one of her toddlers to distract him.

It worked! Brother Rothburn took Isaac Cummings on his knee and began whispering a story into his ear.

Poor kid, I thought. Sacrificed for the cause.

"Well," Sister Laramie continued, "I taught Trust in Sunday School for two years, and I know that we must have covered some lesson concerning the importance of honoring your parents." She stopped to pull a Kleenex from the box next to the microphone. She lifted her glasses and wiped at the small eyes on her taut face. She smacked her lips and sniffed directly into the microphone. "I want to add my testimony of the great job that Sister Marilyn Williams is doing to keep her family active and strong. I hope we can all learn from her sterling example. I also hope that it isn't too late for her children to come around."

I didn't hear the last part of Sister Laramie's testimony due to the fact that Leonard Vastly had decided to make a move for the pulpit. He stepped on Grace's and my toes as he tried to slip past us out of the pew. He accidentally elbowed the head of Sister Barns who was sitting right in front of us. She turned around and gave me a dirty look. I pointed at Leonard, but she just turned away.

We should have stayed away today. We should have gone to another stake, another state for that matter—maybe even have tried out a different religion. I knew that my mother wasn't happy about my dating a girl I had met on my mission. I imagine that there were those who couldn't resist speculating on how Grace and I had grown close when I was a missionary and supposedly unaware of the opposite sex. At first I didn't really care what others might think or say, but it was getting old. I had done nothing wrong. *We* had done nothing wrong. Why couldn't anyone see what a great thing Grace was?

Then Brother Vastly walked up to the pulpit. He talked for ten minutes about being physically prepared for the Second Coming. He bragged about his closets full of beans and Spam, and warned us all that he had also piled away ammo and wasn't afraid to use it on anyone who tried to take away his stuff.

He witnessed to the fact that in his opinion, all prophecy—except that moon turning to blood one, unless you counted last weekend's spectacular sunset—had been fulfilled and that at the first of next year the angels of retribution spoken of in Revelation would come to burn the wicked.

He spoke of a man named Noah Taylor, a visionary guru of emergency preparedness, a veritable fountain of lamp oil for foolish virgins—allegorically speaking, of course. He thanked the Thicktwig Ward Relief Society for bringing Brother Taylor to town to help us all get ready. He also reminded the ward to keep praying for rain. Southdale had been going through a horrible drought over the past year, and if God didn't bless them with some moisture soon, Brother Vastly feared for the safety of his topsoil.

Leonard Vastly was our resident mis-understood. He lived alone in a long single-wide trailer down by Southdale Falls. He was short, spongy, and had big bushy eyebrows. He wasn't exactly heavy, but he was one of those people who refused to let go of his old wardrobe even though he had grown a couple of sizes from when he was younger.

Everything he wore was tight—uncomfortably tight—both for him and for us. I felt pity for his belts and buttons.

Brother Vastly had not always been a Saint. He had joined the Church years ago after he had broken into someone's car and stolen what looked like a purse, but turned out to be a leather tote with scriptures inside. After his initial anger at being cheated out of a purse, he read the Book of Mormon and joined the Church. He was the fabled convert that Church members always hoped would be the result of their stolen Mormon goods. He blamed his criminal past on the fact that his brother used to put straight mayonnaise in his bottle when he was a kid—all that egg had made him rambunctious and deviant.

I had always kind of liked Brother Vastly, despite his many annoyances. He was such an interesting person to look at and listen to. His lessons were off the wall, his ideas were absurd, and his insights were consistently way right of center and unbelievable. He gave our ward color and comical confusion.

After Brother Vastly finished speaking, he came and sat down two benches in front of us. He must have sensed conspiracy in the presence of Grace.

Lonora Leen, the bishop's wife, got up and bore her testimony. It was like a peaceful intermission during a confusing play. She simply testified to the fact that the Lord had helped her through each day. There was no mention of disobedient children or ill-advised marriages, just gratitude and answers to prayer.

For a few moments after her no one got up. Tension grew thick as faces started to wander. The Saints between us and Brother Rothburn sat up again in their seats and Sister Cummings started knocking her kids' books on the floor and asking Brother Rothburn if he'd mind picking them up.

A chair-sitter coughed. Sister Lewis psyched us all out by standing up only to take one of her twins out to the foyer. Someone had to break the suspense. I thought about getting up and bearing my testimony, but judging by Grace's reception so far, I wasn't sure how it would go over.

Someone caught my eye, moving up the aisle to the front.

My relief was short-lived.

It was my mother, Marilyn. She was already moving up the platform stairs. Mom never bore her testimony—I was in for it now. She must have felt a great burning about something to actually get up the nerve.

Mom patted her set blond hair on the sides and smiled weakly. She was wearing a lime green dress with a lace doily collar. She seemed ill at ease, but that wasn't surprising—Mom dreaded public speaking. She had refused to speak at my farewell, let alone my homecoming. It was stage fright. She liked the people in the Thicktwig Ward fine, she just didn't like the idea of talking in front of them.

My mother wore glasses and had a small button nose. She smiled a lot, but it never looked easy for her to do. She had been a good mother, a little more emotionally timid than I felt I needed at times, but kind and concerned about her children.

My mother bore her testimony, sounding like she had

lost a child to war. She thanked the ward for their support. She asked them all to pray for her. It was heartfelt. She worked her way around the story of the prodigal son, mixing up important aspects of the story with the tale of David and Goliath. The part where the prodigal son sold his slingshot for food was particularly interesting. At the end she paused, as if she feared she had gone too far. Changing the subject, she thanked Noah Taylor for his insightful and timely instruction at homemaking meeting last week, and challenged the ward to give him their full support. "December seventeenth is just around the corner," she added in strangely cheery tones. "I'd hate to be caught short."

"Who's this Noah Taylor?" Grace whispered. "And what happens on the seventeenth?"

"I have no idea," I replied.

Mom paused awkwardly again, suddenly said "Amen," and sat herself down. Though I was glad she was through, it occurred to me that she had ended at the worst possible moment. If she could have gone on for just a few more minutes then time would have been up and the bishop could have closed the meeting. Now, however, there was still a five-minute window for Brother Rothburn to work his magic.

I know it was dumb to be so bothered by Brother Rothburn and his never-ending oratory style, but no one could truly understand unless they had actually suffered through it. Brother Rothburn's nickname was Brother "Oh, that reminds me." After almost every sentence he would make some odd connection and go off on some completely unrelated subject. Unfortunately for all of us, he always went off on the *same* unrelated subjects. He rarely said anything new. In fact, I'm certain that, if pressed, a large portion of our ward could recite much of his testimony by heart. For my entire life he had stood up whenever there was a visitor, and gone on and on about everything from Church history to modern-day appliances. He would tell how the golden plates were translated. How the Saints came west. How when he was in the army, his friend Ryan Hinkle was saved from a bullet by a Book of Mormon in his breast pocket. Of course it always took him two minutes to recall Ryan's name. It was something to watch—everyone biting their tongues, dying to shout "Hinkle! Hinkle! Okay? His name was Hinkle!" though no one ever did, it being sacrament meeting and all.

The big hand on the chapel clock moved a minute. Still no one moved. I watched Brother Rothburn notice that there was dead air in the building. He looked at the clock, then at his watch. His head began turning my way. I pushed Grace down as far as I could. Sister Cummings tugged hard on Brother Rothburn's sleeve. He paid her no mind. He was going to take a look around, even if it killed us.

It just might.

Bishop Leen's wife tried to wave her husband up to the stand. She must have been hoping he would close the meeting a few minutes early. But we all knew that wouldn't happen. Bishop Leen was actually part of the problem. He refused to ever end fast and testimony meeting early, but he didn't mind if it ran overtime. He didn't have the guts to tap anyone on the shoulder and tell them to sit down. Sunday School teachers assigned to teach the first Sunday of the month knew to prepare summaries of their lessons, never knowing how much time they would have.

Brother Rothburn began to glance over the crowd. Like a rickety old lighthouse searching for wreckage, his worn eyes skimmed across the reeflike rows. Systematically, he picked his way over the pews, looking for an unfamiliar face. He knew all the regulars rather well. People made it a point to talk to him often so that he would always be aware of the fact that they were supposed to be there. If anyone changed their hairstyle or lost a significant amount of weight they always kept him up to date. No one wanted to take a chance.

I tried not to look nervous as his glance got closer to Grace and me. I didn't want to give it away. Then, like someone else's bad breath, I could feel it slowly wash over me. I stopped breathing. His gaze brushed right past us and moved on, without so much as a hitch. I breathed out. I could see shoulders relax throughout the gathering. But just as his gaze reached the Chavez family, Brother Rothburn glanced back our way as if something had caught his eye. Somehow, he was peering his way over shoulders and around hair.

Bishop Leen began to stir on the platform. He leaned down to pick up his things. He grasped the armrest on his chair to lift himself up.

It was a little too late.

Brother Rothburn had spotted Grace. He smiled as if he had just eaten something buttery. I had been foolish to think we could get away with it. There were only two other members of our ward with red hair. Slowly, like crust-topped lava, Brother Rothburn began to ooze up and out of his seat. Bishop Leen saw him and shifted his weight back into his chair.

Brother Rothburn stood and straightened his tie. He pulled out a hanky and blew into it. He carefully folded the hanky, placed it back into his pocket, and began to amble up to the pulpit. It seemed to take a full five minutes for him to make it up to the stand. He shook the bishop's hand. He shook his counselors' hands, one by one. He stood at the pulpit and instructed the bishop to raise it a bit. Then he asked him to lower it again.

Too high.

Down just a little.

Nope.

Up a little bit more.

Tiny bit more.

Bit more.

Nope.

The bishop gave up in frustration. Brother Rothburn adjusted his microphone to compensate.

Brother Rothburn was old. He had already turned ninety before I left on my mission. His second wife had passed away about ten years earlier and he had lived alone ever since. He didn't do much besides go to church. He went to every scheduled function there was. It didn't matter if he wasn't invited—he went. I couldn't remember a single meeting in my entire life where he had not been in attendance. He had thick gray hair and a big rubbery nose.

His eyes had been blue once, but age had washed them out to a shade that matched his hair. He was tall for a ninety-year-old man, and still got around amazingly well.

"I wasn't planning to come up today," he began. "But I thought, seeing as there is a fresh young face among us . . . Oh, that reminds me. What do you get when you cross . . . oh, what was his name? He was always real outspoken about modesty. Well anyway, I was at the big mall just recently looking for a part to my phonograph, that's a record player for you youngins. They don't seem to make many of them anymore, can't understand why. To me there is nothing more exciting than the scratchy intro on a new 45. We used to get stacks of them and play as many as twelve songs right in a row. Anyhow, I couldn't believe some of the outfits that these kids wear to the mall these days. It seems modesty is outdated. When I was a young boy we used to get dressed up for such things. I hardly went anyplace without a coat and tie. A person wouldn't dream of going to the movies or taking a plane ride in jeans. But I suppose I'm just old and out of it these days. Oh, that reminds me of the story of the stagecoach driver. It seems that this gentleman was interviewing potential applicants for his stagecoach company. The question he asked was how close to the edge can you get? So the first driver, he . . ."

This was terrible. This was worse than terrible. Brother Rothburn was on a long roll and it was all my fault. Every chance they could, ward members turned in their seats to scowl at us. There would be no forgiveness for Grace for coming today, or for me for bringing her. This would last half an hour if it lasted a second.

" . . . And do you know who he picked? The man who could drive the farthest away, that's who. Anyhow, what do you get when you cross . . . now let's see, what was his name. None of you probably remember him, and of course I'm dating myself by bringing him up, but he was a great General Authority with sort of a salty mouth. Bishop, can you recall the name?" Brother Rothburn turned toward the bishop.

"J. Golden Kimball," Bishop Leen answered.

"I do believe you're right, J. Golden Kimball. Now, a lot of people frown on profanity, and well they should. But if you ask me a well-placed swearword can make the impression of twenty plain ones. But I guess you didn't ask me. . . ."

I put my head in my hands.

Fifteen minutes later he began to wrap up. Twelve minutes after that he said something about "In conclusion." And four minutes after that he closed with, "And that's why bonnets were originally called head wraps. Amen."

It was finally over. Heads began to pop up all around like prairie dogs. Brother Rothburn exited the podium and Bishop Leen once again gathered his stuff together by his feet. I was in rapture. I hardly noticed Grace stand and begin to walk to the front. I hardly noticed the bishop sit back down. Before I knew it, however, she was standing at the microphone looking as if she had something to say.

What was she doing? Had she lost it? Didn't she know

the patience of these Saints had already been pushed beyond the breaking point?

I sat stunned in my pew wondering how I would ever live this down.

Bishop Leen was as surprised as anyone. We were already running half an hour over. I heard someone moan out loud.

Grace began. "Brothers and Sisters, I've never been one to know just what the Lord was thinking. It's always been kind of a guessing game with me. But I know He's there, and I . . ."

I don't know how you would describe my relationship with Grace. I knew that I loved her. She said she felt the same for me. But everything between us seemed so discombobulated. In a normal relationship, people date, they cope with uncertainty, and after a while things get clearer. If they're made for each other, they come to the conclusion that love is in the air, in the water, and in the food. They talk about getting married.

Things were running in the opposite direction for us.

I had known of Grace for most of my mission. I was intrigued by the bits and pieces of her she let me see. By the end of my two years I knew I couldn't live without her. But lately, I wasn't so sure.

It was like seeing an intriguing new board game that you instantly want. You fall in love with the colored box and the concept, but when you crack it open you realize that you've got a whole book of instructions to wade through and understand before anything worthwhile is going to actually happen.

That was us. Except our instructions seemed to be written in Spanish.

No hablo eb panola.

Had I asked the people Grace had grown up with to describe her, they would more than likely say she was shy, hard to track, an enigma with red hair. Of course they wouldn't have used the word *enigma*, but stick in "kinda confusing" and you get the idea.

But I had seen Grace differently. I had seen her use her determination in the most self-assured ways. It was as if Thelma's Way had been holding the real Grace back. I had gone there to find myself. But it seemed Grace had needed to get away to discover who she was.

In the two days since we had arrived in Southdale, I had already noticed a difference. She was coming through loud and clear. In fact, I was a little frightened by it. I didn't want to get left behind.

Grace bore her testimony. She talked about how wonderful it was to be in such a huge ward. She said all the right things in all the right ways and by the end of her testimony, the feeling in the room was entirely different.

I just stared at her. She came down and sat next to me. She smiled.

Bishop Leen closed the meeting.

A couple people came up to Grace afterward and welcomed her to the ward. Sister Barns apologized for what she was thinking about Grace at the start of the meeting. Brother O'Shawn informed us that he just remembered that he had a nephew who married a girl he met on his mission and that so far, things had worked out okay.

"You're amazing," I whispered to Grace between well-wishers.

"I'm glad you think so," she whispered back.

It felt as if most folks were suddenly willing to give Grace a chance—most folks besides my mother, that is. She slipped out the back without saying a word.

I mentally notched off week number one.

6

LUCY

◈

Lucy Fall was miserable. For the first time in her life she felt absolutely helpless. Still, she couldn't decide if she was more upset about what she was going through, or by the fact that what she was going through had caused the natural blush in her cheeks to fade. Pale was not on her color wheel.

It had been three days since Lance had walked out on her. He had simply packed his bags and stepped away. That was it. Lucy had known that the marriage was strained, but she never imagined Lance would leave her for someone else.

She threw off her robe and slipped into the bath. Even the warm water didn't cheer her.

Where was her mother?

Where was her father?

How could her folks be in Europe at a time like this? Weren't parents supposed to have some sort of intuition thing going on? How could they not have known that their daughter would need them?

Need them. Lucy needed them.

It was such a demeaning thought.

Lucy had thought Lance was perfect. Sure, he wasn't Mormon, but she had married him knowing that her power of refinement could produce the desired results. Lance had come out to church a few times, but he had ultimately decided that fishing and boating were a lot more fulfilling than church. Apparently, he had also come to the conclusion that marriage was a little too confining. He claimed to have tried, but in truth the marriage had gone downhill right from the honeymoon itself. Lucy had wanted to hold things together for the sake of their image, but it hadn't worked.

And now it was too late. Lance was gone.

She began to panic. Something was happening to her. Her insides were pushing up inside her and tears were streaming down her face. Lucy hadn't cried since the day Sally Moss punched her in the stomach for liking Billy Wheeler. That was the third grade.

Her shoulders shook, her throat released, and she moaned. A sudden anxiety wrapped around her, squeezing the air from her lungs. She noticed the mascara dripping into the tub. Things were going to get messy before the night was out.

7

FACT-FINDING FEAST

That night at family dinner my father tried to keep the conversation light. He asked my sister Margaret twice how school was going, and told us all the score of the high school basketball game three times.

"Forty-seven to thirty-two. Can you believe that?"

All the while, he never once made eye contact with either Grace or me. Dad had been avoiding us ever since he had dropped us off from the airport. Clearly, he didn't know how to handle the situation, and life seemed to go better for Dad when he just ignored the things he couldn't change.

"So, Margaret, how is school going?" he ventured again.

Margaret had just turned fifteen. She was a pretty girl with way too many clothes. I had never seen her wear the same outfit twice. She changed clothes more often than most people brushed their teeth. The Gap had personally called her on her birthday to wish her well, and to inform her that the new jumpers were in. She was short enough to be nervous about her height, constantly praying for a growth spurt, and skinny enough to make all the other girls mad. She had blond hair, blue eyes, and a smile bright enough to make every Aaronic Priesthood holder in our ward simultaneously woozy.

"You've asked Margaret about school two times already," my brother Abel offered.

"I'm just interested," my father defended, while buttering one of his dinner rolls. "Just interested in my little girl. Isn't that right, princess?" he winked.

"School's fine, Dad," Margaret replied.

"Good to hear," my father said, "good to hear. Is there any more jam in the kitchen?" he asked nobody in particular.

My mother got up to check.

"So, Dad," I dared. "Do you know if there are any jobs available at your office right now?"

"You never know what kind of strings your old man can pull for his son."

"I already have a job," I said. "But could you pull a couple for Grace? She'd like to work until the semester starts."

"You already have a job?" my father questioned.

"I'll be working for Brother Barns again starting next week. But Grace could really use some help."

Dad sort of huffed and shifted in his seat. "Well, I'd need to find out a little bit more about this Grace. I can't just hand out a job on the spot."

"What do you need to know?" I asked.

"Well, for starters, what can this Grace do?"

I looked around the room, wondering why he was talking about her as if she weren't there. "Dad, you can talk directly to her. She's sitting right in front of you."

Grace opened her mouth to speak, but before she could say anything, my father hollered, "Marilyn, how's that jam coming?"

My mother came out of the kitchen and began spooning jam onto everyone's plates.

"So, Margaret, how is school going?" Dad asked.

"This is stupid," Abel said, frustrated. "Trust, are you and Grace going to get married?" he asked bluntly.

"What?"

"Dad thinks you're going to get married and ruin your future."

"Out of the mouth of babes," my mother sang as she sat down.

"Now, Abel, that's not exactly how I phrased it," my father backpedaled.

"I know," Abel said, "but I didn't want to hurt Grace's feelings."

"This is ridiculous," Margaret snipped. "Who cares who Trust marries?"

"Wait a second," I tried to say, "why don't—"

"There are certain things that are expected of us, young lady," my mother interrupted, waving her fork at my sister. "If you were doing drugs, do you think your father and I would just turn our backs?"

"Margaret's doing drugs?" my father asked in shock.

Abel began to laugh. I saw him smile at Grace as if to say sorry for all this. Grace smiled back.

"Margaret's not doing drugs!" my mother shouted.

"Good going, princess," my father congratulated.

For a second there was nothing but the sound of chewing.

"Dad, what about that job?" I tried again.

"So how was church today?" Dad asked, ignoring my question.

It was obvious that my father didn't want to talk about a job for Grace. Painfully obvious—Dad never talked about church. He sort of skirted around the fact that he was inactive by never talking about anything related to the gospel. The fact that he had just brought it up was proof positive that he was getting desperate.

"Mom bore her testimony," Margaret informed him.

"This roast is better than ever," was my father's only reply.

"Sister Barns brought an old Book of Mormon to class," Abel tried.

"Patty Barns has really lost weight," my mother commented. "I hardly recognized her in that waisted dress."

"How old was the Book of Mormon?" Grace asked Abel.

I looked at her, thinking about how nice it was to hear her voice at our dinner table.

"I don't know. Old. But not real old, fake old," he answered. "Sister Barns said it was just a copy of the first one."

"I wouldn't mind getting my hands on a real first edition,"

my dad said, happy to have landed on a less threatening topic. "That's quite a piece of American history. Remember Jack Shaw?" he asked no one in particular. "He had that first edition. Boy, he thought he was something else."

"They had a real first edition in Thelma's Way," Grace ventured.

"Where's that?" he asked.

I shook my head. Forget the fact that his own son had lived there for two straight years, or that one of our dinner guests was born and raised there—Dad still didn't recognize the name.

"Thelma's Way," she said, unfazed. "It was a nice copy. It was even signed by Parley P. Pratt."

"You're kidding," my dad said, actually looking at Grace and showing genuine interest for the first time in the entire conversation.

"Nope." Grace smiled. "It belonged to the branch."

"Where is it now?" he asked quickly.

"Who knows?" I piped in. "Someone took it."

"Who knows?" my father said, turning to me. "Did someone sell it?"

"I don't think so. Folks are kind of just waiting for the guilty party to admit they did it."

"Do they know how much it's worth?"

"I told them about twenty thousand," I said.

Dad took a big bite of his roast beef and chewed thoughtfully.

"One sold at a New York auction for over fifty thousand last week," he finally said.

"Well, that wouldn't matter in Thelma's Way. Whoever

has it will probably trade it for a couple cows, or a piece of land. Actually, they'll be lucky to get that. People don't have much use for old books. I'm sure whoever has it would be willing to let it go for something shiny or new-looking."

My father turned back to Grace and smiled.

"Tell me more about your hometown," he said.

Grace knew he had ulterior motives, but she was happy to oblige. She told him about the winding path from Virgil's Find and the chapel where the branch would meet. She told him about the debate the town had had, and how after the food fight the Book of Mormon turned up missing again. She told him how the whole town was waiting for someone to begin spending a lot of money, so as to give away the fact that they had secretly cashed it in. She told him every single thing she knew about the lost Book of Mormon, and all about Thelma's Way.

My father listened to Grace as if she had a doctorate in conversation from Yale (instead of a letter of recommendation from her father concerning homeschool).

Two days later, Dad flew out of town. He wouldn't say where he was going, only that it was very important and that he would be back in a week or so. My mother insisted it was a routine business trip, and that his leaving had nothing to do with the huge fight the two of them had had the day before over Margaret wearing makeup (Mom for, Dad against).

"He has business trips all the time," my mother told Abel and me defensively.

We had no reason not to believe her. At least not yet.

8

BE PRESCARED

NOVEMBER 17TH

As luck would have it, we didn't need my father's name to find Grace a job. Wednesday evening, Brother Victor, the Thicktwig Ward employment specialist, showed up at our house to let Grace know what jobs were available.

Brother Victor was a tiny man. Although he was many years my senior, I always felt tempted to pick him up. He was just so compact. He looked like a miniature human, like one of God's trial-sized samples. He was also one serious ward employment specialist. He had held the position for as many years as I could remember and apparently desired never to be released. Thanks to him, almost no one in our ward stayed out of work long. A few years back, when Brother Treat had been laid off from his job at the carpet factory, Brother Victor worked day and night to find him a job. Brother Treat was actually kind of enjoying the lazy rush of drawing unemployment, but he soon found out that it was more work avoiding Brother Victor than holding down a regular job. He took a position driving one of the city buses that went down our street.

Brother Victor informed Grace that Brother Noah Taylor, the emergency preparation guru from Manti, was looking for someone to answer phones and do the billing for his food storage warehouse. The job would only last until the end of December. It was perfect for Grace.

"I thought it might be," Brother Victor smiled.

Grace called up Brother Taylor and was offered the job on the spot. It was a nice wage with good hours. She was very relieved.

"My work here is done," Brother Victor whispered as he left.

My mother was actually pretty impressed that Grace got the job. I guess she thought it was a socially enviable position—Brother Taylor was the out-of-towner to know.

Later that evening, I walked Grace back to Wendy's for the night. We stood on the unlit porch pretending that it wasn't as cool as it actually was.

"How are you doing with all this?" I asked.

"It's a slight adjustment," she shivered. "But I like it here."

"You do?" I asked, surprised.

"Your family's nice . . ."

"They are?"

Grace slipped her arms around me and put her head on my shoulder.

"That's kind of nice," I said, trying to sound calm.

"Trust," was all she said.

I kissed the top of her head. She pulled back just a bit

so that my lips could meet her on the forehead. Her body shifted and suddenly her soft mouth was on mine. I didn't really know how we had gotten there, but I was not about to complain. I could feel her fingers on the back of my neck. Suddenly it was way too dark out and I couldn't see anything except me kissing her forever. The night spun around me like cotton candy, making my senses sticky and sweet. Grace touched me on the cheek and brushed my right ear with her hand. Then she placed her head back on my shoulder and sighed.

"What was that for?" I finally asked.

"I want to make sure that we're turning into more than just good friends."

Grace kissed me again and then slipped through Wendy's front door. I walked home with a windy soul under a clear sky.

My mom was in the living room pasting pictures into photo albums as I came in.

"Trust, is that you?" she asked, too busy to look up. "You know, I think Grace is real lucky to land that job with Brother Taylor. I hope she's grateful, but then I guess those natural people usually are."

"Natural people?" I asked.

"You know, free spirited. She'll learn a lot under the tutelage of Brother Taylor."

"So what's the deal with this Taylor person?" I asked, curious to know more about this man everyone spoke so highly of, that Grace would now be spending time with on a daily basis.

Mom smeared glue stick onto the back of a photograph and slapped it on an empty page.

"Brother Taylor is an important person," she raved. "He's a direct descendent of some important Church leaders."

"John Taylor?" I asked, making a stab at it.

"No, Tony Taylor," my mother thought. "I believe he was a stake president in Manti. Anyhow, Noah Taylor is going to be the one who saves our whole town."

"From what?" I asked.

"Oh, Trust," Mom replied. "You have so much to learn."

"No, really," I tried. "What is this Brother Taylor going to save us all from?"

"Well, for starters . . . oh, look at this picture of your father," she said, becoming distracted. "I tell you he could turn heads. He had a real sense about him."

"Mom?"

"Yes, Trust?" she asked nicely.

"Brother Taylor, what's he saving us all from?"

"Well, Sister Barns felt that we sisters in the Relief Society should make sure that our food storage was up to date. Times are awful crazy. . . . Look at your father in this one." She held up another picture. "He used to love to fish. He would take me out all the time. He could catch any fish. But he always threw them back." Mom sighed. "That's the kind of man he was—compassionate. He used to be so compassionate."

"And?" I prodded.

"And moral. Why, your father was so considerate of my standards while we were dating."

"Mom," I complained. "I meant, and what else about this Taylor person."

"Well, he's really helping us out. We thought he would come and tell us what to buy and what to store. But then he told us how hard it can be to find places for all that food and water. That's true, you know. We have one of the biggest houses in the ward, and I can't think of an extra foot for storage."

"What about the garage?" I asked.

"Brother Taylor says the temperatures are all wrong. Foods can become stale, or lose their flavor. Now that's funny," my mother paused. "I remember this picture, but I didn't remember your father wearing that shirt in it. I wonder if this photo has changed colors, or maybe someone doctored it up. They can do that now, you know. So who could have slipped into my old photos and changed his shirt color?"

"Maybe you're remembering a different photo," I offered.

"No," she insisted. "This is the one I'm remembering."

"Mom, no one snuck into our house to change the color of Dad's shirt on that photo."

"It's just odd, that's all," she observed.

I'll say.

"So where does this Brother Taylor think you should store your food?" I asked, thinking that perhaps he was a temperature-controlled shed salesman with objectives of his own.

"That's the wonderful part. He's taking care of all of it for us. He's renovated that old warehouse right there on Frost Road to be a climate-controlled food storage wonderland. Oh, here's that picture of Margaret that she hates so much. I don't know why she fusses so. Anyone can tell that's a skin-colored turtleneck and not her chin."

"Ralph couldn't."

"He still would have stopped writing her if I hadn't sent him a copy," Mom said defensively.

"They'd been pen pals for eight years."

"It wasn't my doing."

"He never wrote again after that."

"Germans can be a little touchy."

"So anyhow," I said, trying to pick up the conversation someplace near where it had dropped off. "You take your supplies to Brother Taylor's warehouse and he keeps them there for you?"

"Sort of. Look at your father in this shot. I can hardly remember him looking this relaxed," she said sadly.

"Sort of?"

"We pay Brother Taylor and he buys everything for us," she said, picking up a new stack of photos. "It's really lightened my load not to have to bother with it. It's sort of like time-share food storage. You know, like with the condo."

"What good is food storage if it's down the road?" I asked, starting to feel weird about Brother Taylor. "Besides, aren't you supposed to rotate food storage? What's this guy going to do when his entire warehouse begins to expire?"

"Oh, Trust," my mother cooed. "Look at you. I remember

your birth so vividly. I'm sure glad the shape of your head snapped back."

"Mom, I don't know if keeping your food storage at a distant warehouse is what the prophet had in mind."

"Trust, don't be so cynical," she scolded. "Brother T's from Manti. I'm sure he would know if the prophet disapproved. Besides, Noah Taylor has been blessed with a foreknowledge of when things will begin to fall apart."

"He has?" I asked.

"I guess he had a vision or something—December seventeenth."

"December seventeenth? You mean of this year?"

"Of this year," she said, unconcerned. "That's why everyone's operating in such a huff. Noah's got us all on fire. He's a dedicated man," my mother complimented. "He's even rented an old farmhouse to live in out past the Dintmore Hills because he can't stand to be away from his farming roots," Mom paused to turn the album page. "Now just what is your father doing in this picture?" She laughed. "He had a silly streak, you know. He wasn't always so business oriented."

"I remember," I said. "He was so different when I was small."

"I can't believe it's the same man today," my mother said, suddenly sad.

Mom was silent for a few minutes.

"Are you okay?" I asked finally, feeling as if I should say something.

"I'm fine," she replied. "I just can't get over how much things change, that's all."

"Mom, I'm in love with Grace," I said out of the blue, unable to hold it back.

"Things change," she said again sadly.

I left Mom to her memories.

9

HOLLOW

◇

NOVEMBER 18TH

Lucy couldn't remember ever being happy. She knew that she had grown up pain-free, but that was not happiness. She knew that now. She understood that now. She looked at herself in the mirror and tried to smile.

People were supposed to smile.

Her blond hair looked lifeless and dull, almost as if she had been using a generic-brand shampoo. She couldn't believe that the blue eyes staring back at her were the same ones that had once made Lance weak in the knees.

Lucy hadn't been out of the house in days. She had passed the hours cutting up everything that belonged to or reminded her of Lance. Her home looked like the scratching post of a cat with powerful paws. Lucy knew she needed to begin again, but she just couldn't find a way to let go of the hurt. She sat on the couch and thought about all the horrible things people would soon be saying about her:

"She must have driven him away."

"I guess he had to find companionship elsewhere."

"What kind of failure loses her husband to a waitress?"

She went to the window and adjusted the blinds. Light slipped through, striping her bare arms with contrasts. She thought about summer, and how much easier all this would be if it had happened during a greener month. Even nature seemed against her.

Lance had stopped by the day before to pick up a few more of his things. He seemed so unbothered by everything that was happening. Lucy had locked herself in the bathroom until he left.

"I hate him," she said as she raised the blind to peer out the window.

A white car drove by on the street below. Lucy wasn't sure, but she thought it might have been Trust's. She had bumped into him a few weeks back at the grocery store while shopping with Lance. She remembered now how good he had looked.

What had she ever seen in Lance? Lucy's mind drifted back to life before they had ever met.

A vague memory settled over her, and she smiled.

She could remember being happy.

10

SPINNING COOKIES

NOVEMBER 20TH

Saturday morning my father called to inform us that he'd run into some trouble with his business negotiations. He wouldn't be back for at least another week. He still didn't say where he was. Mother didn't push it.

Grace had begun her job the day before, and was enjoying it. She, like the rest of them, seemed to think that Noah Taylor was an outstanding guy. I had yet to meet him and form a favorable opinion. The two times I dropped her off he had not been around. All I knew was that he was a widower from Manti who wanted to prepare the world for its end.

Southdale was growing even more hectic than usual. The fact that Thanksgiving was less than a week away made everyone feel as if they needed to act a little busier. Stores were hanging Christmas decorations and promoting Christmas items in their usual gloss-over-Thanksgiving fashion. Southdale never did get very cold, but it wasn't usually this dry. The November ground was dry and porous, giving Southdale a ruddy complexion and making us all pray for rain.

I was sort of just kicking around, waiting for this week to end and the next week to begin, when a surprise visitor showed up. I was outside fixing the garage door for my mother when I heard a loud vehicle turn onto our street and tear toward our house. I looked up to see a truck that looked vaguely familiar turn into our driveway.

It stopped a couple feet away from me. The driver turned the engine off, opened his door, and climbed out. As he pulled in, I didn't recognize who it was, due to the sunglasses, but the moment he was standing on the ground there was no mistaking Elder Jorgensen for anybody other than himself.

Elder Jorgensen was a former missionary companion of mine. Out of all the people I had served with, he had been the most dedicated, hardworking, and likable. He was almost seven feet tall, and the oldest in a family of fourteen children from Blackfoot, Idaho. He had abrasive-looking blond hair that was short and spiky. It had also thinned a bit since I had last seen him. He had two big front teeth and a smile that, when activated, hid his ears. I knew now why the truck looked familiar to me. Elder Jorgensen had shown me more than a few photos of it when we had served together. His parents had taken care of it for him while he was on his mission, washing it every week and keeping all the other siblings away.

The last time I had seen Elder Jorgensen was right after he had broken his leg. We had been tracting out in the Thelma's Way woods when he had fallen and snapped his lower leg. It was his accident that provided Grace and me our first chance to be alone when she helped me go for help. There was no doubt in my mind as to why he was my favorite companion.

"Elder," I said, excited to see him.

"Not Elder anymore," he exclaimed. "Just plain Doran. Doran Jorgensen. Of course there's a P there in the middle. P for Peter. But I don't mention that much, seeing how I was named after my uncle Peter who *was* a good guy before he left his wife and kids for a girl half his age. I usually just go by Doran Jorgensen."

I stared at him until he felt further explanation was necessary.

"Doran was the name of my great-grandmother's business."

"Wow," was all I could say.

"She made brooms," he further explained.

I almost said "Wow" again, but I had used that up already.

"I remember your first name," he bragged. "Honor."

"Actually it's Trust," I laughed.

"Those virtues confuse me."

I hugged Doran and then stood back an appropriate distance.

"So what are you doing here?" I asked.

"Just got done with the mission," he said proudly. "Finished honorably, of course."

"Of course."

"My folks were kind of smothering me so I thought I'd

take a road trip and visit some of the ex-companions. Wanted to show you guys my truck."

I walked slowly around his vehicle, pretending to admire it and know exactly what I was looking at.

"It's just like the pictures," I observed.

"Yeah," he sighed proudly, following me around. "So, you want to go for a spin?"

Not really, but I said, "Sure."

Doran looked at the dirty work clothes I was wearing. "Maybe you should change."

"Really?" I asked, thinking that he had to be joking.

"I just steam cleaned the upholstery."

I changed clothes and we drove through Southdale acting like we owned the place. Doran took a corner quickly, throwing me up against the passenger-side door. I looked for a seat belt and was informed that he had just removed them.

"Why?"

"They were old and fraying," he hollered. "I special ordered some new ones but they won't be in for a few weeks."

I hoped I would live to see them.

"Isn't this great?" he asked.

"Yeah," I yelled over the engine roar.

He stopped abruptly at a red light, causing my knees to press up against the dashboard. The small plastic elk head he had hanging from his rearview mirror dangled wildly.

"Hey, whatever happened to that girl in Thelma's Way?" he asked.

"Grace?" I asked back.

"Yeah, Grace. Too bad about her doctrinally incorrect name."

"We believe in grace, Elder."

"Doran."

"We believe in grace, Doran."

"So what happened to her?" he asked, apparently not wanting to get into a gospel debate at the moment.

"She's here," I informed him.

Doran looked around the cab of his truck. "I'm sure she is, Trust. You always did act a little funny about her."

"Not here in . . ."

The light turned green and we sped off noisily. Doran spotted an empty parking lot with hundreds of speed bumps. He turned sharply and began bouncing over all the long asphalt lumps. Our heads knocked against the roof of the cab as he swerved and plowed over more of them. Doran laughed as if this was as fun as life could possibly get.

"Listen," I tried to reason. "Could you slow it down a little?"

"Watch this," was his reply. He pulled into a dirt field next to the parking lot and began spinning circles, his big tires grinding loudly as I became wedged against the passenger door. Dirt was spraying everywhere. He honked his horn and "Yee Hawed," in celebration of diggin'. The thought struck me that Elder Jorgensen and I really were very different. When I had served with him, I thought the talk about his truck was kind of folksy and endearing, and I had seen his enthusiasm as a positive missionary tool. Now those two things combined were going to kill me. I held onto the door handle and tried to act as if I were having fun. I could see other cars along the road staring at us as we spun donut after donut in the dirt. I was surprised that Doran wasn't too dizzy to drive. He had obviously done this before. He kept on turning, picking up speed.

I was just about to suggest we move on to something less noisy and mind-numbing, when I shifted in my seat and accidentally pushed the handle on the door. Like a Pringles can, it popped open, blowing me out. I flew through the air and onto the hard dirt ground, crumbling into a six-foot-two bent-up heap of human.

My head hurt. Earth exploded all around me as my mind began to grow dark. The last thing I remembered was the sound of Elder Jorgensen's musical truck horn playing "La Cucaracha."

II

KICKING 'EM
WHEN THEY FALL
DOWN

NOVEMBER 25TH

The person who invented hospital food must have been a patient himself, admitted because he was an abnormality of nature and had no taste buds. I pushed my piece of turkey away in unsavory disgust.

This was the worst Thanksgiving ever.

I had attempted to be gracious by telling Grace and my family that they should not bother about me and to go on and celebrate at home.

The nerve of them to listen.

I had been in the hospital for over four days now. The concussion that I had sustained by falling out of Elder Jorgensen's truck left me in pretty bad shape. Today was actually the first day that I had begun to feel almost normal again. After I had been thrown out of the truck,

Doran rushed me over to the hospital where I had lain unconscious for days. When I had come out of it, Doran was leaning over me, shaving the hair on the right side of my head.

"What are you doing?" I whispered.

"Don't worry," he said. "Just rest."

I should have worried. When I really came out of it a day later, one side of my head was bald. I would have been completely bald if it hadn't been for a nurse stopping him mid-strand. Doran claimed he was just trying to help, shaving my head in case they needed to perform surgery.

I was so glad Doran had come to Southdale to visit me.

Grace had spent all of her evenings by my bedside. She read to me and talked to me even though my side of the conversation was often lacking. She would tell me all about her job and how Brother Taylor, or Noah, as she had taken to calling him, was really working hard to get this town up to speed.

Doran felt so bad about everything that he had decided to stick around until I was completely better. He had also been kind enough to volunteer to take Grace to and from work each day.

According to my sister Margaret, Grace was beginning to fit in. The ward had really come around ever since Noah Taylor had given her a job. The only person who was still having a hard time was my mother. She just could not accept the fact that Grace might someday be her daughter-in-law. I'm sure my father would have been struggling with it too, if it weren't for the fact that he still wasn't around. He would call my mother every few days to let her know that he was all right, but he wouldn't say what he was up to, and he wasn't rushing home. It wasn't that big of a deal to my mom; business was business, and if providing for the family meant that he had to be away for a couple of weeks, then so be it. That was all well and good, but I couldn't help thinking it was awful strange for him not to come home for Thanksgiving.

Thanksgiving afternoon, Doran brought Grace over for a visit. Then he left us alone so we could speak.

Grace looked great. Southdale seemed to sit well with her. She was wearing faded jeans and a smile that seemed to suggest she still liked me, regardless of my half-missing hair and attractive gown.

"You look good," she said, sitting down on the side of my bed.

"Not as good as you," I replied.

Grace leaned over and kissed me. Despite my hospital breath we both seemed to enjoy it.

"I'm sorry about all this," I offered. "I was supposed to be helping you adjust to Southdale."

"Doran's helping," she said.

"Doran's the reason I'm here."

Grace's red hair looked so dark that day. She had also cut it a few inches shorter. The way the ends of it lay across her dark T-shirt had me fixated. A sense of something washed over me. Grace was changing on me, and it was no longer subtle. Like a dam that was bursting after years of a slow leak, she wasn't holding back anymore. A personality, a presence that had been stored away all these years was emerging in full force. She wasn't the same person I had known in Thelma's Way. It scared the heck out of me—she was already more than I could comprehend, and the possibility of where she could end up blew me away. At the same time, it thrilled me beyond words.

"Well, I shouldn't stay long," Grace said. "Your mother wants me to help her with something, plus Doran needs to speak to you for a moment alone."

"He's not carrying any razors is he?"

Grace laughed.

"Have they told you yet when you get to go home?"

"Hopefully in a couple days."

"I can't wait," Grace smiled, her pink lips causing my monitors to jump.

She leaned over and kissed me again.

"I think I love you," I said.

"I thought you might," she whispered, giving me her standard reply.

Grace slipped out of the room and Doran came in. He shut the door and pulled up a chair beside me.

"Hey," he said, straddling the chair backwards, his long legs pushing his knees up to his chin.

"Hey," I said, wishing that I was still talking to Grace.

"You feeling better?"

"A little."

"Sorry about the hair," he apologized.

"It'll grow back."

"That's where you're lucky," he tried to joke. "Mine's thinning out, never to return."

I pretended as if I hadn't noticed.

"You okay?" I asked him, noting that he seemed a little nervous.

"Actually, Trust, there is something I wanted to talk to you about."

"All right."

"I don't think you'll think so."

"What is it?"

"Well, I feel real bad about what happened to you. Real bad. You know you were my favorite companion and everything. I learned more from you than anyone else."

"Thanks."

"You're welcome. Now here you are in the hospital because of me. I shouldn't have taken those seat belts out."

"These things happen," I consoled.

"I'm glad you feel that way. Anyhow, I really do think that things happen for a purpose. God doesn't stir something up for nothing. I had an uncle that got hit by lightning and lost his sight. Two weeks later he got hit by a car and passed away. My mom's always thought that God took his sight away so he wouldn't see it coming. Do you understand what I'm trying to say?"

"I think so," I lied.

"Good," he said with some relief. "Well, I think something good might just come out of all this."

"Are you thinking of something specific?" I asked.

"Actually, now that you mention it, there is one thing. You know I've been wanting to help you out," he rambled. "I just feel awful about all this."

"You said that."

"I helped your mom with that garage door you were fixing."

"Thanks."

"Don't mention it," he said with a faint smile. "I took Abel shooting with his BB gun. We didn't hit anything, but there was some bonding going on."

"He's a good kid," I said, wishing he would get to his point.

"I've been driving Grace to and from work."

"That's great."

"There's more. It seems as if I have fallen in love with her," he said quickly. "I didn't mean for it to happen, but what could I do. Her, me, driving back and forth in my truck. I'm only human."

I couldn't believe what I was hearing. It was like Donald Duck saying he now liked Minnie Mouse. He had no right—Minnie belonged to Mickey. The analogy wasn't that great, but I was on a lot of medication at the moment.

"Did something happen between you and Grace?" I asked, dumbfounded.

"Oh, no," he insisted. "I haven't even touched her."

"Have you talked to her about this?"

"Nope. She's usually too busy talking about you."

I breathed a sigh of relief.

"Well, I'm glad you brought this up," I exhaled dramatically. "I guess it might be best if you just went back to Idaho before your feelings get too strong for her. I'm sure my mother can get Grace to and from work. Besides, I won't be in here that much longer."

Doran just stared at me.

"You *are* leaving?" I asked.

"Trust, I don't know how your parents raised you, but my folks have always told me to follow the prophet. And the prophet has said that every young returned missionary shouldn't waste any time getting married."

"But he didn't tell you to marry my girlfriend."

"Maybe not exactly."

"Doran."

"I love Grace, Trust. I didn't come here right now to bow out, I came here to tell you of my intentions. I plan to marry Grace in the Idaho Falls Temple as soon as she says yes."

"Is this a joke?" I asked, beginning to get a little bothered by it all.

"This is no joke, and those are my intentions," he said, standing.

"Grace is my girlfriend," I debated. "She came here so that the two of us could figure out our future together."

"Things change," he said firmly. "I just thought I had better be honest with you about all this. I'd better go."

"But . . ."

He was gone. It was the most ridiculous thing I had ever heard. Elder Jorgensen and Grace. The idea was so absurd that I wanted to laugh. The phone in the room rang. I picked it up to find my mother on the other end.

"Trust, is Grace still there?" she asked.

"No," I answered. "She just left with Doran. Why?"

"Nothing really," she answered guiltily.

"Mom, what is Grace going to help you with this afternoon?" A growing sense of concern was coming over me.

"I suppose I can let you know now," Mom gave in. "The missionaries in our ward are looking for people to practice their discussions on. I thought Grace would be perfect. They should be here in a few minutes."

My mother was so sneaky.

"Mom, just because Grace fell for me while I was serving a mission doesn't mean she's going to fall in love with one of those elders."

"Trust, I'm just trying to help Elder Nicks and Elder Minert learn their discussions."

"Mom, they've both been out for over a year and a half," I argued. "I'm sure they know their discussions by now."

"Elder Nicks is from Arkansas."

"What's that supposed to mean?"

"All I'm saying is that Arkansas is a lot closer to Tennessee than here."

I'm sure that in my mom's mind this all made perfect sense.

"Grace is going to know exactly what you are trying to do, Mom."

"Trust, I don't think it's very nice of you to second-guess your mother."

"So where are they going to teach her?" I asked.

"I thought I'd let them do it in the den, it's much more private."

"Mom."

"I'll keep the door cracked," she defended.

"You're not going to sit in with them?"

"Oh, I'd just be a fourth wheel."

"Mom, I'm in love with Grace."

"I'm sure you think you are. I'd better go," she said. "I wanted to warm up some leftovers for the elders. Happy Thanksgiving, Son," she added.

Click.

This was just perfect. First Doran was staking claim, and now my mother was throwing our poor missionaries into the pot.

A nurse came in and messed with my IV for a bit. I asked her for extra drugs and she didn't even smile.

The world was a cold, cruel place.

The nurse left, and a few moments later I heard a soft knock on the door.

"Come in," I said dejectedly.

In walked Lucy Fall.

If Moses himself had come to visit I could not have been more surprised.

"Lucy? Is that you?"

"Hello, Trust," she said, her demeanor softer and more subdued than I had ever remembered. "Can I come in?" she asked.

I should never have said yes.

12

CONTRITION

◈

Lucy Fall moved through the hospital doors and out into the November cold. She pulled her wool scarf tightly around her neck and breathed in deeply. Thanksgiving had turned out a little different than she had predicted. Of course, the entire month of November had not gone as previously planned. For the first time in her life Lucy was having to adjust to change.

The divorce was already going through. Lance didn't want to waste any time getting it all over with. Apparently he had other matters on his mind. Brunette matters. Lucy was as anxious as he was to finish it. She wanted nothing more than to be done with Lance. He had been a bad decision, with a costly outcome.

Lucy found out from a friend about Trust's accident, and that he was staying at the Southdale University Hospital. For the last few days she had wanted to stop by and visit him, but it had never felt right until today. She wanted to tell him how sorry she was about all that she had put him through, and apologize for the way that she had treated him in the past. Her intentions were forgiveness.

Bare trees twisted in the wind as Lucy crossed the street and approached the parking lot. A few leftover leaves swirled around her feet like they were connected with string. She reached her car and got inside quickly. The wild air howled, angry over her getting away.

Even in the hospital gown and with a half a head of hair, Trust looked good. He represented everything Lucy had given up and now wished to have back. He had been glad to see her, fumbling even.

Lucy had forgotten about the effect she had on him.

Lucy hung her head as she sat there in her car. Once again the tears came. Her shoulders shook and her eyes poured. As she had done so often in the past weeks, she just let it happen, feeling better after it passed.

Things were changing for Lucy, and this time possibly for the better. It seemed as if for the first time in her life she was recognizing a real soul within herself.

Was that possible?

Lucy had no real intention of taking Trust back. She had heard that he was interested in a red-headed girl named Grace whom he had met on his mission.

Funny, Lucy thought, Trust had not even brought this Grace girl up tonight.

Lucy started her car and slowly pulled out and away.

13

INFILTRATION

Roger passed the potatoes and smiled. He had never seen so much food in his entire life. Mounds of it rolled over the table like foamy waves. Bowls the size of bathtubs were bursting with cheese-covered confections and piles of meat. His eyes sized it up as his stomach trembled. This was his third Thanksgiving dinner for the day.

"Are you certain no one else will be joining us?" he asked Sister Watson for the second time.

"Certain." She smiled. "Just you and me. Now, where was I? Oh, yes, when I turned twelve my mother changed my name from Cindy to Melinda."

"I thought your name was Mavis?" Roger asked.

"That's a whole other story," Sister Watson replied. "We'll go into that later."

Roger Williams tried to remain calm. These last couple of weeks had not been easy for him. He had thought that it would be so simple to just walk in, find the Book of Mormon, and walk out. That had not been the case. It had taken him two days just to locate Thelma's Way. And now here he was after weeks of combing the town with nothing to show for it. He had had some success in convincing the locals that the book really wasn't worth that much and that they had been misinformed about its real value, but that was it. He could not comprehend how his son Trust had managed to live so long among these backward people. There had been moments when he even considered just giving up his quest, but he wanted that first edition Book of Mormon. And he felt confident that once he located it, he could talk whoever had it out of it for next to nothing.

He could afford to hang on a little longer.

The locals had allowed him to use an upstairs room in the Thelma's Way boardinghouse. It wasn't too bad a setup from which to operate. He had drawn out maps and prioritized the people in town most likely to help him find the elusive first edition.

Most everyone in the area believed the Book of Mormon was still around. Roswell Ford had informed him that the entire town was watching each other closely for clues. But President Heck thought maybe the heavens had taken it back, just like they did the golden plates.

Roger was betting on Roswell's theory.

The search continued. Information wasn't hard to extract because these people loved to talk. Plus, Roger had made it even easier for them to do so by tearing a small piece of paper up, writing the word "Press" on it, and sticking it in the brim of his hat on his way into town.

Everyone bought it.

Roger claimed he was a reporter from out west, one who was looking to chronicle the history of Thelma's Way in a book. Not a single person in Thelma's Way was shocked by this. Most folks wondered why it had taken the west so long to come around.

He had made no mention of the connection between him and Trust. He didn't want to complicate things by having people get sentimental and nostalgic on him. It was obvious, however, that Thelma's Way loved his son. Roger found himself growing proud of the boy he had grown so distant from.

" . . . I think you should dedicate an entire chapter—no, section—to the pageant that I wrote and . . ." Sister Watson was blabbering.

A sudden knock at the door silenced her for a moment.

"Well, who in the . . ." Sister Watson mumbled as she got up, more than mildly bothered by the interruption.

Sister Watson was decked out. She had on her nicest dress and her best-fitting wig. She was also wearing more makeup than a non-circus performer should be allowed to wear. Her attempts to impress Roger Williams were going unnoticed, however, and now someone had the gall to disturb their conversation.

She stepped to the door and flung it open. Framed by the weather-worn doorjamb was Toby Carver, holding a plate of food and wiggling his neck to look around her into the house.

"I've got company, Toby," Sister Watson insisted.

Toby ignored her by stepping inside. "Thought I might bring something by for Mr. Williams here," he explained.

Roger turned in his seat to face him.

"We've plenty of food," Sister Watson scolded.

"Well, I also just thought of something that might interest Mr. Williams."

"What is it?" Roger asked, setting his fork down.

"Well, you was asking 'bout that Book of Mormon, and where to find it."

"Yes," Roger said with excitement. "Did you find it?"

"Sort of," Toby bragged.

"Sort of?" Roger demanded.

"Well, not that exact one, but I went down to the church in Virgil's Find and borrowed one of their extra copies for you. Them's the same words inside."

Toby Carver handed an inexpensive blue-covered Book of Mormon over to Roger.

"I marked a couple of my favorite parts for you," Toby said proudly.

Roger forced a smile. It took everything he had inside not blow up in Toby's face. The last thing he needed was a worthless modern copy of the Book of Mormon. These people were impossible.

"Thanks," he managed to say. "But it would really make my history of your town complete if I could see, or maybe take a picture of, the real first edition."

"It's lost," Toby informed him.

"I know that," Roger said, frustrated. "But I'm sure someone could find it."

"Yes, Toby," Sister Watson said. "Why don't you go look for it and leave Mr. Williams and me alone."

"If I found it, could I hold it up for the picture?" Toby asked.

"Of course," Roger brightened. "In fact, you tell everyone that whoever finds it, I'll put their picture on the front of the book."

"The front?" Toby asked reverently.

"The front," Roger punctuated.

Toby Carver smiled, slowly took two steps backwards, and raced off.

"That book will turn up now, sure as rain," Sister Watson said. "Who in their right mind wouldn't trade a dusty old book for the chance to be on the cover of a new one?"

Roger Williams smiled. Things were looking up.

14

DIZZY

NOVEMBER 26TH

The next morning the doctor informed me that I should be able to go home within 24 hours. I was ecstatic. I had been a little concerned about the whole Doran-and-Grace thing. Not that I thought she would actually leave me for him, not that he was a real threat, but it just made me nervous to have a gung-ho returned missionary spending all his time in pursuit of my girlfriend while I was chained to an IV.

Grace dropped by Friday afternoon after work. She sat on the edge of the bed and read to me from the newspaper for a while. It was one of the nicest moments of my life. Then she proceeded to bring me up to speed on the ward's current events.

Noah was continuing to drum up sales for his food storage time-share, and Grace was beginning to speak about him in far too glowing terms. Apparently everyone was really happy he was around. Everyone except Leonard Vastly, that is. Two weeks ago, Leonard Vastly had been singing Noah Taylor's praises—not anymore. Word on the ward was that Brother Vastly was beginning to feel Noah Taylor was encroaching on his status as the number one hoarder in Southdale. Brother Vastly did not like that. He had worked long and hard to be known as "That crazy man with all the food." Too hard to let some yahoo from southern Utah with a fancy warehouse come in and bump him from power. So, in an effort to one-up his new rival, Brother Vastly had completely sealed off his single-wide trailer with heavy clear plastic tarps and duct tape, vowing not to come out until the first phase of his food storage ran out. After a couple of hours, he had been forced to cut an air hole, but aside from that minor glitch he had completely cut himself off from the world. He called it his "Bio-Doom." He was funding his little project by collecting his retirement ten years early. He hated to give up his livelihood, but some things were worth it—this was for the betterment of society. Grace told me he kept the curtains on his bay window open so that scientists and interested civilians could study and watch him in this great endeavor of self-reliance. No one had complained about him taping up his house, but a couple of his neighbors protested the open-curtain policy. Now, by order of the mayor, his curtains were to remain closed after six in the evening. No one wanted to know *that* much about him. Brother Vastly communicated to the outside world via ham radio and hand signals.

"Won't come out at all?" I asked in amazement.

"That's what he signaled," Grace replied.

Grace told me all about the missionaries who had come

over to practice their discussions on her. According to her, my mother could not have been more obvious about her intentions if she had tried. She had played soft music on the home stereo and served hot cocoa with chocolate mints while they taught Grace the discussion. Elder Nicks and Elder Minert were a little embarrassed, but they had been good sports.

"So, I guess they won't be coming back?" I asked.

"Actually," Grace said, "I was hoping I could hear the rest of the lessons. With you by my side, of course. I don't know if Thelma's Way really afforded me the chance to learn much about the Church."

"How about if I teach them to you myself," I offered.

"You'd get too distracted," she smiled.

"Hmmm," I mused, staring at her.

Grace stood up, signaling that it was time for her to go.

"How are you getting home?" I questioned.

"The bus."

"So did Doran tell you?" I asked.

"About being in love with me?" She smiled.

I nodded.

"Not in so many words, but this morning at six o'clock he was outside my window singing."

"You're kidding?"

"No," Grace laughed. "Wendy threw one of her cats at him. He got pretty scratched up. Then when he drove me to work, he kept playing country slow songs and looking over at me. I thought maybe it would be best if I learned how to use the bus system."

"Sorry about him," I apologized.

"He's harmless enough," Grace brushed it off. "He kind of reminds me of Leo back home."

I hadn't thought about it, but Doran and Leo Tip did have a lot in common.

"You just have this effect on men," I smiled.

"Boys," Grace joked while leaning over to kiss me.

She kissed me longer than usual. I'm sure I would have resisted, but I was a helpless patient strapped to a hospital bed.

Saturday morning I was released from the hospital. For insurance purposes, I had to ride in a wheelchair to the front door where the nurse then dumped me out and wished me well.

My mom and Grace had come to pick me up. Grace helped me into the car as if I were an invalid grandfather.

"I'm really okay," I insisted.

"Let me help," she said, slipping her arms around me.

I obliged. I was happy to be going home.

15

SIGNS O' STRESS

That night, before bed, I sat in the kitchen watching my mother reiron my father's shirts. She carefully went over each one. She would take one from its hanger, lay it across the ironing board, and press down on it as hard as she possibly could.

"They get wrinkly just from hanging," she fussed.

"Mom, are you going to be all right?" I asked.

"I'm fine," she insisted. "Happy as a . . . happy as a clam."

"No news from Dad?"

"Oh, I'm sure he'll call when he gets a chance." She pressed so hard with the iron that I thought she would rip the shirt. "You know how busy he gets."

"Busy doing what?"

"Business stuff."

"Where?"

"Honestly, Trust, what's with all the questions?"

"I just think it's weird that Dad's been away for so long.

He missed Margaret's recital, and Abel's play, and Thanksgiving."

"He was there in spirit," Mom pointed out. "Besides, if I recall correctly, a certain someone else missed those things as well."

"I was in the hospital," I defended.

"And your father is on business."

"Mom, who are you trying to protect?" I argued.

She set the iron down and steam hissed out angrily. "Trust, there are things about marriage you can't yet understand," she said harshly.

"I'm not fifteen," I pointed out.

"You just don't understand how your father and I operate."

"So tell me."

"This isn't the time, Trust."

"You know, I can remember a time when you and Dad were different," I told her.

"I'm ironing," my mother said, as if she were eating a good meal and I had just begun to talk about some graphic surgery.

"I really thought Dad would come around while I was serving my mission," I said reflectively. "Do you know that he only wrote me four letters the entire time?"

"He works very hard to keep this family comfortable," she defended.

"You don't look so comfortable," I observed.

"Trust!" she said, slamming down the iron. "I don't appreciate you talking to me like this."

"I just meant that with all the things you and Dad can afford, our family still seems lacking."

It was no use. I had lost her. Mom had slipped into her "I'm not going to talk about anything emotional" mode.

"So how is Grace liking the missionary lessons?" she asked.

"Actually," I sighed, "I wanted to talk to you about that too."

"Abel's getting tall, isn't he?" she said, blatantly changing the subject again and focusing only on the shirt in front of her.

I stood up, kissed my mother on the cheek, and went to bed.

16

THE PROBLEM WITH WIDOWERS

NOVEMBER 28TH

Sunday morning we all rode together in my mother's van to church. Grace had even talked Wendy into coming with us. She and Wendy had really gotten along well, despite their age difference. I think Grace was happy to have a woman to talk to, and Wendy was thrilled to have anyone to talk to. The only other time Wendy had ever come to church with us was for my mission farewell over two and a half years ago. I had forgotten what she looked like in a dress. Common courtesy prevented me from laughing.

When we pulled up to the building, the parking lot was already full. Cars and minivans covered the ground like bulky sequins on a black rug. As we were walking into the building it became obvious that folks no longer feared or felt bad about Grace. Everyone would greet my mother, comment about my half-shaved head, and then trip over themselves to say hi to Grace. I couldn't believe it.

"What did you do to these people?" I asked Grace quietly.

"They just feel sorry for me," she brushed it off.

Wendy didn't really want to go into the chapel, so she decided to stay out in the foyer and sit on the soft, boxy couches. When I told her that the foyer was sort of reserved for parents with fussy children, she told me she loved kids. When I reminded her that she really didn't like children, she told me that her opinion of children had changed ever since she saw that one movie about that one kid that saved that whale. I decided not to reason with her any further.

Grace and I entered the chapel and picked out a private pew on the side. It would have been a nice place to observe the meeting, but Sister Cravitz walked over and insisted that we join her.

Sister Cravitz was the Thicktwig Ward's unofficial mother. She watched over and kept track of every part and person within our fold. She felt most comfortable with her big nose wedged forcefully into everyone's business. She wasn't a pretty woman, but she wouldn't have made a completely ugly man. She styled her hair in a tight bun that was flat and perfectly round. She wore huge orthopedic shoes and the same skirt every week, alternating it with her rose-colored blouse that matched, and her orange-colored one that didn't. Sister Cravitz had celebrated her sixty-ninth birthday about a month ago. She had no kids, and her husband was buried in the Southdale Memorial

Park right next to the maintenance shed. Although Sister Cravitz made it her business to be involved in others' lives, it was generally understood that she didn't like people.

Now here she was, doing an uncharacteristic thing like inviting Grace and me to sit next to her during church. I was shocked. Two weeks ago she had acted as if Grace were a virus sent to infect us, and now she was letting her sit closer to her than she had usually allowed her husband to sit. It must have been because she felt pity for me and my recent accident.

It's fun to pretend.

I knew full well it had everything to do with Grace. I was amazed. It had taken me almost the entire two years of my mission to recognize the effect Grace had on me, and here she had been in Southdale for only a few weeks and people were already falling all over themselves to get to know her. After we were seated, Sister Cravitz pulled out her change purse that was filled with white Tic-Tacs, and offered us some. I took only one, not wanting to appear greedy. Once again I was astounded—Sister Cravitz didn't share her Tic-Tacs with just anyone. The only time I could even remember her doing so was when she had been forced to sit by Brother Vastly in Sunday School during one of his garlic health blitzes. Of course she didn't actually give him Tic-Tacs—she threw them at him.

Sister Cravitz took a Tic-Tac for herself and then snapped the clip shut on her coin purse. She sucked the marrow out of the mint, and then turned toward Grace.

"I hear you're doing wonders for Brother Taylor," she said. "I'm not quick to hand out compliments, but I'm usually first to say 'job well done' when the task at hand is accomplished properly."

"Thank you," Grace said.

"Being prepared is a mighty task," Sister Cravitz lectured. "A mighty task indeed. This city has got a real leg up on adversity thanks to Noah Taylor. What are you most frightened of, dear? Drought, or fire?"

"Both," Grace answered politically.

"How about you, Trust? What do you fear most?"

I paused for a moment to give the appearance of contemplation.

"No need to answer," she insisted. "I can read your mind."

I was just about to apologize for what I was thinking when she guessed . . .

"Fire."

"You're right." I played along.

Sister Cravitz smiled and pulled out her coin purse again. Suddenly we were her best friends.

Sister Morris began to wrap up the prelude music and Bishop Leen stepped up to the pulpit. He ran his light fingers through his faded hair and pushed his skin-colored lips to the microphone.

I looked at my program to see how the meeting would run today. There was one youth speaker, Jeffy Smith; a musical number by the Rose kids; and a nonyouth speaker, Noah Taylor. I looked up at the stage to see if I could spot Grace's employer, but from our position, I couldn't see anyone sitting on the other side of the pulpit. I wanted to meet Brother Taylor and thank him for everything he had done for Grace. I still wasn't convinced he was as honest as everyone said he was, but the positive effects he had had on my girlfriend were worth setting aside any personal misgivings.

Doran came in the far doors and sat down across the room from us. Coming in five minutes late had allowed him to make something of a dramatic entrance. He was still pursuing Grace. It was as if the heavens had commanded him to persevere. He was that committed. The fact that Grace had made her feelings for me clear made no difference to him. In Thelma's Way, with him as my junior companion, I had been so happy about the strength of his will. Now it was beginning to make me uncomfortable. Doran had moved into a small apartment across town and sent Grace a copy of his personal mission statement. I couldn't remember the whole thing, but a couple of lines still stood stiffly in my mind.

". . . I will better myself by loving you. I will seek to find resolution by committing myself to the idea of being eternally proactive with my lady . . ."

Doran was wearing a gray suit that accentuated his gangly figure. He had on a cowboy tie and boots that he had tucked the legs of his pants into. His spiky hair was gelled down and parted perfectly in the middle. He looked at us from across the room and sighed. I felt sorry for him. I knew what it was like to love Grace from afar. I could only imagine how hard it would be to know that she cared for someone else. I needed to be more compassionate with Doran.

After the sacrament was administered, the youth

speaker, Jeffy Smith, talked about honesty and how his aunt was in jail for mail fraud. I watched Sister Smith hide her head as her boy aired their dirty laundry without a thought. At least we knew he had written his own remarks. Jeffy then reported on the Scouts' last camp out and announced that anyone who may have ended up with an extra mess kit needed to return it before his big brother found out he had borrowed it.

Amen, I think.

The Rose children sang "In My Father's House Are Many Mansions." It was a lovely number, but as it progressed I could hear Brother and Sister Carp growing angry in the pew behind us. It was no secret that the Carps and the Roses didn't really get along. The Roses were a very well-to-do family. Brother Rose was a partner with one of the largest law firms in the state. He was also the school board president, and had been elected Father of the Year twice. His family drove the nicest cars, had the nicest house, and were constantly talking about their huge summer home in Wyoming. Well, Brother Carp didn't have a summer home. In fact, thanks to a bad business deal, he and his family were back living with his parents in their duplex. Brother Carp claimed it was temporary and that they were only going to stay with his folks until he could get his financial feet back on the ground. Well, that was two years ago. Now, instead of looking for work, he chose to pick apart those who actually had some—Brother Rose being his favorite target. The Roses had tried to get along with the Carps but whatever they tried seemed to backfire. So Brother and Sister Carp continued to grow more and more bitter, biting at the Roses whenever possible and finding offense in nearly everything they did. Now here were the young Rose children singing "In My Father's House Are Many Mansions." Brother Carp missed the analogy completely, thinking that the Roses were simply bragging about their summer home. He stood up and stormed out.

I took a moment to self-righteously contemplate how someone could possibly be so offended by something so simple.

The Rose children finished singing and sat down. I watched someone get up and walk to the podium. I watched that same someone claim that his name was Noah Taylor and that he was happy to be speaking today. There had to be some kind of a mistake! This man didn't look like a Noah Taylor—he looked more like a Mr. "I'm everything every woman could ever want in a man and then some." The Noah Taylor I had imagined was a gray-haired old man from Manti, Utah. A widower with a bad hip, a long beard, and a tendency to go on and on about how rotten our society had become. You know, Noah . . . Noah Taylor. What stood before me was something altogether different.

"That's Brother Taylor?" I whispered to Grace, hoping the answer would be anything but what I knew it was.

"That's Noah," Grace said without taking her eyes off him.

This was just awful. Noah Taylor was a good-looking man. He had short brown hair that seemed just clean-cut enough to indicate that he was orderly, and just tousled enough to show that he wasn't worried about what others thought. He wore a sweater with a tie that only a woman would pick out. He looked to have a few years on my twenty-three. I suspected he was pretty close to thirty. He smiled and made a bad joke about food storage that every member of the congregation laughed at.

I didn't think I liked Noah Taylor.

"I thought you said he was widowed," I said.

"His wife died a year and a half ago." Grace frowned. "Isn't it sad?"

I was grieving.

Noah talked all about the last days, and how God was hoping that we were watching for Him. He laughed, he cried, and he convinced even me that he was too good to be true. He pitched his effort to prepare everyone, pleading with the members to let him help organize them.

After sacrament meeting was over, Grace insisted that I meet Noah personally. She dragged me up onto the stage to wait at the end of the line. I ran my fingers though my half-missing hair, hoping he would think it was some sort of cool new style and knowing that he probably wouldn't. Every woman in the ward was frantically trying to thank Brother Taylor for his inspiring words. Our neighbor, Sister Lewis, was talking with such animation to him that she seemed to spit all over everyone. Sister Cravitz hugged him twice, and Sister Johnson spent a good four minutes questioning him about the shelf life of chocolate drink mix vs. fruit punch. Eventually the adoring throngs thinned out and Grace and I approached.

"Grace," he said with far too familiar an inflection. "How'd I do?"

"Great," she replied. "I wanted you to meet Trust."

I stuck out my hand to say, "Hey."

"It's nice to finally meet you, Trust," he said as if on cue.

"Likewise." I nodded.

"Grace has sure been a lifesaver at the warehouse," he complimented. "Thanks for bringing her out here."

"I thought you were old," was my only response.

"Well, I feel old," Noah said, looking at me queerly.

"Probably not as old as I thought you were," I said kindly.

"How old did you think I was?"

"I don't know," I said, sincerely trying to sound friendly. "I sort of pictured you looking like Moses, or Colonel Sanders."

"The chicken guy?" Noah asked. "Is that how Grace has been describing me?" He laughed.

"Trust really hit his head hard when he fell out of that truck." Grace playfully defended me.

"Well, I'm glad to see you're feeling better," Noah said perfectly. "I'd better run now," he added. "Sister Treat wants me to look at her wheat."

He was smooth.

Noah walked down from the podium, shaking people's hands and patting them on their backs. The confidence the guy radiated couldn't be contained on the North American continent, let alone in the room. I couldn't believe that someone with the first name of Noah could be so suave. Grace smiled at me knowingly.

"Colonel Sanders, huh?" She laughed.

"What?"

"You're not jealous, are you?"

"Me jealous of him? I mean, just because he's good-looking and sort of stylish. . . ."

"He does look nice today, doesn't he," Grace reflected. Darn that sweater.

"I'm just wondering why you never mentioned what he looked like before."

"I didn't think it was important," she teased. "Besides, you know I'm not really into good-looking guys."

"Thanks," I martyred, as we began to walk down from the stand.

I was going to go on and on about how hurt I was, milking it for all it was worth, when suddenly there was Lucy. I actually hollered, making myself look guilty.

"Ahhhhh!"

"Hello, Trust," Lucy said, obviously pleased by my reaction.

Lucy looked great. No, better than great. She looked as if she had tossed aside her old self and was now emerging as something completely new and fascinating. Her blue eyes had been so shallow, but now they looked deep and cloudy. I could tell that the last little while had really worked her over and was forcing her to look at life differently.

"Lucy, what are you doing here?" I asked, still startled and standing in front of Grace as if to hide her. It was a bad move.

"I'm back in my parents' home," Lucy informed us.

"They'll be out of the country for another month still. I wanted to come to church so badly. Lance didn't really approve of me going."

Grace squeezed my arm harder than necessary as she stepped out from behind me.

"Oh, yes," I fumbled. "Lucy, I would like you to meet Grace Heck. Grace, this is Lucy Fall. She's an old friend of mine."

"Nice to meet you," Lucy said dispassionately.

"Nice to meet you, Lucy," Grace replied kindly.

I thought now would have been a good time to end this discussion, but Lucy felt otherwise.

"Well, Trust, you look better than you did the other day," she commented, digging my grave by big, huge shovelfuls. "Your hair's growing back nicely."

"The other day?" Grace inquired.

I tried lamely to cover my tracks. "Didn't I tell you about Lucy stopping by the hospital?"

"I don't remember you mentioning that." Grace smiled.

"I just stopped by to say hi to Trust," Lucy explained. "Ever since Lance left, I've been so lonely. When I heard that Trust was in the hospital, I thought it might help me feel better to visit an old friend."

"Who left?" Grace asked.

"My husband, Lance," Lucy said sorrowfully. "Or I guess I should say my ex-husband. The divorce has already gone through."

"I'm sorry to hear that," Grace consoled.

"It's better this way," Lucy sighed. "Well, I should get

going," she added. "I just wanted to say hi again, and thank you for cheering me up."

"No problem," I lied.

"It was nice meeting you, Grace."

"You too, Lucy. I hope things work out for you."

Lucy managed a smile.

Grace stood there still holding my arm tightly as Lucy walked away. I was in for it. I had meant to tell Grace about Lucy, but it had slipped my mind. There was no way I could ever be interested in Lucy again. She was just an old friend who needed some comfort. It would be wrong of me to simply abandon those in need because they were beautiful ex-girlfriends that I used to obsess over.

"She seems nice," Grace said coyly as we both watched Lucy wander off.

"I meant to tell you about her stopping by the hospital," I tried.

"I'm sure you did."

"Seriously."

"I believe you," Grace toyed with me. "That's too bad about her marriage."

"Isn't it," I said, trying to sound sincere.

"She sure is pretty," Grace observed. "She's even more beautiful than her picture."

"I hadn't noticed," I said, quickly adding, "and what picture have you seen of her? I don't remember ever having shown you one."

"There was one in your house."

"Where?"

"That's not important," Grace insisted.

"Seriously," I persisted. "I didn't know we had one around."

"There's that one," Grace said. "On that table by the nook."

"Oh," I said, not realizing that we had a nook.

"So were you trying to hide me from Lucy?" Grace asked accusingly as she moved on. "You're not embarrassed by me, are you?"

"No," I said, slower than I should have. "It was just a reflex. Like a spasm or something."

"A spasm?"

"Or something."

"Oh."

"Really, I get them all the time."

"How attractive," Grace joked.

"I mean they're not real noticeable."

"We'd better get to Sunday School," Grace said, changing the subject. "Wendy's probably still waiting in the foyer."

As we walked out of the chapel, Wendy was nowhere to be seen, but Doran was waiting for us. He stepped up and addressed Grace.

"Hello, Doran," she replied.

"Grace, I was wondering if you would accompany me to Sunday School?" He stuck his arm out eagerly for her to latch on.

"Actually—" Grace began to say.

"I know you're still seeing Trust," he interrupted. "But I'm just asking for thirty minutes of your time. If you don't feel differently about me after that, then I'll try another approach."

"Doran, don't you think this is a little—" I was interrupted.

"You know," Grace said, "maybe I'll take you up on that, Doran. Trust needs a little time to think about his reflexes."

Grace took Doran's arm and walked off down the hall. I stood there in the now-empty foyer feeling like a pair of glasses on a blind man—worthless. The two full-time missionaries, Elder Nicks and Elder Minert, came down the hall and walked up to me.

"Have you seen Grace Heck?" Elder Minert asked.

"No, why?" I asked despondently.

"My companion wants to get her address so he can write her when he gets home."

Elder Nicks blushed.

"She went that way." I pointed.

The two elders skipped off toward the Relief Society/gospel doctrine classroom. I walked outside of the church building, across the street, and all the way home. When everyone got back from church, Grace went directly to Wendy's house without even stopping to check in on me. She also skipped our family dinner, not even bothering to call to inform us that she wasn't coming. When I walked over to her place later that night, Wendy gave me some lame excuse about Grace already having gone to bed.

I was beginning to worry.

17

A LITTLE CLOSER

◇

Few things had ever stirred up Thelma's Way as much at the offer of having their picture put on the front of a book did. Everyone was trying frantically to locate the missing Book of Mormon.

By default, Roger Williams was actually doing the town a great favor. For so long most of the members in the area had been inactive. Now everyone was asking President Heck for forgiveness, and begging him to be assigned to as many home teaching and visiting teaching families as possible. To the locals this seemed like the best way to get into people's homes to take a look around. People were showing up at each other's houses with pies and bread and lessons that required them to stay for a while. Folks were even teaching those that had already been taught, bringing the home teaching percentage to 140 percent, and visiting teaching to 112. In two days the attitude of the entire valley had changed. And in the process everyone was forgetting why they had stayed away from church. Sure, they all knew that the reason people were visiting them was because of the Book of Mormon, but they didn't care. It was just so nice to be getting along.

Sunday morning sacrament meeting was packed. The branch presidency had to call upon the members to bring lawn chairs and grain drums for people to sit on. They lined the aisles with makeshift seats and large quilts. They were sprawling out on the floor and sitting on each other's laps. Even the seats up around the podium were filled. President Heck sat with Toby Carver and Leo Tip looking out at the biggest crowd they had ever drawn. And Roger Williams sat on the other side of President Heck as the branch's guest of honor.

President Heck stood up and began the meeting. "Brothers and Sisters," he said. "Never in the history of Thelma's Way has there been so many members at one sacrament meeting. Now I ain't so backwards as to pretend why you're all here, but I'm sure God is happy to see you, even if it's greed that brought you in." President Heck cleared his throat and sniffed his nose.

"Now this last week was Thanksgiving," President Heck continued. "It's a time to remember the pioneers. I hope that while you were all eating you took just a tick to think about those poor people that founded this great country. I know I did. I also took time to think about each of you, and be thankful for your company. But I suppose I'm most thankful for my family. The wife can harp a bit, and Digby ain't doing as good in math as I'd like him to. But they're blood, and I'm grateful to 'em," he said elegantly.

"We miss Grace," he continued. "She didn't actually hang around the home as much as we'd like her to done do, but still we miss her. Why just last night Narlette was talking about her. Isn't that true, Narlette," President Heck asked out to his daughter in the crowd.

"Yes, Daddy," she hollered back.

"Kids can be so sweet sometimes," President Heck pointed out. "And I'd be mighty neglectful if I didn't say that we miss Elder Williams. That boy did more for this meadow than I care to recap. I don't think there is a soul here that didn't have some conversation or interaction with Elder Williams. He was good stock."

Roger Williams tried to stare passively out at the crowd. There had still not been a single person in Thelma's Way who had made the connection between him and Trust.

President Heck put both hands on the pulpit and straightened his arms. "I feel inspired to be honest with you," he went on. "This Book of Mormon thing makes me a little jittery. Not since I gave up smoking for the final time have I been so shaky about something. I don't really like us all smiling at each other just so that we can peek up our neighbors' knickers. But I feel a comfort knowing that this book-writing Roger Williams has the same last name as our Elder Williams. I know we're not supposed to be sniffing around for signs, but this one smells right. I figure if the Williams name has done us right once, then the Williams name will do us right twice."

The congregation began to whisper amongst themselves, commenting enthusiastically about how much sense this made.

After the services, Roger Williams headed back to the boardinghouse to rest in his room. He had a couple of hours before he needed to go over to Sister Teddy Yetch's home for dinner.

Roger's shoulders hung heavy as he walked. This whole thing was taking way too long, and each hour longer seemed to make things more complicated. He hoped with all his heart that it wouldn't be someone like President Heck, or Sister Watson, or Toby Carver, or Narlette, or CleeDee, or . . . he hoped that whoever found the Book of Mormon would be someone that he had not begun to grow attached to. Roger didn't know if he could honestly look them in the face and take it away.

This Thelma's Way was one strange place.

18

FOREWARNED

NOVEMBER 29TH

Monday morning I called Grace at 7:00 only to find out that she had caught the bus to work an hour ago, and that Wendy didn't take kindly to being woken up any hour earlier than eight.

Then I called Brother Hyrum Barns to see about the job he had promised me two weeks ago.

"Actually the position's filled, Trust," he explained.

"But I thought that—"

"I needed someone a week ago, and well, you were all banged up," he rationalized. "I didn't know if you would be able to handle the workload when you did get better."

"It's only paper filing," I laughed. "I could do that with my eyes closed."

"I'm just nervous about having someone who busted his head alphabetizing my files. I've already given the job to that tall boy from Idaho."

"Doran?"

110

"Don't blame me, Trust," Brother Barns pleaded. "I had an opening and Brother Victor filled it for me."

I didn't blame Brother Barns or Brother Victor—I blamed Doran. I hung up the phone and began to think about other possible jobs and how much Doran was complicating things. I could hear the doorbell ring downstairs. A few moments later my mother hollered at me to come down.

Bishop Leen was in the living room tapping his foot and glancing about.

"Hello, Trust," he noticed me.

"Bishop."

"I was wondering if I could visit with you a moment?" he asked.

I nodded and we sat.

"Normally this kind of thing would be handled by your elders quorum president, but he was scared to tell you."

"That bad, huh?" I asked, my blue eyes clouding.

"Well, it all depends on how you look at it. You see, Brother Leonard Vastly needs a home teacher, and no one's willing to do it. It seems that everyone sort of feels like Brother Vastly and Noah Taylor are enemies. And well, no one wants to give the appearance of siding with Leonard Vastly."

"And you think I do?" I asked.

"Well, Sister Cravitz said you seemed a little jealous of Noah Taylor yourself. You and Leonard would have something in common . . ."

"Why would I be jealous of Noah?" I asked.

"Now, I'm not saying jealous exactly. I'm just saying

that you're mad because he seems to have more going for him at the moment. Big business, great personality, plus he's been spending all that time with Grace. She really is an exceptional girl, by the way."

"Thanks."

"Anyhow, by your helping Leonard Vastly you would be showing Noah that you're not afraid to take a stand."

I couldn't believe what I was hearing.

"Bishop, I'd be glad to home teach Brother Vastly, but I'm not doing it to spite Noah. He seems like a nice enough guy."

"All right," the bishop winked. "That's what we'll tell the others."

"Really, I have nothing against Noah."

"I read you loud and clear."

"Actually, I don't think you do," I said, frustrated. "I'm happy that Grace is working for him."

"Denial's a hard pit to climb out of," Bishop Leen counseled.

I put my head in my hands and sighed. "Is Brother Vastly still living in his 'Bio-Doom'?" I asked.

"Unfortunately, yes," the bishop said, standing. "And he still vows to not come out until Noah Taylor is proven wrong. Of course, Sister Morris swears she saw him at the dollar movies the other night wearing a wig and fake glasses."

Things just kept getting better.

"So, will you accept the assignment?" the bishop asked.

"Of course," I replied.

"Good," he said, verbally slapping me on the back. "Now, is there anything else I can do for you?"

"Actually, yes."

"Shoot."

"Well, I was—"

"Hold on a moment," he interrupted. "Is this going to take real long? I'm due over at the planetarium for some indoor pruning."

"It shouldn't."

"Shoot."

"Well, Bishop, everything aside, doesn't this Brother Taylor thing bother you just a bit? I mean, should we really be putting ourselves into his hands? Food storage time-share? How much do we even know about this guy?"

"Listen, Trust," he said kindly. "I understand why you're worried. But I talked with Noah Taylor for a long time when he first came to town. I e-mailed his father who used to be a stake president. This December seventeenth thing is more of a gimmick than a genuine scare."

"That's not how the ward is acting."

"Trust," he tisked. "I've seen this before. Young men returning home from their missions to discover that everything running exactly the way it was before they left is suddenly wrong."

"It's not that," I protested. "I just don't think we should be putting our fate in Noah's hands."

"Nothing will happen on the seventeenth. Nothing except for everyone in our ward being completely prepared for what may actually come later on. Is that so bad?"

"I guess not. But don't you think people should have their stuff in their own homes?"

"Noah Taylor is only going to be around until the end of December," he lectured. "Southdale isn't his permanent home. He'll go on to some other town that's in need of preparation. I suspect right now he's just organizing our supplies in that warehouse for the time being. When he leaves, people will have to find a new place to store their stuff. This is a good thing, Trust."

"I hope so."

Bishop Leen looked at his watch. "I should be going. Good luck with Leonard Vastly. He's really a good guy, just a little weedy between the ears."

Ten minutes after Bishop Leen left, Sister Barns, the Relief Society president and wife of my would-have-been employer, showed up to ask for permission for Grace to participate in their date auction coming up on December the ninth. All the proceeds would go to help those in our area who couldn't afford to pay Noah to get themselves prepared. The auction was actually a farce, a big setup, where folks would simply bid on their wives or girlfriends in an effort to help the needy. Afterwards, all those who had successfully bid would get to participate in a big group date in the cultural hall.

"I thought we weren't allowed to have fund-raisers," I questioned.

"Well, we've invited all the Scouts so that we can call it a Scout activity."

I told Sister Barns that the decision to be bid on was Grace's, and that I would bid high if she agreed to it.

"I think you'll have some competition," Sister Barns smiled. "That boy who's working for us sure is sweet on her. And Brother Treat seems to think that Grace would make the perfect girl for his Leon."

"Leon's only seventeen," I laughed.

"That's old enough to group date," Sister Barns chirped.

"Sister Barns, Grace is twenty-three."

"Love can fill tremendous gaps."

Something was wrong. The entire city of Southdale had gone goofy. I should never have brought Grace back unmarried. We should have gotten hitched back east and then come west. Better yet, we should have gotten married and stayed back there. Her presence here was making everyone, including me, crazy.

"I thought this auction was just a setup?" I questioned. "Don't we all know at the outset who will take whom home?"

"In theory," Sister Barns clucked. "But the potential for someone to outbid you is always there."

I shook my head.

"Leon's been working at the Shoe Stop, after school," she added, hinting that Leon might have money to spend on Grace.

"Sister Barns, Grace and I are loosely engaged," I explained. "We just haven't set a date yet."

"Satan looks for the cracks," she said. "Then he wiggles in and destroys the foundation."

"What?" I asked, wondering what she was talking about.

"Long engagements are a first-class invitation to failure. Don't R.S.V.P., Trust. Don't R.S.V.P!"

"We're not actually engaged," I tried to explain. "Just loosely engaged."

"Well, then I see no harm in Leon or Doran staking claim."

Sister Barns stood, thanked me for the nice conversation, and left.

I spent the next hour trying to call Grace at work. No one ever answered. After twenty-four attempts, I gave up.

I was not feeling good about things.

19

APPLYING STUCCO

Monday after work Grace came straight home and found me. She apologized for not coming over to Sunday dinner. She apologized for going to Sunday School with Doran. She apologized for not calling me earlier in the day. And she told me I was all she had thought about for the last twenty-four hours.

It was a start.

"Let's take a drive," she suggested.

We drove up into the Dintmore Hills and parked above the Scarsdale Meadow. There were literally thousands of hills there. Some of them were tall and rolling, others were jagged and flat. Each one of them had an official name— an early settler had gone to the trouble of labeling them all. It would be impossible to remember all the names, but we were now parked on top of Georgia, one of the best-known mounds. Georgia was high and rounded at the peak, and she also provided the nicest view of the largest meadow within the hills.

The afternoon was turning to dusk, and tiny clouds slid across the sky like ice on an iron. Grace held my hand in silence. She looked great at night. Her dark red hair and deep eyes were more mesmerizing than a single flickering flame against the blackness.

Pale stars began to appear in the fading blue.

"Sister Barns came by today," I said, starting the conversation.

"I bet I know what she wanted," Grace replied, gazing at the sky. "Nothing like an auction to make a woman feel important."

"So she called you?"

"Yep."

"Are you going to do it?"

"I guess so," Grace replied. "After all, I know who will win me. Plus, it will help Noah out."

"Oh," was all I said.

"It still bothers you that Noah's not some old prophet-looking guy, doesn't it?" Grace poked.

"Not really," I said, mentally crossing my fingers behind my back.

"You're a poor liar." Grace smiled, turning to look at me.

I looked into her eyes and forgot all about Noah Taylor. In fact, I forgot everything I had ever known except for how to form this next sentence.

"So, are you glad you came?" I asked her.

"Here?" she asked, meaning the top of Georgia. "Or here?" she said, putting out her hand and indicating Southdale.

"Here," I replied, with my hand as well.

"Umm hum," she said, biting her lip. "This has been the best time of my life."

"Do you miss Thelma's Way?"

"A little," Grace admitted. "The sky out here is too open, and your river doesn't hold a candle to the Girth. I miss the meadow and the miles of trees. And I . . ." She laughed at herself. "I guess I miss Thelma's Way more than I thought."

We both sighed.

"Do you actually think anything will happen on the seventeenth?" I questioned.

"Noah does," Grace answered.

"Do you think he's an honest guy?"

"I guess so, why?"

"I don't know," I answered. "I just think it's kind of creepy, him acting like he knows something that no one else does."

"The important thing is that he's getting people prepared," Grace defended him. "Back home in Thelma's Way, folks wouldn't dream of not having decent food storage. Everyone's always out of work, or struggling, but they always have food put away. Here these people . . . well, they . . . I don't know."

"We're too comfortable to care," I said for her.

"Exactly."

We sat on top of Georgia and watched some animals run across the dark meadow. The headlights of our car gave them definition for a brief moment.

"You know, we should probably talk," I pointed out.

"I thought we had been," Grace said knowingly.

"I mean about the more important things. Sister Barns said that long engagements were a personal invitation for Satan to crack our foundation."

"I didn't know we were engaged."

"That's sort of what I meant by talking."

"Are you asking me to marry you?" Grace questioned with a little less enthusiasm then I felt the moment deserved.

"I don't know." I blew it.

"Well, let me know when you've made up your mind."

"I don't want to rush this," I said defensively.

"I see."

"I'm just thinking of you."

"Thanks."

"I thought maybe you needed more time."

"Maybe I do."

Daylight faded completely, turning the sky from denim to dark. Grace and I sat together quietly listening to the night. I thought about Lucy, and how up until two years ago I had always imagined myself marrying her. Now I couldn't see myself with anyone besides Grace. It didn't matter if my mother objected. It didn't matter that she wasn't rich, or socially influential. The only thing that made sense was us. But we still had not set anything in stone. For some reason it was hard for us to verbalize what we both believed to already be.

"You know," Grace said softly after a few moments of silence, "I've never driven a car before."

"Never?"

Grace shook her head. I don't know why I was surprised by this. There were no roads in Thelma's Way and no cars besides the homemade one that Leo Tip had built. I guess I just figured she would have driven in Virgil's Find at some point in her life.

"You want to learn?" I asked.

I had barely gotten the question past my lips when Grace began crawling over me to switch seats. We struggled with each other as we changed places.

"We could have used the doors," I pointed out.

"That was a lot more fun."

I had to agree.

I showed Grace where all the pedals were and how the stick shift worked. She started the car, pushed down the clutch, and pulled the stick shift into reverse.

"Let up slowly on the clutch," I instructed.

The car bucked, rocked, and then sputtered out.

"What did I do?" she asked.

"Nothing really. It just takes practice."

So we practiced for the next few hours. Eventually, Grace got the hang of it. She flew down the dirt road in utter bliss, spraying rocks and dirt behind us. The Dintmore Hills were actually an ideal place to practice driving. There were hundreds of dirt roads and very few other vehicles around. I was just about to suggest we begin making our way home when the car coughed and died. Grace coasted to a stop at the side of the road.

"What happened?"

"I'm not sure," I replied. "Try to start it again."

Nothing.

"Switch places with me," I suggested.

Grace climbed over me, kissing me as we passed. The car wouldn't start. I flicked on the car light to better read the gas gauge. Empty. We had been so busy having fun that I had forgotten to pay attention to how much fuel we had left.

"We're out of gas," I said plainly.

"Sure," she said seductively. "You're obviously not the gentleman I thought you to be."

"You were driving," I pointed out. "I'm the victim here."

"So what should we do?" Grace asked, smiling.

"We could stay here for a while and wait for help," I suggested.

We both looked at each other, taking in our intimate enclosure.

"That's probably not a wise idea," Grace said, blushing under the dome light.

"We could walk."

We both jumped out of the car. Grace buttoned up her sweater and took my hand.

"At least it's not raining," she said optimistically.

"Doesn't your Noah live somewhere out here?" I asked.

"My Noah?" Grace glanced at me.

"Well, he's not mine," I guffawed.

Grace laughed to make me feel funnier than I really was. "He lives somewhere out here in an old farmhouse," she said, "but I have no idea where."

"Good," was my only reply.

The dirt road shifted beneath our feet like dry cereal,

each step crunching loudly. Grace leaned her head against me and talked—about life and love and the amazing things that had brought both of us to this point. At the risk of sounding unflattering, time with Grace reminded me of my old bike.

My family had not always been so well-off. As a child I remember my parents struggling to make ends meet. We had lived in a little house across town right next to the Southdale Dairy. It seemed like I never had the things other kids did. I remember wanting a bike so badly for Christmas one year. I begged and begged, knowing that the best way to get Santa to cough up the goods was to strong-arm my parents. Christmas morning I woke up to my worst nightmare. I had gotten a bike, but it was a used one—a girl's model with a long seat and a low middle bar. I could tell that there had once been pom poms on the handle-bars, but in an effort to appease me, Santa had trimmed them off. It was purple, white-wheeled, and bigger than any of the bikes my friends had.

My world crumbled.

Mom and Dad tried to make Santa look good by saying nice things about the bike. They acted like there was absolutely nothing wrong with it. Afraid of tarnishing their opinion of the fat guy, I kept my feelings to myself. My friends, however, let their opinions be known, teasing me like mad. They called me "Tricycle Trust," because they couldn't come up with a nickname that rhymed with "purple two-wheeled girl's bike."

One evening after a particularly heavy teasing day I returned home crying. My father sat with me on the front porch and tried to cheer me up. He told me not to worry about what others said, and that my big bike was actually faster than any of my friends'.

Dad was right. The next day I discovered that I could outride any of the neighborhood kids. There wasn't a single bike that could touch me. In one afternoon, everything changed. I went from "Tricycle Trust" to "Trucking Trust, the Fastest Kid on the Block."

As we walked, I told Grace about my bike and how she sort of reminded me of it. What had once been viewed as out of place became the envy of the town.

Grace stopped walking. It was so quiet and so dark.

"You know, you're a weird guy," she said. "You really are."

It wasn't quite the reaction I had been hoping for.

Then she kissed me, setting things right.

We walked a while longer. Half an hour later when we finally spotted headlights, we were both a little disappointed. Two teenagers in a beat-up pickup stopped and gave us a ride. We rode in back with a big dog named Glue. They dropped us off at a gas station on the edge of town. It was past eleven o'clock. When I called my mother, she acted bothered but agreed to come get us after she went to the trouble of getting dressed again.

As Mom drove us home, she went on and on about how Elder Minert and Elder Nicks had been by to schedule a time to teach Grace the second discussion. Mom asked Grace if Wednesday evening at around seven would be okay.

"That would be fine," Grace answered.

"Oh, and Trust," my mother chimed, "I volunteered you to help Sister Barns set up the stage for the auction on the ninth. I hope that's okay."

"That's fine," I said. "When does she need me?"

"I told her you'd be at the church Wednesday around 6:45."

I should have guessed.

Grace squeezed my hand and offered her condolences in the form of a long stolen kiss. Mom spotted us in the rearview mirror and coughed wildly. We then listened to her talk about morality the rest of the ride home.

20

SINKING

The big empty house made Lucy even more depressed. She listened to the clicking of the clock and the barking of a dog somewhere far away. Things were only getting worse. It seemed to take everything she had simply to crawl out of bed in the mornings.

She had called her parents in France, desperate for some counsel and compassion. But Lucy's mom and dad were far too busy traveling to pick up on the dire straits their daughter had coasted into. They seemed to have little advice. They told her to buck up and move on.

Life had turned into one giant bruise.

Lucy had been pleading with God to help her. She had even tossed out her standard prayer phrases in exchange for words so honest they made her weep. Her knees were tired and her head was throbbing. She didn't want to be alone anymore with who she used to be. She didn't want to go on.

She would have called her parents' home teacher to ask

him for a blessing, but their home teacher was Leonard Vastly, and according to the lifestyle section in the local paper, he had sealed himself up in plastic sheeting for the time being. Lucy didn't know where to turn. She glanced over the ward list, looking for someone whom she would feel comfortable getting a blessing from. Truth be told, she had not actually been the kindest person to most of the names in front of her.

Abraham, Ronald and Lynn

Lucy had made fun, more than once, of Sister Abraham's choice in clothing. Her wardrobe made it so easy. The white shoes after Labor Day had been too much for Lucy to overlook.

Aston, Kim and Mary

Lucy had been fairly clear about how she felt concerning a man having the name "Kim."

Baull, RoyAnn

Lucy had talked both behind and in front of RoyAnn's back. Words like "spinster," "old maid," and "loser" came to mind.

The list went on.

Lucy had been such an awful neighbor. She pushed her head into her pillow. The expensive cover and imported goose feathers did little to comfort her crumbling self-esteem. A small twinge of inspiration fell upon her as she wept. She sat up and turned to page three of the directory.

Williams, Roger and Marilyn

In God she would trust.

21

BIO-DOOM

◇

NOVEMBER 30TH

Tuesday morning I got up early and went to pick up our stalled car. I gassed it up and drove it home for my mother to use. With no employment yet, and little will to look, I decided to go pay Leonard Vastly a visit. My mother had already gone for the day and I couldn't find my father's car keys, so I decided to take the bus—it seemed so socially conscious. Grace had been using the bus on and off for the past week, and if it could take her where she was needed, then I felt certain it could serve me just fine.

I found a few dollars and walked down the road to the bus stop. Fifteen minutes later, I was almost to Brother Vastly's place. Brother Vastly lived about five miles straight up the street from us. But his home was about a half mile away from where any bus would go, so I had to make the last leg of my journey on foot.

Leonard lived on the edge of an upscale subdivision. He owned the only mobile home in this part of town. He had brought his single-wide in about fifteen years back, inspiring the locals to make more restrictive zoning laws. Luckily for Brother Vastly, such laws couldn't touch what was already in place. His single-wide stayed, making him the king of the only factory-manufactured castle anywhere in the area.

When I first spotted his place I was amazed. The entire mobile home looked like a huge wad of trash. It was wrapped in plastic and streaked with duct tape. I spotted the bay window and the open curtains through the cloudy plastic. It looked as if Brother Vastly were sitting at a desk typing something. I watched a couple cars pass and stare. Someone honked, prompting Leonard to raise his hand and wave politely.

I sauntered up to the window and knocked on the glass. Leonard turned and peered out at me with excitement.

"Hello, Trust," he hollered through the plastic layer covering his window. His muffled voice was hard to make out.

"I came to visit you!" I hollered back.

"I'm sealed in," he signaled.

"Me, your home teacher." I motioned to myself.

The heavy plastic made Brother Vastly look distorted and fuzzy, but I could see him scratching his head as if in thought. Then he looked out the window to see if anyone else was around.

The coast was clear.

Leonard signaled for me to come around the back side of his trailer. I walked around, finding nothing but a sealed-up single-wide. I looked about as if I were missing something. I was just about to return to the window when I felt someone pulling on my ankle. I looked down to see one of Brother Vastly's arms reaching out from under the plastic at the bottom of his home. He pushed apart a metal section of the underskirting and stuck his head out.

"Brother . . ." I started to say.

"Shhhhh," he said quickly. "Crawl in here where we won't be observed."

Happy no one was around to see, I got onto my knees and crawled under the plastic and through the skirting. We scooted on our stomachs for a few feet, and then popped up through a trapdoor that Leonard had made out of a huge linoleum square in the center of his kitchen floor. Once we were up into the house I looked around at all the food rations he had stored. I had never seen so much food and supplies crammed into one place. It looked like the complete inventory of at least two grocery stores. And the place smelled like garlic mixed with kitty litter.

"Whoa," was all I could say.

"I've spent years getting things just right." He beamed.

I looked around and once again settled with just, "Whoa."

"Now, in here we're a fully functioning sphere," he began to inform. "Break your leg? I got you covered. There's a fully stocked infirmary in the master bathroom and two satellite first aid kits located in here." Leonard pointed to the cabinet above his refrigerator as if he were a stewardess giving safety instructions, "and here." He signaled to a drawer underneath his kitchen bar. "Hungry?" he continued. "Enjoy one of thirteen kinds of grain I've got stitched into the fabric of the couch."

I looked over at the lumpy sagging couch and tried to act impressed.

"You think Noah Taylor's thought of things like that?" he asked determinedly.

"No," I replied in all honesty.

"Thank you. Now, say the government's gone mad," he spat, "the computers are down, and there's a foreigner with a hungry family at the back door."

Brother Vastly caught his breath.

"Open the oven," he demanded.

I was actually scared to.

"Just open it," he insisted. "The energy's off. I stopped being a victim to electricity days ago."

I slowly opened the big oven door to discover that he had removed all the insides and hollowed the entire thing out back into the cabinets. I could see a couple of boxes of crackers and a small pillow in there.

"It's my hiding place," Leonard explained. "Who'd ever think to look in the oven?"

"Don't you . . ." I began to ask.

"Save the praise for later," he said, holding his hands up. "There's more to see."

Brother Vastly led me down the hall to the master bedroom.

"So you've got a house full of food, your couches are stuffed with grain, your walls insulated with soup mix, and most of the crawl space beneath your abode is filled with dehydrated bananas and apricots."

Brother Vastly paused for effect.

"Big deal. What separates the men from the morons in

the competitive field of food storage is water. That soup mix is going to go down awful dry unless you have some H_2O to bring it to life. Look away," Leonard instructed. "Look away."

I turned my head, but I could hear him punching in a code on the door lock leading to the master bedroom. I thought it rather silly to have an expensive door lock on a cheap particleboard door. A chime sounded and he opened up the door. I turned to find myself staring at a big, above-ground swimming pool. The pool was filled with water, the weight of which was so great it had broken the flooring out beneath it and was sitting a good foot and a half beneath the rest of the mobile home foundation.

"She's resting on cases of apricots," he informed me. "Floor gave way right after I filled her up. Luckily I had already put my cans underneath it. God cares for the sparrow."

"That's a lot of water," I said, expecting he'd like me to say so.

"Think Noah Taylor's got that kind of liquid holed up?"

"I couldn't say."

"Well then, let me do it for you. No. Plus, we're on a well here. Water's pumped into this pool, continually restocking me. If times get real hard I can even bathe in it. Don't tell a soul about this," he insisted.

"I won't."

"I'd hate to have people begging me for sips."

I figured he could put an end to that just telling them he swam in it.

"What kind of water storage do you and your family have?" Leonard asked me.

"I'm not sure," I said ignorantly. "If we have any I'm sure my mom's storing it with Brother Taylor."

Leonard shook his head sadly. "Our ward is wading into some dangerous territory. I'd hate to have the lights go out and *my* fruit and date bars be ten miles away."

"Wouldn't we all," I tried to joke.

"I like you, Trust," Leonard approved. "I like your attitude. Your good looks make me a little skittish, but you seem to have a solid head. Although I must admit I don't care for the radical hairstyle," he said, referring to my shaved head. "Come here," he continued, waving me back down the hall.

"How's the carpet feel?" he asked.

"Fine," I said, although I realized for the first time that it was a tad lumpy.

Back in the kitchen, Leonard leaned over and pulled back a section of the carpet where it met the linoleum. I could see hundreds of Ziploc baggies filled with what looked to be red licorice.

"A lot of people are saying to themselves, 'I've got twenty cases of wheat, and four cans of elbow macaroni, I'll live off of that,'" he said dramatically. "More power to them. But what good is living if you can't soothe the sweet tooth every so often?"

"Pointless," I said, playing to his vanity.

"Pointless indeed. That's why I've lined the entire low-traffic areas of my carpet with red licorice. Don't like the black, never have, leaves a real pasty taste in my mouth."

Brother Vastly smacked his lips, acting as if he had just ingested something pasty.

"Now, the heavy-traffic areas are lined with beef jerky," he continued. "Your walking around is actually tenderizing my beef. Of course, I got turkey jerky in the laundry nook, but the traffic isn't as heavy in there."

Leonard's wrinkly, dirty clothes stood as witnesses to the truthfulness of his last statement.

"Any questions?" he asked.

"Where do you sleep?" I wondered, knowing that the master bedroom was filled with a pool, and the other bedroom was the bedless bay window room I had stared through from the outside.

"Sleep," he guffawed. "Sleep is nothing but a weak man's mandolin."

I had no idea what that meant, but I left it alone, asking only, "So you don't sleep?"

"I take fatigue prevention every three hours. I sprawl out on the bags of wheat flour I have stored next to the couch there."

"Why don't you just sleep—"

"Fatigue prevention," he corrected.

"Why don't you prevent fatigue by lying on the couch?"

"Trust, you've got a lot to learn," he said, shaking his head. "Why, even a tenderfoot must know that flour is softer than grain. Better back support too."

"Well, you certainly have gotten prepared," I complimented.

"The way I see it is there are no real emergencies for

those who are fanatic," he espoused. "I read that some-where. Any other questions?" he asked.

"Actually, do you have a bathroom I could use?"

"I'd love to let you, but I took the toilet out of the mas-ter bathroom to make room for the infirmary, and I've unhooked the guest room toilet so that I could plant wheat in the bowl."

"So where do you . . ."

"I've got a solar compost behind the fire wall in the infirmary."

I didn't want to know any more, so I said nothing.

"So then I guess you have a message for me?" Leonard said, changing the subject.

I could think of lots of things I would like to tell him, but I had no prepared message.

"Not really," I replied.

"Didn't you say you were my home teacher?"

"That's true, and—"

"Have a seat then. I'm spiritually weak due to the fact that I can't come out to attend church. I asked Bishop Leen if I could get someone to bring the sacrament to me, but he said no. It's a real shame when people who stand for a cause get overlooked."

"Pity."

"I gotta do what I gotta do," he insisted.

"So how long do you really plan to stay in here?"

"However long is necessary."

"And what determines that?"

"Noah Taylor. If his December seventeenth doom date is accurate, then maybe I'll come out soon after the carnage and destruction die down. But if he's wrong, which I'm thinking he is, I'll just stay here for a spell to prove my point."

"And your point is?"

"People don't need people."

"So would you rather I leave?"

"Actually it's kinda nice to have someone around."

"Well, if it makes you feel any better, I think everyone is wrong to put so much stock in what Noah Taylor is saying. He's just a man like you or me. He has no right or privilege to know the future for us."

"Sister Cravitz told me you'd fly off on him," Leonard said.

"What?"

"She radioed me a while back and told me about you being jealous of Noah."

"I'm not—"

"We're the only ears here," he said, pointing to his.

"Really, I'm not—"

"Listen, Trust, lying to yourself is the same as lying to another."

I was being chastened by a man with licorice-lined carpet.

"I guess this Grace girl you brought to town is really stirring things up," he went on. "You know, Southdale really needs a little mixing. Especially the members here. We get a little stale stuck out here away from all the other western Mormons. It's nice to have Grace waking us up a bit."

"She's not really doing anything," I said, baffled.

"Exactly," he replied. "Exactly."

"No really, she just works for Noah."

"You know, I used to have a sister-in-law with red hair," he reminisced. "She was the most exasperating person. She was all about money. Couldn't get enough of the stuff. Her husband, my brother, was working three jobs and had an adult paper route. That's different than a juvenile route. The adult routes usually cover a large area and require a car. Anyhow, she left my brother about three years back, no, no I take that back. It was right after Ned had that work done on his teeth, so it would have to have been about six years ago. My goodness, how time flies."

I was glad he thought so.

"Left him for a car salesman," he went on. "I'm sure she drives a nice vehicle, but does she have the amount of food security I do? I don't think so. So, Trust, what's your message?"

"Well, I really just wanted to make this first visit a get-to-know-you kind of thing. I actually didn't think I'd be allowed to come into your 'Bio-Doom.'"

"I am a self-contained ecosystem, but if I need to bend the rules to help out my new home teacher, than so be it."

"Do you think you might bend the rules to come to church?"

Brother Vastly laughed. "You know, that sense of humor of yours might be just the thing to help you hold on to Grace."

"My relationship with Grace is doing just fine."

"Remember, a lie to yourself . . ."

"I know, I know."

"Trust, this is awkward, I understand," Leonard said, putting his left foot high up on a crate of no-name green beans and making it almost level with his belt. "It's unnatural for a home teachee to teach the home teacher, but I'm going to give you a little advice. Put your personal safety first."

"I'm not sure I agree with that," I replied.

"Line upon line," he saged. "Line upon line."

"I'm pretty certain the Savior would want us to put others before ourselves."

"I'm sure He would," Leonard defended. "You've missed my point completely."

"What's your point?"

"I don't want to get into specifics." He shifted uncomfortably.

"I'd better get going," I said, standing up.

"Listen," he insisted. "Before you go, I want you to try something I made. It's an all-natural dried fruit bar I call the 'Lenny' because it rhymes with 'skinny.' If you ate these all the time you'd be pretty skinny—cleans the body out completely. Not that you need it—you've actually got a nice shape considering you've only been back from your mission a few months."

I wanted to list all the reasons why I didn't want to try a "Lenny," as well as point out that "Lenny" and "skinny" didn't actually rhyme, but I felt it was my priesthood duty as his home teacher to indulge him in this wish.

Leonard rushed off down the hall and into the pool room. He went inside. I heard splashing, a door open, a door close, more splashing, and a fairly mild swearword. A few moments later, he emerged with a plate of unwrapped fruit bars, the bottom half of his pants wet. I didn't dare ask. The fruit bars were brown and abrasive-looking.

"Take one, and shove another in your pocket for later if you'd like."

"One's fine."

Brother Vastly picked up a second and pushed it into one of my pockets for me.

I bit into the bar in my hand reluctantly. It was worse than I had anticipated. It was like eating a piece of pulpy chalk.

"You know, a while back I heard this story," Leonard said. "This woman made a cake at the start of every month and then would serve it to her home teachers when they came over. If they came at the beginning of the month, it was fresh. If they came near the end, it was stale."

"I just got assigned to you yesterday," I complained, wondering why I had to eat a twenty-seven-day-old date bar because of it.

"These aren't a month old," he said merrily. "I made these about four years ago. I haven't had a home teacher since the boating incident. I'm sorry, I can't see why a seven-year-old kid should get a life jacket before me."

I just stared at him.

"My last home teacher owned a boat," was all he said by way of explanation.

"Do I have to leave the same way I came in?"

"Excellent question, and yes. I'll also need you not to tell the others that I let you into the Bio-Doom. I don't want folks thinking I'm some sort of noncommitted freak."

Heaven forbid.

"I'm here for the long haul," he said. "Of course, if you showed up for your next visit with a couple cases of soap, I wouldn't be sad."

Brother Vastly picked up the linoleum-square trapdoor and waved me over. Then he waited for me to finish my fruit bar. I shoved the whole thing into my mouth and swallowed. He gave me the okay sign.

"Thanks for coming by, Trust. I'll remember these kind acts when I'm enjoying my mansion on high."

"Thank you," I said, wanting only to get out, and maybe get a drink. I would have asked him for one, but I was afraid he'd retrieve it from the pool.

I crawled across the dirt, out the skirting, and through the plastic. It was nice to smell the open air again. I walked through the neighborhood and to the bus stop. There was no one else waiting at the moment, so I just stood there patiently by myself. When the bus arrived, the doors opened to reveal Brother Treat behind the wheel. Brother Treat had driven a bus ever since Brother Victor had found him the job. I had never actually ridden on his bus, but he had talked often of how hard he worked to keep this town running smoothly.

"Brother Treat," I said, happy to see him.

"Trust," he replied coldly.

I stepped up to get on and he drove forward a couple feet. My foot knocked into the side of the bus, the door no longer directly in front of me. I stepped over and looked at Brother Treat. He motioned as if to say, "oops." I tried again, and once again the bus moved forward. I tried again, this time a little more quickly. He moved the bus up six feet. I ran to try to get on, and he moved it a good twenty feet. I walked slowly up to the bus, the people currently riding on it staring at me. I'm sure that they, like me, were wondering what was going on.

Right before I got to the door I hollered out, "What's the matter?"

Brother Treat didn't answer.

I stepped toward the open door, and once again it started to creep forward.

"Brother Treat!"

I didn't know Brother Treat that well. He and his family were "overflow Saints," meaning they sat in the folding chairs at the back of the chapel. Years back when there had been a fuss between the bench sitters and the chair sitters, it had been Brother Treat who had been wounded by Sister Cravitz, prompting him to pour bleach all over her prizewinning azaleas. Brother Treat had a nice face and bad hair. He was tall and unusually thin for a bus driver. Due to a bet involving a skateboard and stairs in his youth, he had false teeth—teeth that he would occasionally take out and publicly clean. Actually, he was a rather quiet man who, aside from the bleach episode, had never shown much gumption. Excluding, of course, the time he accidentally stepped on another Scout's pinewood derby car—a car that was in competition with his son Leon's.

Leon.

I had forgotten that Sister Barns had mentioned Leon's supposed crush on Grace. Certainly this strange bus episode couldn't be about that, could it?

"Brother Treat," I hollered, the bus doors about eight feet away from me at the time. "This isn't about Leon and Grace is it?"

I had barely gotten the words out before the bus doors slammed shut and Brother Treat took off for good, exhaust billowing into my face.

I couldn't believe it. I waited around for another bus but none came. I began walking home, stopping only twice: once to get a drink and use the bathroom at a small business along the way, and once to see an early afternoon movie about a spy with a lisp.

What? I had nothing else to do.

When I arrived home, it was already beginning to get dark. I looked over at Wendy's house and saw that Grace's bedroom light was on. I thought about going directly over and visiting her, but I decided to wash up from the day's activities first.

The second I walked through the front door of my house, my mother yelled at me to call Sister Cravitz. I did so, only to find that Brother Vastly had just radioed her to tell her that the date bars he had served me were actually small fire-starter bricks he had made, and that he was terribly, terribly sorry. I held my stomach and pulled the one he had pushed into my pocket out. I had thought they tasted rather woody. I flipped it over and over in my hand, contemplating the day I had just completed. Then I called Grace and invited her over for dinner.

We ate in the living room in front of a roaring fire, compliments of Brother Leonard Vastly.

22

WHO WOULD HAVE THAWED IT?

Thelma's Way was driving Roger Williams mad. The town had turned into one happy batch of Mormons, partly because of him. Who would have thought that an uninterested member such as he could be so instrumental in bringing souls back into the fold? Folks had often told him about how hard Elder Williams had worked to beef up the branch. And yet, Trust's efforts had yielded little fruit. Now here, with a few lies, Roger seemed to have brought most of the flock back home.

Roger wasn't sure if this strengthened or weakened his newly rekindled testimony. He was also having a hard time not getting frustrated about the still-missing Book of Mormon. His efforts, despite reactivating the members, had produced nothing. Roger had done everything he could think of. He had even considered praying for help. It was a thought he pushed quickly away.

Roger sat himself upon one of the chairs on the boardinghouse porch. Paul Leeper emerged from around the corner and bid him good afternoon.

"Paul," Roger greeted.

Paul Leeper was the once-famous once-apostate who had caused the town so much trouble. He was a skinny man with a thick helmet of hair and scrunched up facial features. Whereas Paul had once been a loudmouthed troublemaker, he was now just a loudmouthed local.

"Any luck finding the book?" Paul asked.

"Nope," Roger stretched. "Not even a decent clue."

"I just saw it over at . . . nope, that's not true." Paul caught himself.

Paul was working hard these days to stop his habit of perpetual lying. It wasn't easy. This, after all, was a man who had once claimed to have invented grease. He had also bragged about being at the Council of Nicaea where he had helped pick out and edit the original books of the Bible.

"I think that old Book of Mormon might be lost for good," Roger sighed.

"These are some big woods," Paul added.

Lupert Carver came toward the boardinghouse from across the meadow. He appeared to be dragging something behind him on a leash. As he got closer, it became obvious that what Lupert was pulling was a stiff dead dog.

Paul leaned against the porch rail and looked out at him. Roger raised himself from his seat and gazed as well.

"Lupert Carver," Paul hollered. "What are you up to?"

Lupert slid the dog up to the boardinghouse and stopped.

"You remember Bushy, here?" Lupert asked.

"I thought he died years ago," Paul gaped, stepping off the porch and crouching down by the dog. Roger stepped down as well.

"He did," Lupert shrugged. "I couldn't stand to bury him so I stuck him in my mother's deep freeze. Mom found him this morning while rummaging for some frozen sausage. She's not real happy with me."

"I suppose not," Paul sympathized.

Roger lightly kicked the frozen dog with the toe of his shoe.

"My father saw a movie where they froze someone till they found a cure to fix 'im," Lupert explained.

"Movies ain't real life," Paul lectured. "I guess you'll need help burying him."

"Maybe," Lupert answered. "But I thought I might prop him up in the sun and see if he thaws out alive."

"Now Lupert, boy," Paul said sternly. "Once a dog is dead, no amount of sunning is going to bring him back to life."

"That's what my pa said," Lupert lamented. "A course, he wasn't positive about it. He went to Virgil's Find to look up if it's true."

Roger Williams simultaneously shook his head and smiled. Lupert Carver was a great representation of what he was up against here in Thelma's Way. It was as if these people remained in a constant state of slow, childlike innocence.

Roger watched as Lupert walked over to the middle of the meadow. The ground was snow-covered and dirty. Lupert propped Bushy up in the center of the clearing. The dog stood frozen stiff, staring at the boardinghouse as if it were a fat pheasant. After Lupert had stood the dog up, he turned and walked back toward Roger and Paul. The moment his eyes were off of Bushy, two of Leo Tip's wild dogs tore out of the woods, ran up to the frozen dog, and quickly and almost silently dragged their once-friend out of the meadow and back into the trees—like a hand playing jacks, they had swooped down and taken what they wanted.

Roger and Paul stood there with open mouths. Lupert stepped up to them unaware.

"Maybe if he thaws just right," Lupert said hopefully, turning around to gaze at his dog that was no longer there.

"Where's Bushy!" Lupert yelled in a panic. "Where'd he go?"

Paul put his hand on Lupert's arm and tried to think of something honest to say. Roger helped out.

"He's gone to heaven."

"No kidding?" Lupert smiled.

"No kidding," Roger answered.

Lupert bowed his head in reverence. "They sure took him quick," he observed.

"Heaven knows a good hound when they see one," Paul comforted.

"I knew God was up there," Lupert wowed. "I just knew it. I gotta tell Mother." He beamed, turned, and ran off.

Paul put his hand on Roger's shoulder.

"Our secret?" he asked.

Roger nodded. He would have said more, but for some reason his heart was doing flips and turns within his chest. It pumped wildly. He tried to rationalize what he was feeling. Thelma's Way had tossed him around like a bin full of lottery balls. The tragic (or magic) of this place was overwhelming. To think that an accomplished man like himself could be touched by a thawing dog and the faith of an ignorant child was baffling.

True, he had witnessed one miracle after another while staying in Thelma's Way. He had been there when Annie Holler had given birth to twins. He had watched Janet Bickerstaff get baptized in the freezing Girth River and witnessed Frank Porter regrow hair after applying a new salve that Sister Lando had concocted. Memories came crowding in on him both hard and soft.

Roger Williams sat down.

23

CONVERSATIONS WITH THE COMPETITION

DECEMBER 1ST

Wednesday evening I left Grace at my home and drove my mother's car to the church building. The Southdale chapel was rather spooky-looking at night. Actually, it was rather spooky looking during the day. It had been built before the Church started using molds. The east side of it was brick, while the west end was wood siding and stucco. As far as buildings go, it had the personality of a pudgy toddler. We loved it, we were happy to have it around, but we wished it would photograph better.

In front of the chapel there was a steeple which stood alone, circled by a rose garden and rising incredibly high above the ground. The steeple had been added to the chapel grounds about five years ago. Before that, we had been a steepleless people, relying only on the pitched roof to point us toward heaven.

The steeple was supposed to be half the height it actually was, but someone had messed up during the installation of it, ordering and installing one that towered high above all the other steeples in town. The Lutherans had complained, and the Baptists had written a letter to the local paper pointing out our poor taste in putting up such a blatantly offensive edifice. I think I agreed with the Baptists. The tall metal steeple looked like a radio tower sitting in front of our house of worship—a radio tower with hair. You see, the top of our tall steeple was flat and round, providing a perfect place for a single bird's nest. Well, a not-so-single bird had built one years ago. That bird had lived there until it was struck by lightning. The bird itself caught fire and toppled out of the nest, its feet tangled up in the fibers of its own creation.

There the dead bird dangled. Many tried to knock it down, but nobody was successful. Marcus Leen, Bishop Leen's youngest son, had even chosen the task of removing it for his Eagle Scout project. He had made elaborate plans to extricate it, building scaffolding around the tall steeple and crafting a very long stick to push it off with. He got close, but the winds at that altitude made it too dangerous to proceed. A few of the priests at the time had tried to knock the bird down by throwing rocks. That effort ended in two broken windows and a stray cat that didn't think too kindly of Mormons.

So the dangling bird had stayed until nature concocted its own remedy. One morning it was gone, the wind having dislodged it and carried it away. If you squinted, you could still see bits of nest up there, but no fowl had chosen to build since.

I walked into the building and straight to the cultural hall. Sister Barns was already there bossing a couple of the young women around.

"Trust," she said as I walked in. "I'm so glad you came."

"Thanks for asking me," I replied, unable to think of anything else to say.

"Listen," she squeaked. "I need this ramp to be solid. There's going to be a number of single women walking on it and some of them, well, let's just say that a few of these choice women, well, what I'm trying to get at . . . God doesn't make everyone petite."

"I'll make it strong," I smiled.

"Good. Now, I asked Noah Taylor to help you out. I hope you don't mind."

"Not at all."

Sister Barns looked around and then leaned in toward me. "In my opinion you've got much nicer shoulders than he does," she whispered, as if I needed some bolstering up.

"Thank you," I whispered back.

Sister Barns blushed.

"Noah's in the Relief Society room, picking out support beams," she informed me and turned back to what she was fiddling with before I arrived.

I walked to the Relief Society room and found Noah leaning against one of the tables talking to a rather mature seventeen-year-old girl who looked in need of a strong lesson on modesty. He was making jokes and complimenting her on her nice smile. He was wearing another sweater.

I cleared my throat.

"Hello," Noah said, startled. "I didn't see you there. You could have given this old man a heart attack."

"You're not so old," the young girl teased.

"Not according to Brother Williams here," he smiled, referring to my Colonel Sanders remark.

"So is this the wood we'll be using?" I pointed, wanting to get the project over with.

"That's right," Noah clapped. "I hear that you and I are a team tonight."

"I heard the same thing," I said back.

"Well, this will be great," he smiled falsely. "I've been wanting to get to know the guy Grace calls 'Trust' a little better."

The young girl finally realized she wasn't going to get any more personal attention from Noah and wandered away. Noah and I picked up a couple pieces of wood and carried them into the cultural hall.

"So how is Grace doing at work?" I asked.

"She's great, Trust, a real gem. I don't know how I would get all of this together without her."

"I'm glad," I said honestly.

"Listen, Trust, I'm not going to pretend that I don't hear all the whispering," he said softly to me. "I know that people here are talking about all the time Grace and I spend together," he said in a friendly tone. "I just want you to know that I have absolutely no interest in her whatsoever."

151

I didn't know what to say. A couple moments ago I was bothered about the possibility of him liking Grace. Now I was bothered by the reality that he might not.

"Excuse me?" I asked.

"She's a nice girl, but I would never pursue someone like her. So, set your worries aside."

"I wasn't worried," I insisted.

"Trust, when you've been in the business as long as I have, you get used to these girls that see you as more of a hero figure than just a regular guy."

Noah Taylor was one pompous person.

"I'm not sure I understand what you're saying," I said, giving him a chance to reword what he had just worded.

"How old are you, Trust?"

"Twenty-three."

"I'll be thirty in June."

"What does that have to do with anything?"

"Southdale is fine," Noah patronized. "It's a nice city, but it's not the real world. Live a year in L.A. or New York. Then you'll know what I mean."

This was the dumbest thing I had ever heard.

"I've been to both those places," I said defensively, adding to the stupidity of the conversation.

"Great," he said mockingly. "Now let's get this walkway done."

We crawled under the walkway on our backs and began to work with the wood to shore things up. There was cloth skirting all the way around, leaving Noah and me in relative privacy.

"So how did this date of December seventeenth come

about?" I asked while shoving wood up into the underside. I expected some great larger-than-life story, but instead I got the truth.

"Well, as I've told the people here, I had a dream where the heavens parted and showed me. But I like you, Trust. You seem like you've got things figured out so I'll level with you. I made the whole thing up. It's a nice way to make some money and, if you like, I could figure a way to include you. Get people spooked and they'll pay through the nose, if you know what I mean."

There was a moment of awkward silence while the words I had just heard sunk in.

"What?" I asked in disbelief.

"Come on, Trust, you're smarter than that. Admit it. It's a way to get them off their duffs. They get excited about something for a change and it doesn't hurt us any either." He turned his head and smiled. "In fact, December seventeenth is perfect timing, really. It sets me up to take one of those less expensive winter cruises when I'm through here. A penny saved is a penny . . . well, you get my point."

"I can't believe you're saying this," I said, anger beginning to build.

"Oh, Trust, you should be happy," he offered. "There's no way I could ever be interested in some pale redheaded girl when I can have my pick of all the bronze women in the Caribbean, or maybe Tahiti. That would be nice. What the heck, I'll be loaded. I'll just spend a month at each." He chuckled and went back to wedging wood supports into place.

I was absolutely dumbfounded. If someone had just informed me that in a matter of minutes all my limbs would fall off and everyone I ever loved would leave me, I couldn't have been more shocked. Sure, I didn't like Noah, and yes, there had been twinges of jealousy, but I had never suspected that under that tousled hair and big sweater there lurked such a truly horrible person. This was fraud to the highest degree, and somewhere in the last mound of garbage he had spit out, my subconscious had heard fighting words.

Poor Noah.

I'm not sure what it was. Perhaps it was all the stress I had gone through in the last few weeks. Maybe it was Elder Jorgensen and his relentless pursuit of Grace. Maybe it was Southdale and their gullibility to buy into Noah's plan. Maybe it was all the pent-up emotions I had held back on my mission—the companions I had bit my lips and counted to ten for. My mother, my father, my half-shaved head, my most recent concussion. Maybe it was the drought, or the season. Or perhaps it was the fact that I had still not fully digested Leonard Vastly's fire-starting brick. Or maybe, just maybe, I was flashing back to Thelma's Way, and the time Elder Weeble had bad-mouthed Grace on the front of the boardinghouse steps. I had wanted so badly to stick up for Grace, to wrestle Elder Weeble to the ground and demand him to take it all back. I had restrained myself due to the fact that I was a missionary at the time, and that I needed to act the part.

I was no longer a missionary.

I sat up quickly, banging my head on the underside of

the walkway. Then I lunged at Noah. His smug smile quickly vanished. He was obviously a man who was used to little resistance. I jumped on him, hitting him in the face as he desperately scrambled to get out from under the walkway. I pulled on his pretty sweater, dragging him back under. Then he screamed and kicked at me like a sissy grasshopper with huge lungs. I could hear footsteps running into the cultural hall. I grabbed Noah's arm and pushed it up behind him. He screamed again, ripping his arm out of my grasp and frantically crawling out from under the walkway. I followed right behind him, not yet satisfied with the amount of damage I had caused. There was a small crowd of onlookers now. Sister Barns rushed up to the fleeing Noah and grabbed his hand.

"What's going on here?" she demanded.

Before Noah could answer, I pulled my right arm back and threw a punch directly into his right eye. Noah seemed to fly backwards out of Sister Barns's grip. He fell with a thud to the ground, his rear end sliding across the gym floor until he came to a stop against the wall. I stood there with everyone looking on in astonishment.

The young woman who had been talking to Noah earlier ran to his side. She then yelled at one of her friends to bring her a wet towel. Noah stood, embarrassed about what had happened and by all the attention he was receiving in the wake of it.

"I demand to know what's going on here," Sister Barns stamped.

"Ask him," I said, cooling down, already beginning to regret what I had done.

"Well?" She turned to Noah.

"I'm not sure," he said innocently. "I told him that Grace was doing such a good job and he went ballistic."

"That's not true," I tried.

"Trust, I think it would be better if you left now," Sister Barns said, pointing toward the far door.

"He's duping you all," I insisted. "He told me so himself. Said he's going to enjoy spending all the money you're foolishly giving him in the Caribbean."

Noah looked shocked.

"Trust," he said calmly. "Lying about this isn't going to make it any better. I forgive you for hitting me. There's no need to make this situation even worse."

"Tell them what you said about Tahiti," I demanded, not sounding like I made much sense.

Everyone just stared at me, pity and shame painting every self-righteous mug in the room. I looked at Sister Barns, who was still pointing toward the door.

"Sister Barns," I tried.

She replied by pointing with even greater fervor.

As I walked from the cultural hall, I could see everybody begin to huddle around Noah Taylor. I picked up the pace, hurrying from the building and out to the parking lot.

I needed to get to Grace before Noah did.

24

SWAPPING WOUNDS

By the time I had arrived home, Noah had already called and spoken to Grace. Grace met me in the entryway of my house, leaving the full-time missionaries who had been teaching her tucked back in the den. She claimed that Noah had called to apologize if he had done anything wrong, and that he felt just awful.

"Tell Trust I'm sorry if I said something that offended him. I thought we were just having a friendly conversation," Noah had weaseled.

"Grace," I groaned. "He's a phony."

"Trust."

"I'm serious," I went on, taking off my coat and setting my keys down in the small dish by the door. "He told me he's only doing this for the money."

"He said that exactly?" Grace asked, obviously torn between believing Noah and believing me.

"Those weren't his exact words, but he's out to make fools of everyone."

"I just don't—"

"Believe me?" I finished for her.

"I've worked with him, Trust. He's not like that."

"What's he like?" I asked in frustration. "Cute? Handsome? Funny?"

"You're being stupid," Grace said boldly.

"I'm trying to tell you the truth, but you just want to take 'sweater boy's' side of the story."

"Let's talk about this later," Grace said softly.

"Why? So you can go to work and get all the details from him?"

"Trust, have I ever given you reason not to trust me?" she asked firmly.

"No, but . . ."

I was interrupted by the missionaries. Apparently they had heard enough from their listening point back in the den to sense that it might be best for them to leave. They came slinking down the hall, hoping to slip out unnoticed.

"You guys don't need to leave," Grace told them.

"Well, we just remembered . . . uh . . ." Elder Nicks said, unable to conjure up what he had just recalled.

"Yeah," Elder Minert tried to help. "We just remembered."

"I'll call you tomorrow, Grace?" Elder Nicks asked forlornly.

"That'd be great," Grace said. "I'm sorry about tonight."

"Will you be okay?" Elder Nicks asked, looking at me suspiciously.

"She'll be fine," I insisted.

The two elders took their cue and cleared out.

"Listen, Grace," I tried to reason once they were gone.

"You have to believe me. Noah is in this for himself and no one else."

"I'm sorry. I just don't believe you."

The words hit me harder than anything in my life ever had. I felt like a crash test dummy that had been shot from a cannon directly into a cement wall. My head collapsed as my ego tucked and folded. How could Grace not believe me? How was it possible that in such a short time Noah Taylor could cause her to turn on me?

"You don't believe me?" I asked incredulously.

"Trust, I just know that Noah . . ."

"No way," I cut her off. "Don't give me the 'I just know' line. For a year I've loved you. Now Noah walks in here and you instantly decided that he's right and I'm wrong."

"He told me, Trust," Grace said soberly.

"Told you what?" I asked, angry.

"He told me how you threatened him into leaving town."

"Ha," I laughed. "And you believed him?"

"We should talk about this later," Grace said.

"Much later," I replied, so disgusted with all of it that I wasn't thinking straight. "Maybe I'll be back tomorrow. Maybe." I turned and stormed out, slamming the door behind me. I stood on the front porch waiting for Grace to come out and stop me.

She never did.

My coat and keys were inside, and there was no way I was going to put my pride through the kind of pummeling that going back in would induce. I stormed off into the night, having absolutely no idea where I was going.

25

BE THOU BUMBLE

◇

I wandered around Southdale until about eleven o'clock. I refused to go back home, confident that Grace would be watching out of her window for me to come slinking back. I had no money, no credit cards, and the cold was only getting stronger. I thought about going to another member's home and asking for shelter. But I figured word of Noah's and my disagreement had already been properly spread around. I didn't think anyone would agree to shelter a known miscreant.

At 11:30 I finally gave in and decided to do the one thing I had been avoiding all night. I made my way over to Leonard Vastly's Bio-Doom. I knew that Leonard didn't have an extra bed, but he did have a vacant couch, and I had remembered his home being warmer than the naked outdoors.

I walked quietly through the posh neighborhood surrounding Leonard's bubble house. Then I approached the plastic-covered monstrosity and tapped lightly on the window that I believed was closest to where Leonard slept. I was worried about making him mad by awakening him from his fatigue prevention, but I was now tired enough not to really care.

I tapped louder.

Nothing. I walked around to the bay window and knocked some more.

"Psst! Leonard, it's me, Trust."

No answer. I walked back and down to the master bedroom window and tried rapping there, thinking that perhaps he was taking a late bath in his water supply. Not a single sound came from within. I looked around at the dark night and decided that now would be a perfect time to break the law. I snuck over to where Leonard had let me in before. Then I dropped to the ground and crawled under the plastic covering and beneath the mobile home skirting.

It was pitch black below. I tried to feel my way around, finding cans and buckets blocking almost every way. Eventually I felt the trap door and pushed up and into Leonard's kitchen. It was almost as dark inside as underneath. I located the couch and sat down. Then I called out Leonard's name a few times, hoping he would answer.

I would have walked around and searched the house for him, but I guess I was too tired. The thought occurred to me that he may have been balled up in his oven hideout. If that was the case, I could wait until morning to find out. I leaned back on the grain-filled couch and fell asleep.

What seemed like only moments later, but in reality must have been a couple of hours, I was awakened by the sound of the hinged linoleum swinging open. My eyes were adjusted enough to the dark to see that it was Leonard. He came up through the floor pulling what looked to be a couple of grocery bags. Then he closed the floor and opened the refrigerator door. Light flooded the room, silhouetting Leonard as he stood in front of the fridge looking in. From this perspective, I could tell that he had put on a few pounds while living off his low fat fruit bars. I was also surprised to see that his refrigerator had electricity. According to Leonard, he had shut off all current so as to not be a servant to energy.

Brother Vastly began to unload groceries into the refrigerator. Then he shut the refrigerator door and walked right past me. He picked up a huge cardboard box to reveal a TV set. He turned it on and backed up toward me to take a seat on his couch.

"Hey," I warned as he bent to sit.

"Whoaaa!" he screamed, throwing the soda he had in his hand into the air and jumping on top of the bags of flour lying on the floor. In the light of the TV, I watched him scramble frantically for something.

"Brother—"

Before I could finish my sentence, gunshots began to ring out wildly. I slid off of my seat and pushed my back up against the base of the grain-filled couch, thinking about what an absolutely pathetic way to die this was. I could see the headlines already: "Local boy buried by bullets and barley." After a couple of seconds, however, I realized that I was still alive. I looked up just as Leonard threw something across the room at me. I jumped up, running out of the way

162

and knocking Leonard into a huge bag of flour. The bag ripped and exploded all over the two of us and the TV. Brother Vastly slipped away from me and fell to the floor. He folded into a fetal position mumbling something like, "Must protect the soft innards." I rolled him over and stared at him.

"Brother Vastly, it's me, Trust."

He slowly opened his eyes and gazed at me in astonishment.

"Trust?" he asked as bits of flour continued to flutter to the floor.

"Yes," I said with great relief.

"What the heck are you doing in my dome?" he whined, straightening himself and sitting up. Then he leaned over and pressed the stop button on his home stereo. The sound of gunshots ceased.

"Clever," I observed, indicating his method of home security.

"I never much cared for guns," Leonard said, embarrassed.

"I won't tell a soul," I promised.

"So, what are you doing here?" he cleared his throat, trying to act tough.

"I had no place to go, so I came here. When you didn't answer I crawled in the way you showed me. I'm so sorry."

"'Sorry' is nothing but a lower form of flattery," he said, leaning over and pushing himself up.

"Well," I tried, "I didn't mean to break into your beautiful palace."

"Thank you," Leonard nodded.

I stood up straight and dusted myself off.

"So why can't you just go to your home?" Leonard asked.

"Grace and I sort of got into a disagreement, and . . ."

"Say no more," Leonard insisted. "We've all been there."

Falling flour shimmered under the light of the infomercial now showing.

"I'm sorry about the mess," I apologized. "I didn't think you'd react so hastily."

"I'm a pro at reacting," he pointed out.

"What about your neighbors?" I questioned. "I'm sure they heard the fake shots. Won't they call the police?"

"Don't worry about the police," he piffed. "I've been through this before."

About two minutes later, as we were picking things up, we heard a car pull up outside Leonard's home. There was a loud rap on the front door.

"Leonard," a male voice called out.

Leonard unlocked the front door and pushed it open as far as the plastic covering would allow. Through the four open inches I could see flashing red and blue lights, as well as the blurry profile of a big man. Leonard flipped on an inside light, once again giving away his current power connection to the local electric company.

"What seems to be the problem, officer?" Leonard yelled.

"Could I come in for a moment?" the cop asked.

"It's best that we don't corrupt the bubble," Leonard insisted.

164

"Leonard," the cop seemed to pleadingly whine.

"Everything's okay," Leonard comforted. "I thought there was an intruder. Turns out it was just someone from my church."

Even in the dark outside I could see the cop shake his head.

"It was only a recording," Leonard added.

"We went over all this before, Leonard," he said mournfully. "We can't have you waking up the neighborhood every time a noise worries you."

"I know, I know," Leonard said, bothered. "But aside from some scattered wheat flour things are in order."

"Leonard," the cop begged.

"Sam," Leonard whined, apparently more familiar with this lawman than he had let on.

"Just no more noise. Promise me?"

"I promise," Leonard said begrudgingly.

"And finger crossing doesn't count this time," the cop said, frustrated.

I looked down at Leonard's hands just as he was uncrossing his fingers.

"All right," he consented.

Leonard shut the door and turned to me.

"Sam was married to my sister Tina for a couple years. They broke up when Tina and my two older sisters went into business together. The business went bust about three months into it. People just aren't interested in competitive hopscotch or the gear that goes along with it. Anyhow, now Tina won't talk to either Nina or Linda. My younger brother Fidel did manage to get us all together for a family picture, but I'd be a dishonest man if I didn't admit that Tina's smile looks a little strained." Leonard pointed to a big family photo hanging on the wall behind him.

"You sure have got a lot of family," I commented.

"Mother loved children," he said solemnly.

"Well," I sighed. "I've caused enough trouble for one night. I should probably just leave."

"Nonsense," Leonard huffed, the flour on his skin making him look like a frosted cookie. "You're in need, and I'm an enabler. I've got a spare couch with your name on it."

I looked over at the empty couch he was referring to. It was covered with flour and sagged above the floor like an exhausted sumo wrestler.

"We'll throw a blanket over it and it will be as good as new," Leonard said optimistically.

We both worked for a few minutes cleaning the place up to the point of being sleepable. Leonard then retrieved a couple of blankets from the back room and handed me two of them. I spread mine out over the couch and then lay down. Leonard reclined on his sacks of flour eating ice cream out of a small carton and watching some TV show with an elderly detective who was able to see into the future. I probably would have drifted off if it had not been for him constantly interjecting, criticizing, and picking apart the show he was watching:

"That's impossible."

"A real detective would never leave his gun lying around."

"Oh, how convenient."

"Who wrote this drivel? I could have written a script

ten times this good. In fact, I just might. Where's my pencil?"

I wanted to fall asleep so that I could wake up and have this night be ended, but Leonard was just too vocal. I had never seen a grown man get so worked up over a TV show. Except for maybe when the locals in Thelma's Way would watch *Days of Our Lives* and argue over story lines and plot closures. After listening to Leonard complain for a while, I sat up and gave in.

"Not tired, huh?" Leonard asked.

"I guess not."

"Grace worrying you?" he questioned.

"A little."

"Women," he spat, sending flecks of ice cream across the room and onto the TV screen.

The store-bought ice cream he was eating reminded me that Leonard had not been around when I arrived. I decided to stick my nose into his business.

"So where were you earlier?" I asked. "I thought you never left the dome."

"What do you mean?" he asked back.

"When I got here you were out."

"I must have just been in the back room," he said defensively.

"I saw you come up from the floor with groceries," I laughed. "I helped you put the last of them away."

"Trust," he said calmly. "A lot of people are counting on me. You wouldn't want to be the one to let them down, would you?"

"I'm not going to tell anyone that you went out."

Leonard *Whhheeewwwed*. "I appreciate that," he said. "You're thinking of the greater good."

"If you don't want to stay in here then why don't you just quit?"

"And look stupid?"

I bit my tongue.

"Noah Taylor would have a heyday if I gave up," Leonard continued. "He's just looking for a chance to make me look bad."

"Noah Taylor is a fake," I added.

Brother Vastly looked at me with pride. "You've really turned out to be a fine young man."

"Seriously," I ignored him. "The whole reason I'm here now is because of him. He told me in confidence that this December seventeenth thing was all just a big scam. And when I confronted him in the open he claimed I was just making it up because I was jealous."

"He does have that hair thing going on."

"I'm not jealous of Noah Taylor," I said, frustrated.

"It's just you and me, Trust. You and me."

"He's a crook."

"I believe you."

I suppose I should have been comforted by this, but there was surprisingly little personal fulfillment in the knowledge that Leonard Vastly was mentally aligned with me.

See, everyone? I told you I was right. If you don't believe me, just ask Leonard Vastly, the man over there in the plastic-covered single-wide.

"Thanks, Leonard," I lamented.

"I'll tell you what," Leonard said, setting his ice cream down. "What would you say if we helped each other out. We could make it our mission to expose Noah Taylor as the fraud that he is. You and I could be like a team of do-gooders righting this horrible injustice."

I must have done something incredibly bad in my pre-mortal life.

"I don't know," I said. "I don't think we really are the most believable witnesses at the moment. No one's going to listen to a single word we say."

"You've got a good point." Leonard hummed.

"I shouldn't have walked out on Grace," I scolded myself.

"We all live with regrets," Leonard agreed.

My list was growing longer and longer.

26

DIAL TONE

It had taken a few days for Lucy to work up the nerve to call Trust. She had debated every point and position that she could think of, only to come to the conclusion that she had nothing to lose. Her father was still out of the country, her home teacher was locked up in a mobile home, and there was simply no one else she would feel comfortable receiving a blessing from.

The phone rang and Abel answered.

"Hello," he said.

"Hello," Lucy replied, willing herself to go on. "Is Trust at home?"

"Nope," Abel said flippantly. "Who's this?"

"Do you know when he'll be back?" Lucy asked, ignoring his question.

"Can't say for sure. He stormed off about two hours ago. I don't think he's coming back."

"Ever?" Lucy asked, distraught.

"Well, he's got to come back sometime," Abel duhhed. "I just don't think he'll be back tonight."

"Is your mother at home?" Lucy asked, desperate.

"She went to sleep an hour ago."

"Oh."

"Is this that girl that Trust used to date?" Abel asked bluntly.

Life was just too much for Lucy at the moment. Here she was, the bitter taste of swallowed pride still in her throat, and hitting up against little brother syndrome. With each rise and fall of emotion, God was becoming more and more distant to her. She could see little purpose in a creator who relished the slow discomfort of his children. What good was a world where those in need were victims of petty particulars like schedules and missed opportunities? Why would a fair God put her in such a hopeless place?

"Hello," Abel said sarcastically. "Are you still there?"

Lucy hung up the phone by throwing it across the room. It slammed up against her vanity, smashing it into a dozen pieces.

The irony was completely overlooked.

27

FIT TO BE TIED

Roger Williams was becoming increasingly concerned. He was no closer to finding the Book of Mormon, but he was starting to . . . no, it couldn't be. Not a single decent tip had come from the promise of being on the front cover of his fictitious book, but he still . . . it just couldn't be. He had interviewed dozens of people, visited too many homes, and the only thing he seemed to have discovered was . . . it was too unbelievable to admit.

Roger Williams was beginning to care for these people.

He didn't know what it was. Maybe it was the water. Maybe it was the air. Whatever the reason, the valley of Thelma's Way had seemed to soften his heart and leave him less polished than he preferred to be. Out of fear he packed his bags and planned his exit. The first-edition Book of Mormon wasn't worth losing his sense of identity for.

Before he could escape Thelma's Way, however, he had

promised to help Ed Washington get his motorcycle across the Girth River.

The Girth River ran along the far side of the Thelma's Way meadow. It was thick, deep, and relatively bridgeless. There had once been a usable bridge, but it had been burned down years earlier after Paul Leeper led most of the Mormons astray. The burned bridge now spanned the river like an incomplete and charred set of Lincoln Logs. The only way across the Girth these days was to use one of the community rafts. You had to take your raft to the head of the river and paddle furiously across before the current washed you out of town completely. In his quest to find the Book of Mormon, Roger Williams had crossed the river many times. He had actually become quite good at it. So good, in fact, that now that Ed Washington wanted to get his motorcycle over to the other side, he looked first to Roger for help.

Foolishly, or fatefully, Roger agreed.

Ed owned one of only two motor vehicles that the town had to its name. He had been given the old motor-cycle by Digby Heck after Leo Tip gave Digby his piece-meal car that he had built himself. There were no real roads for Digby to drive on, but he liked to circle around the boardinghouse acting better than all the poor people on foot. The motorcycle was actually a far more functional mode of transportation for this town. Ed rode it daily down the thin footpath that connected Thelma's Way to Virgil's Find. Ed was currently enrolled at the College of Virgil's Find, taking mostly electives until such a point that he could decide what he wanted to be when he grew up. Most folks felt that Ed had better hurry up and figure it out, seeing how he had just turned forty-five and wasn't getting any younger, or smarter, for that matter.

Well, today was Wednesday, and Ed had no classes. He decided to fill his time finding a way to get his motorbike across the Girth River so he could try out a few of the trails over there. To the best of anyone's knowledge, which really wasn't saying a whole lot, no one could remember any motorized vehicle being driven on the other side of the river.

Ever.

Ed sensed a personal challenge.

Unfortunately for Roger Williams, Ed's personal challenge required the help of others.

"Why don't you just ride around in the meadow like usual?" Roger asked. "There's plenty of ground to travel here."

Ed shrugged his shoulders. "I don't know. I suppose the urge to go where no man has gone before and all is getting to me."

"But folks have actually gone there before," Roger informed Ed.

"Sure they have, on foot."

"Actually, Ed, I was sort of heading out for a bit. I've got some things to do."

"Please," Ed begged him. "Pete said he'd help, but you know how Pete is. He's not exactly an expert on things like this."

"All right," he relented. "I'll help you, but it'll need to be quick."

Roger and Ed headed out across the meadow. Ed walked his motorcycle and theorized about how best to get a heavy piece of machinery across a swollen river.

"I was thinking catapult," Ed said enthusiastically.

"I think you're thinking too big," Roger replied.

Ed smiled happily, taking it as a compliment.

"How about just going real fast and hoping the motorcycle will skim across the top of it," Ed suggested.

Roger grinned. "That's impossible, Ed."

"Yeah," Ed shrugged. "That's what I was thinking."

Roger and Ed reached the banks of the Girth near the burned bridge. Eighteen-year-old Digby Heck was there, throwing a long rope with a rock attached to the end of it into the current.

"Digby." Roger acknowledged him.

"Mr. Williams, Ed." Digby looked up from his rope, then pulled the rock back in and tossed it out across the river again.

"Do you mind if I ask what you're doing?" Roger asked.

"Mind? Shhheeesssh, why would I mind? I'm just dragging the river looking for the Book of Mormon," Digby shrugged. "I figure if we ain't found it on land, then maybe I'd find it under the river."

"Actually," Roger said, "if someone had put it in the Girth, it most likely would have been washed downstream by now."

Digby laughed. "That's a good one, Mr. Williams."

"Listen, Digby," Roger said, using his deepest, most authoritative voice. "Do you think Ed and I could borrow that rope for a moment?"

"I suppose I can stop searching for a few secs."

"What'd you got in mind?" Ed asked Roger.

Roger answered by laying the motorcycle on one of the bigger rafts and tying it down with the rope Digby had been using. Ed and Digby just stood there as if their hands and arms were painted on.

"Think it will float?" Ed asked after Roger tied the last knot.

"There's only one way to find out," Roger replied.

Together Ed, Digby, and Roger pushed and pulled the raft to the edge of the river. But just as they were about to test it out, Roswell Ford approached them, drawn over by his own curiosity.

"Now just what is you three dinking 'round with?" he demanded, his old head wobbling as he spoke.

"Ed wanted to get his bike over to the other side," Roger explained.

Roswell spotted Pete Kennedy and Toby Carver across the meadow. They looked to be pushing around a dead squirrel with a long stick. Roswell whistled loudly.

"Toby, Pete," he hollered. "Head over here 'fore Ed and Digby kill Mr. Williams." Roswell then wagged his wrinkly right pointing finger in Roger's face. "You can't put me on the front of your book if you're dead," Roswell said, sharply reprimanding him.

Toby and Pete scurried over to the bank.

"Ed's wanting to get his motorbike over to the other side," Roswell informed them.

Toby and Pete looked at each other.

"He could use your help," Roswell spat.

"I was thinking that we could tie this raft onto another and then paddle the both of them across," Roger suggested.

"Now, in a perfect world, that just might work," Toby mused. "But the Girth would pull both rafts downriver before either made it."

"That's true," Pete said.

"Well then, we could stretch a rope across the river and try pulling the thing over," Roger brainstormed, getting caught up in the challenge of it.

"That'd be a mighty long rope," Ed said.

"It could work," Toby commented with excitement. "Teddy's got that rope she used to hang dry all them towels she found at the dump."

"It still doesn't sound right," Pete said.

"Why don't you just ride your bike over here in the meadow?" Roswell questioned Ed. "You're always going 'gainst the flow. Does your mother know you're doing this?"

"I'm over forty years old," Ed said defensively, his dander flaring at the mention of his mother.

"Well, does she?"

"I'm my own man," Ed argued.

"All right, you two," Roger arbitrated. "Let's not get ourselves all worked up. It shouldn't be too hard or too big a deal to get this motorcycle across the river. Doesn't anyone here have a rowboat or a canoe?"

"Jerry Scotch bought a real nice one a few years back," Toby said.

"And?" Roger asked.

"He forgot to tie it down and it floated downriver and over the falls. Splintered into a million pieces."

"It takes two weeks to count to a million," Digby Heck chimed in.

Everyone just stared at him.

"Learned that in homeschool," he explained.

These people were impossible. How Roger could have ever grown to care about them was beyond belief. This was the laziest, most backward place he had ever visited. There were probably lost tribes in Africa that would find this place repressive and slow.

Roger was about to throw in the towel and leave the task at hand to Ed and the others while he slipped out of town. His resolve was thwarted, however, when Ed suddenly slapped himself on the forehead. Ed's eyes lit up as an idea of gigantic proportions rumbled through his brain.

"Now, why didn't I think of that before," Ed said excitedly. "Toby, does Wad still have that big piece of pressed wood?"

"Of course," Toby answered as if it were ridiculous to think of someone ever giving up such a thing as a large piece of pressed wood.

"You got them big bricks still?" Ed asked Pete.

"They're over behind the boardinghouse," Pete reported.

"Good."

"What's the plan, Ed?" Roger asked.

"You're all gonna feel real silly that you didn't think of it first."

"Spit it out," Roswell demanded.

"I'm going to jump the river," Ed beamed. "We'll build a little ramp, and then I'll sail over to the other side."

Everyone *oohhed* and *ahhed*, embarrassed that they themselves hadn't thought up such a solution. Everyone except Roger Williams.

"Ed, you can't jump the river," Roger said. "That's no different then just riding across it. It's impossible."

"This is a time for support, not mutiny," Roswell scolded.

"Think about it, Ed," Roger pleaded. "This motorcycle can't go over ten miles an hour. And even if it could go a hundred, that still wouldn't be fast enough to fling it across the Girth."

"We'll see," Ed insisted.

"Yeah." Roswell slapped Ed on the back. "We'll see."

"Say something, Toby," Roger begged, knowing Toby was a tad more levelheaded than the others.

"I'll spread the word," Toby said. "I bet we could get a right nice crowd to witness this."

"D'you think?" Ed smiled excitely.

"You'd better bring your bandage," Roger said, disgusted, referring to the Ace bandage that Toby doctored the entire town with.

"Oh, you of tiny faith," Toby commented as he ran off to alert everyone about today's spur-of-the-moment festivities.

Within half an hour, most of Thelma's Way had gathered down by the river. Pete and Wad dragged out his big flat board and Digby, with the help of his little sister Narlette and sturdy Sybil Porter, brought out a few big cinder blocks. Then they constructed a makeshift ramp and aimed it toward the river. Roger Williams had thought about just leaving town. Getting out while the getting was good. But he felt compelled to stick around and witness the outcome of this manmade tragedy.

To make things even more spectacular, Ed tied several pieces of long rope to the back of his bike. He figured once he was airborne and flying across the river, the ropes would flap around in the wind creating a visual wonder like few in these parts had seen before. Folks lined both sides of the path leading up to the ramp. Toby tried to get everyone to hold hands and form a sort of course-marking fence, but Roswell refused to hold hands with Jerry Scotch, claiming that Jerry had never really cleaned up since the taffy pull the town had put on a week back. And Sister Watson was not about to give widowed Frank Porter any ideas by putting her mitt in his. So no one held hands, except for Leo and CleeDee, Wad and Miss Flitrey, and Philip Green, who held his own—but that was mainly to hide the extra finger on his right hand that he had only recently become ashamed of. It's funny how something can be neat at age seven and awkward at age sixteen. Paul Leeper was on hand, taking lots of pictures so he would have proof of this occasion when and if people ever doubted it.

Ed revved up his engine and rode over toward the boardinghouse so as to be able to get the necessary speed required to help him make it across. Everyone watched Ed work up the nerve to make the run. He drove in a few circles near the boardinghouse. He waved at all those standing near the river and across the meadow. Then he faced his motorcycle toward the ramp and gunned it. The bike took off from underneath him, went a couple of yards by itself, and then fell to the ground. Ed picked himself up and ran over to it. He waved to everyone to indicate that he was all right. Everyone waved back.

Roger Williams was sick in the stomach.

Roger figured there was no way Ed could come out of this unscathed. He hadn't even gotten near the ramp and already he had fallen over. Ed got back on the bike and started it up again.

This was it.

The rusted old motorcycle choked and coughed as it tried desperately to get above ten miles an hour. The crowd held its breath as Ed closed in on the ramp. When he finally got there, the motorcycle barely made it up the incline. It reached the top and sort of rolled over on its side, flinging Ed onto the river bank. Well, not actually flinging him, but it was far fancier than saying he rolled limply off of the bike and landed in a goofy-looking heap in the mud. The motorcycle itself splashed in the water near the shore. Everyone just stood there speechless. Ed floundered around on the banks of the river, moaning and flapping like a sea lion who had just been harpooned in the ego.

Everybody ran to Ed's aid. All the fuss really wasn't necessary, seeing how Ed had sustained no more than a couple little scratches and bruises. Roger Williams stepped back from the crowd to watch. Toby and President Heck disassembled the ramp and carried the large flat board over to Ed. They laid it down by him and rolled him onto it. A number of men and boys grabbed hold of the edges and lifted him up, carrying him about like an open-faced sandwich. The entire crowd marched off toward the boardinghouse. Roger just stood there staring at the motorcycle that was still lying in the water. Young Narlette Heck was the only soul around. She wandered up to Roger.

"Ed's not real smart," she commented.

Roger just smiled. Two weeks ago, this girl had been a bothersome pest. Now, however, he found her almost endearing. Although she was at least five years younger than Roger's daughter Margaret, he saw a lot of similarities.

Roger needed to get home. It had been too long.

"The motorcycle's slipping," Narlette said, pointing to the bike that was now beginning to be tugged by the current.

Roger looked around him, wishing for someone he could send to grab it. Not a soul was in sight. Everyone was inside the boardinghouse by now helping Ed dress wounds that didn't need dressing. Without a word, Narlette ran to the bank and tried taking hold of one of the ropes that was tied to the back of the bike. It was no use, she wasn't strong enough, and the motorcycle kept sliding forward.

"Help," Narlette struggled. "It's slipping."

"Just let go," Roger hollered.

"Ed needs it for school," Narlette yelled.

Roger shrugged in frustration. He ran to help. The motorbike seemed to be floating—the large foam seat and gas tank seemed to make it more buoyant than anyone could have predicted—but it was being dragged in the current at a pretty good clip now. Roger couldn't help thinking as he got his shoes wet that this whole day could have been salvaged if Ed had only known of the floatability of his bike.

The rope began to whiz through Narlette's small hands, burning her palms and bringing tears to her eyes. Roger stomped into the water, grasping for the back wheel. The rubber slipped from his grip. He stumbled, pushing the bike farther into the river. Narlette gave up and let go. Roger would have done the same. He could, after all, easily afford to buy Ed another motorcycle. Unfortunately, his leg had become tangled in the dangling ropes. He stood up and tried to brace himself, hoping he had the strength to hold the thing still.

He didn't.

The weight of the bike pulled him over as it continued its rush downriver. He could feel his wet clothes growing heavy. He thrashed at his jacket, fighting to rip it off.

"Narlette," Roger yelled, again losing his footing. "Narlette!"

The motorcycle caught in the fast-moving belly of the river. It whipped and turned, picking up its already speedy pace. Once again Roger was pulled under.

"Mr. Williams!" Narlette screamed. "Mr. Williams!"

Narlette took off running toward the boardinghouse. Her feet scraped loudly against the December ground. When she reached the others, it took almost a whole minute for her to catch her breath and get the words out.

Roger Williams was in trouble.

28

TEACH YE ADEQUATELY

◇

DECEMBER 5TH

Sunday morning I received a call from Brother Morose, the Thicktwig Ward Sunday School president. He solemnly explained that Sister Winters was under the weather. He then told me that I would be teaching gospel doctrine today. I felt like I needed to say thanks for being picked.

"Thanks."

"I'm hesitant to ask you," Brother Morose whispered. "What with all the talk of you and your bad decision this last Wednesday."

"Excuse me?"

"Noah Taylor is a respected visitor."

"Noah Taylor is a—"

"Respected visitor," he reiterated. "And you, Brother Williams, seem to have let your emotions get the best of you. But that's neither here nor there. Today is Sunday, and I'm giving you an opportunity to redeem yourself."

"Thanks," I said again.

"The lesson is on Alma, chapter 32."

"Okay."

"It's largely about faith. And seeds."

"I'm familiar with the chapter."

"A few lessons back the topic was repentance," he snipped. "Pity you couldn't have taught that one."

"Well, I—"

"Good-bye, Brother Williams."

Click.

The last couple of days had not been my finest. When I returned home from Leonard Vastly's on Thursday morning, I found my mother crying at the kitchen table. She was not expecting me and was very embarrassed to be caught knee-deep in actual emotion. When I asked her what she was upset about she refused to answer me. When I asked her if it was concern for my father that was making her cry, she just hollered at me and warned me about prying into other people's business.

Mom was worried about Dad.

It really was no great surprise. We were all pretty concerned about where Dad had gone and when he would come back. It had been well over a week since he had last called. Mom was beginning to fear abandonment. It was no secret that my parents' relationship had not been one of marital bliss these last five or six years. They had begun drifting apart when my father threw himself into building up his tiny empire. Consequently, many important parts of our family had grown soggy in the wake of his neglect. But for him to simply walk out on us seemed unbelievable. And the thought of him just walking out on his business and all he had created seemed absolutely unfathomable.

Grace and I had not had much of a chance to talk about what had happened between her and me. I had tried to get her to go out with me on Friday night, but she kindly brushed me off, claiming she had volunteered to help Sister Barns collect food donations for the auction. When I told her I would be happy to come along and help, Grace told me that Sister Barns had specifically requested that I not come.

So I asked Grace out for Saturday night. She said she would like to, but that the missionaries were coming over to Wendy's to teach her the third discussion. When I asked her if I could join her, Grace explained that the elders were frightened of me, and that it would probably be best if she did this alone.

We were losing big chunks of ground. Our once full relationship was thinning, making what we had feel bald and barren. Alopecia of the heart. I didn't know quite what to do. I had called Wendy and asked her if she could please let Grace know how sorry I was about hitting Noah, and asked if there was any way I could make it up to her. Wendy answered by listing all the things that Noah Taylor did better than I.

It was an embarrassingly long list.

"But I grew up with you, Wendy," I argued.

"Maybe we've grown too familiar."

"Wendy, what are you saying?"

"It's over, Trust."

"What's over?"

"I don't know," Wendy admitted. "I've just wanted to say that for a long time and I've never had the chance."

Doran was continuing to pursue Grace. He had gone to a recording studio downtown and made a tape of himself singing a song he had written for her. It was called "Amazing Grace." He parked his truck outside of Wendy's home and blasted it on his truck's beefed-up stereo system. His voice wasn't as bad as his song-writing abilities:

Amazing Grace how fine your face,
How nice your body too.
I think it's time you changed your mind
Give that other guy the boot,
Give that other guy the booooooooooot.
Dooodoodoo, ooohwaahhwahhhdiddy.
Etc. etc.

Things were just getting more and more confusing. So Saturday afternoon, I bought Grace a card and made Abel deliver it to her. It was one of those cards that guys only buy when they know they're in trouble. There was an angel on the front with a poem underneath. On the inside, there was a broken heart with a big bandage on it. Like I said, under normal circumstances I would have gone with something a little more classy, a little less desperate.

With Abel reporting back that the card had been successfully delivered, I spent Saturday evening with my sister Margaret, shopping for sweaters at the Gap. I wasn't willing to admit defeat just yet.

Margaret and I returned home from the mall to find a

note from Noah taped to the front door. He was basically apologizing for having done anything to offend me and pleading for my forgiveness. This guy was unbelievable. He didn't flinch. For days I had felt nothing but rage and disgust for the man; now I found myself actually wondering if I could have somehow misunderstood him. I replayed our conversation in my head, finding nothing open to any other interpretation but that he was a jerk in nice guy's clothing.

I wanted desperately to talk to someone about everything going on in my life, but my only real confidant at the moment was Leonard Vastly. And even though I was beginning to sort of like the guy, I wasn't about to start sharing secrets with him. Besides, the only way I had to talk to him was by visiting his garlic-scented doom dome. I considered calling President Heck in Thelma's Way. Chances were he was hanging around the boardinghouse and I'd be able to catch him. But President Heck was not only a friend, but he was also the father of the girl that I was currently stewing about.

Saturday night I went to bed feeling more lonely than I had felt in a long while. I stared at the ceiling for hours, running all the things that were bothering me back and forth across my mind. I eventually fell asleep in uncertainty.

After I got off the phone Sunday morning with Brother Morose, I put on my new sweater and yelled down the hall for Margaret and Abel to hurry up. Church started in half an hour, and I didn't want to be walking down the aisle late. I was already feeling conspicuous enough in my new outfit. I didn't want to give anybody anything extra like arriving late to use against me. When I got downstairs, my mother informed me that she wouldn't be going to church.

"Are you feeling all right?" I asked her.

"I'm fine," she insisted, looking at me. "I just don't feel up to going. And your sweater doesn't match your tie."

I left that discussion right there.

Grace knocked on the back door and Margaret let her in.

She looked as beautiful as usual—her hair full and loose, her green eyes not letting on to the fact that she knew just how pleased I was to see her. I stared at her, taking in all the subtle changes she had undergone since being here. It wasn't that she was fading into someone else, or that she was shedding her old self to take on the new. Who she was and had always been was just getting more polished in Southdale. As if Southdale were toothpaste with whitening agents. She had moved up at least seven shades, currently residing at a brilliance two notches above blinding. The only real tainting she had sustained was her willingness to take Noah's side over mine. But with the things I had done, I couldn't completely blame her.

Grace took my hand.

"Thanks for the card," she said.

Who can resist a bandaged heart?

"You're welcome," I said humbly.

We got into my mother's car and drove over to the chapel. It was a wonderfully nice day for December. The sun was out, and on the ride over, I spotted at least three pedestrians brave enough to sport shorts on a warm winter morning. The sky was clear above Southdale, making the world seem that much wider and that much warmer. Suddenly, I felt self-conscious about my sweater.

I watched a small plane streak across the blue, two thin trails of smoke behind it. From down below, it gave the illusion of being the toggle on a smoky sky zipper.

The church parking lot was about two-thirds full when we arrived. Everyone was walking in past Bishop Leen, who was out front with a couple of deacons trying to extract a kite that had become tangled up in our steeple over the weekend. They were having very little luck.

Before we reached the building doors, Sister Cravitz stopped us and asked if she could talk to me alone. Grace went in with Abel and Margaret to save us seats.

"What can I help you with?" I asked as we stood outside.

"Your hair's getting better," she observed.

"Thanks. Did you need something?"

"Well, I'm aware of how things are going with you and Grace, and I'm afraid I took a little liberty," she said, as if she had just swiped a hotel towel or taken a salt shaker from some restaurant.

"Do you want me to help you put it back?" I asked, trying lamely for humor.

Sister Cravitz just scowled. I mean that as a statement of fact like "grass is green" or "the sky is blue." Sister Cravitz's face only had one gear. She never smiled, she just scowled.

"Trust," she said. "I'm doing you a favor."

Warning bells began to ring. The last time Sister

Cravitz had done me a favor I had found myself signed up and committed to teaching orphans how to make piñatas at the Southdale orphanage.

"I have a niece," she continued.

"Sister—"

"Hear me out," she said, holding her wrinkly palms up at me and flashing the deep, long life-lines that she was always bragging about. "Cindy, that's her name, Cindy Finders. She's a relative on my side. Doesn't have the Cravitz name, but she has a nice share of the Cravitz's levelheadedness. She's also served a mission in Spain. Speaks pretty Spanish though I can't understand a word of it."

"Sister Cravitz, I'm honored, but—"

"Trust, you're a sharp-looking man. I've always thought that. I can't say that I'm giddy about all your choices, but I'm well aware of how handsome you've become."

I hadn't thought I could become any more uncomfortable.

"Grace and I—" I attempted to say.

"I know," she said soberly. "Things aren't the best for you and her. So that's where that liberty I took comes in. I e-mailed my sister back in Georgia, and she's going to see about getting me a picture of Cindy for you. I know, I know, it seems mighty shallow to swap pictures, but you can't be too careful these days. Did you see who Margaret Chad married?"

"Actually, I did, I—"

"Well, I suppose he's got really nice insides. Anyhow, I don't have a single picture of Cindy past the age of twelve, and honestly, Trust, she didn't bloom until at least three years after that. I could have sworn I had a picture of her in a sweater and poodle skirt, but my sister tells me I'm getting Cindy mixed up with pictures of myself when I was a girl."

"Oh." Dear merciful me.

"My sister says she'll get me a current picture of Cindy," Sister Cravitz went on. "Who knows, there might be one in the mail as we speak. In turn, however, Cindy needs a picture of you."

"Really, Sister Cravitz," I tried to inform, "Grace and I are doing great. I'd hate to get this Cindy involved when I'm already committed to someone else. Do you see what I mean?"

"So, do you have a picture?"

I don't know what I was more bothered by, the fact that Sister Cravitz wasn't listening to me, or the fact that she thought me to be the kind of person who carried around a picture of myself.

"I don't," I answered.

"No big deal," she scowled. "I brought my camera."

From her huge handbag, Sister Cravitz pulled out the oldest-looking camera I had ever seen. It had a giant lens and an accordion-like body that seemed to blend with the folds of her old hands. On top of it was a big row of square flash bulbs.

"Stand up against the building and I'll snap a couple of you."

"Sister—"

"Trust," she scolded. "Let's make things happen."

"But I need to get inside."

"It will only take a moment," she insisted. "We've got a good five minutes before church starts."

"Actually," I insisted, "I'm teaching gospel doctrine today and I wanted to set up the room before sacrament meeting."

"Set up your room? With what?" She called my bluff.

"Um, I was going to see if the library had a tablecloth or something."

Sister Cravitz eyed me suspiciously.

"They've got two of them," she said. "Donated them both myself. I must say it's sort of refreshing to see a man take the time to pretty up a room. Doctrine sits much easier when there's a homey feeling about."

"Isn't it the truth," I agreed, slipping away and into the building.

Sister Cravitz followed me in. I began heading straight for the chapel before she informed me that the library was the other way. I begrudgingly went to the library and checked out one of Sister Cravitz's tablecloths. I ran to my classroom and threw the tablecloth over the table. Then I hurried into the chapel. I took a seat by Grace just as the prelude music stopped.

"I missed you," Grace said kindly.

My sweater was working its magic.

Sacrament meeting was rather uneventful. Brother Jack talked about gospel hobbies, and how we Saints would be best to avoid them altogether. He then went into great detail about how he had mapped out the stars and made timelines of all prophecy dealing with the last days. His conclusion was that Noah Taylor's December seventeenth date was off by maybe two weeks, give or take a day.

I had noticed that Noah was not around this morning. I knew that he visited other wards, and had even been peddling his services to some of the other denominations in town. I figured he was simply off doing the fraud thing. My thoughts of him continued to mellow. Sure, he was a two-faced phony, and yes, this December seventeenth thing was made up, but at least he was getting our ward prepared. I'd have to hope that a few wrongs would make this all right.

After sacrament meeting everyone drifted off to their classes, flowing down the halls like leaves in a crowded gutter. Grace came with me and took a front row seat in the classroom where I would be teaching. I wrote a couple of things on the chalkboard as people continued to stream through the doors and fill up the room. By the time I turned around, we had a full class. I stood there in relative amazement. I had thought that most people would avoid my classroom when they saw that it was me teaching. Instead it was like a feeding frenzy. The smell of blood had drawn a nice-sized crowd. Even Doran was there; he had taken a seat right next to Grace. He and she exchanged a few words as Brother Morose looked at his watch and coughed, calling attention to the fact that I was running two minutes late.

"Good morning," I began. "When I got the call to teach this morning I was excited to find out that we would be covering Alma, chapter 32. So if you would all . . ."

Brother Morose raised his hand.

"Yes," I responded.

"Usually we begin class with a prayer, Trust," he said as if he were auditioning for the part of an undertaker.

"Of course," I apologized. "Sister Barns, would you mind?"

She obviously did, looking visibly upset about me picking her. Of course she really had no choice but to say yes. If she said no everyone would be forced to spend the entire class period wondering just what she had done to prevent her from praying. So rather than suffer the wondering imaginations of her fellow classmates, she stood and prayed.

"Amen," the class said in unison.

"Thank you, Sister Barns," I nodded. "Now if everyone would please open their scriptures to Alma, chapter 32."

People pulled out their scriptures and opened them as if they were presents they had received from a cheap aunt. I could tell this was going to be one enthusiastic class period.

"Before we begin," I started, "could I get those of you who have already read the lesson to please raise your hands?"

Three arms went up. I acted like I was okay with this, counting the three hands slowly to make it seem like they were more.

"All right, Brother O'Shawn," I asked. "Could I please get you to tell the class what the definition of faith is?"

"Well," he said, clearing his throat. "I think what Alma is trying to say in this chapter is that if you lose sight of the

Savior, your vision, or your spiritual eyes as it may, becomes blinded. Making us less than our Father expects."

"Okay," I replied, suddenly remembering why Brother O'Shawn was never called on in class. "So the definition of faith is . . . ?"

"I'm not sure you can put a definition on it," Sister Treat replied for him, trying to sound intellectual.

"Actually, you . . ."

Sister Cravitz's hand went up.

"Yes," I motioned.

"Would it be possible for you to remove your sweater?" she asked.

"What?"

"Your sweater," she insisted. "I just don't think your skin will photograph well against it."

"Really, Sister Cravitz, I'm not sure this is the appropriate—"

"Faith is believing in something not seen," Brother Morose spoke out.

"Thank you," I sighed. "Believing in something unseen. Sister Luke, will you read verse 28 for us?"

"Can I say something first?"

"All right," I nervously agreed.

"I don't know if many of you remember Richard Dot. He was in this ward about ten years ago. Tall, sold trampolines, kept gum in his pockets for the Primary children."

A number of heads nodded.

"Well, he used to tell that story about that father in the manhole."

"I remember," a few members said.

"I'm not great at retelling other people's tales, but the story was about a father who was down in a manhole fixing or cleaning something. And I guess his little daughter came to visit him one day. She was delivering a message, or just stopping by. Well, either way, when she looked down the hole all she could see was pitch, dark, black darkness. Close your eyes," Sister Luke instructed us.

Everybody except Grace and me quickly closed their lids. We used the sudden privacy to make eyes at one another.

"Imagine a darkness ten times stronger," Sister Luke continued. "Now open your eyes."

Everyone opened and blinked like blind men receiving sight.

"Well," Sister Luke went on. "This girl's father told her to jump down into the manhole and he would catch her. Remember, she couldn't see him. Then this little girl . . ." Sister Luke paused to find a Kleenex in her purse. Unable to locate one, she settled for a crumpled grocery store receipt. She dabbed her moist eyes. "I'm sorry, but this part just kills me."

She was not alone.

"Anyhow," she continued. "This little girl just jumps down and her father catches her. Blind faith, Brother Williams, blind faith."

Brother Rothburn raised his hand and I pointed toward him.

"If you don't plant a mustard seed, you can crush it to make mustard."

I wasn't sure where that had come from. Luckily no one was really listening anyway.

"Thank you, Brother Rothburn, and thank you, Sister Luke. I think that's a great example of faith," I said with less than complete honesty.

"Wait a second, Brother Williams," Sister Leen said, coming to life. "Why would a caring father ask his young daughter to jump in a deep dark hole?"

"I think it's just an analogy."

"Well, it's a poor one," Sister Leen huffed. "Besides, what kind of work does a man do down in a manhole? The one in the alley behind us is filthy and infested with cockroaches."

"I hate to say it, but this warm winter's not going to help that," Brother Rothburn commented.

"I think the point is," Sister Luke defended her story, "often we have to take spiritual leaps into dark places."

"I thought God was a God of light," Brother Treat said.

"I have been reading this book by a Mark Lemon," Brother O'Shawn began talking. "In it he tells about how this life is all just a giant computer program and we all are a virus. I find that very interesting, and not entirely contrary to doctrine."

"Is Mark Lemon one of the General Authorities?" Sister Leen asked.

"No," Brother O'Shawn replied. "Actually, he's not a member at all. But if you remember, the thirteenth article of faith talks about us seeking after all good in all things."

"That doesn't sound good to me," she said.

"Well, in context it's—"

"Sister Luke," I interrupted. "Would you please read verses 30 through 33," I motioned, desperately trying to bring the lesson back on track.

Sister Luke begrudgingly read the verses. Then we all sat there in silence for a moment. I raised my finger as if to make a point and was temporarily blinded by the flash of Sister Cravitz's antique camera. A giant blue dot now hovered above everything I saw. Old Sister Timmons looked normal, but everyone else had suddenly aged.

"Sister Cravitz," I began to protest.

"I think it's an interesting use of the word 'the' in verse 28," Brother Morose interrupted, backtracking just a bit and speaking louder than I felt was necessary. "'The' can mean so many things, but Alma clearly meant it to say 'the word.' Not 'a word,' not 'thee word,' not just 'word,' but 'the word.'"

My word.

"Interesting observation," I commented. "I think that every word in the scriptures actually can—"

Sister Cravitz shot picture number two. I held my hand in front of my face, trying to will my sight back.

"Don't mind me," Sister Cravitz said.

It was too late for that.

"Let's read the next couple of verses," I said, discouraged about how poorly my lesson was going. "Who would like to read?"

Sister Cravitz raised her hand.

"Please," I acknowledged.

"Actually, I just wanted you to move over in front of

the chalkboard more, those curtains behind you seem to wash you out."

"Please, no more pictures," I pleaded.

Sister Cravitz snapped one more.

"Okay," she then agreed.

I caught Grace smiling, and suddenly it wasn't all that bad.

"Grace, will you read verse 34?" I asked.

Grace did so.

"And 35?"

She did.

"And 36?"

"Brother Williams, I advise that you break up the reading," Brother Morose scolded. "People lose interest if they are not involved."

"Sister Laramie, would you please read verse 36?"

Janet Laramie read the verse and then told a short, unrelated story about a niece of hers that had recently had such a hard time finding a modest prom dress.

"Thanks," I sighed. "We're running out of time and I wanted to get the main point of this chapter across. And that is that Alma wasn't . . ."

Brother Rothburn raised his hand. I hung my head, realizing that now I would never be able to make my point.

"Yes," I said in defeat.

Brother Rothburn stood up, indicating that he had more to say than the circulation in his sitting legs would allow. "When the Saints assembled in the Kirtland Temple, most people thought that they had achieved Zion. But as we all know, Zion was far from established. I've got a cousin that moved to Missouri just so that he could be ready—"

"Brother Rothburn," I interrupted. "Since you're standing, would you mind giving us a closing prayer?"

"Not at all," he said, having been properly tricked.

Ten minutes later class was dismissed.

"So?" I asked Grace after the room had emptied.

"You did great," she replied affectionately.

"I used to think the branch in Thelma's Way was so weird," I remembered as I put my things into my bag. "Brother Rothburn's almost as bad as Jerry Scotch."

"I don't know," Grace debated. "I just think that time has faded your memory."

"I'm sorry about what I did to Noah," I apologized as we walked out together.

"I know," she replied. "You just don't know him."

"I know he's not telling the truth."

Grace was quiet. We parted ways in front of the foyer bulletin board. Grace went off to Relief Society, and I stood around to read what was posted. There was a fireside coming up on manners, taught by a Dr. David Nuckols. There would be a stake choir retreat in two weeks at the Dintmore Lodge. Members were encouraged to bring both their voices and spouses. And, of course, there was a large piece of orange poster board encouraging folks to get prepared before the seventeenth. In big letters on top of the poster it said, "Those prepared will be spared."

By the time I had finished reading all the posted information, priesthood had already begun. Not wanting to interrupt, or at least trying to make myself believe that was the reason, I stepped outside to enjoy the beautiful day. I walked down the side of the building and sat down next to a big tree that was growing by a row of bushes. The sun smashed through the leaves above, making me look cracked and broken. The large park across from the church was filled with people playing and acting as if Sunday were Saturday. A couple kites flew low in the thin December sky. I was just beginning to feel guilty about not going to priesthood when a pair of hands came up behind me and covered my eyes.

"Guess who?" the voice said, the inflection letting me know it was Leonard.

"Leonard."

"Not so loud," he whispered.

I turned around to see Leonard Vastly. He looked like I had last seen him, except now he had what appeared to be magnets strapped all over his body. He was crouched down behind the tree and leaning into the bushes. He had on a hat and dark clothing so as to be less obvious.

"What are you doing?" I asked.

"I came to talk to you," he said softly, wincing ever so subtly.

"What's with all the magnets?"

"This Bio-Doom isn't exactly a moneymaker," he said. "I'm looking into a few business opportunities."

"Magnets?"

"Multilevel magnets. They help balance out your electrolytes," he said as if rehearsed. "These on my ankles help firm up my skin. The ones on my forearms are actually rearranging the molecules in my hands to make me stronger. How about you, Trust, have you noticed a lack of energy in your life lately?"

"I'm not buying any of your magnets, Leonard."

"They're your electrolytes," he said, as if I were condemning myself to poor physical health by not taking him seriously. "I'll leave you with this," he offered. "These magnets have changed my life. I can't imagine . . ."

Leonard paused and then pulled a pamphlet from out of his shirt pocket. I could see him read a line to himself, trying to remember what to say. He pressed a hand to his head as if in pain.

"I can't imagine a pain-free day without them," he finally finished.

"Are you okay?" I asked, noticing that he was wincing quite a bit.

"I'll be all right," he said bravely. "It's just a little headache."

"Did you take some aspirin?"

"Phhheww," Leonard scoffed. "Aspirin is so passé. I've got a four-pound magnet in my hat. That'll cure it."

I tried not to smile.

"So, did you come to sell me magnets?" I asked.

"Nope, I did some checking on this Noah Taylor."

"And?" I questioned.

"Clean as a whistle," Leonard puckered. "Everybody that ever knew him loves him."

"I just don't get it," I mused.

"If it's any consolation, neither do I."

It wasn't.

"Well, I just want you to know that I'm on the job,"

Leonard said, patting my shoulder. "How's the women frontier?"

"Grace and I are doing okay."

"Good."

"How's the Bio-Doom?"

"It's not easy living in a fishbowl." Leonard tisked. "It can be awful restricting being cooped up 24 hours a day."

"You're not there now," I pointed out.

"I burned some dehydrated broccoli and had to get out for a while."

"Well, I'd better get back to priesthood. Do you want to come?" I asked.

"I'd love to," Leonard said. "But I'm a victim to commitment."

"We've all got our crosses to bear." I smiled.

Leonard was gone.

I stepped back inside, hoping to salvage some bit of Sunday. But as I was walking down the hall Doran stepped out from the nook that the nursery door created and stopped me.

"Can we talk?" he asked.

"Sure."

"Listen," he said kindly. "I really think we should work this Grace thing out. It's not doing either one of us any good to go on like this."

"I agree."

"So I've come up with a plan," he said quickly, as if hoping to get his idea in before I could stop him. "I'll date her on the T-days, that would be Thursday and Tuesday. Then I get to bring her to church every other Sunday. I get one Monday a month, or two, if it's a month with five Mondays. I'd like an occasional Saturday evening, but I've talked with the full-time missionaries and they have her scheduled for the next three."

"Doran," I began to protest.

"Hear me out," he begged. "She'll still technically be your girlfriend, I'm giving you that. I'll refer to her simply as a friend until such time as she is willing to upgrade me to steady, or even fiancée."

I like Doran Jorgensen, I always had. I loved the way he tackled everything in his life with such openmouthed, wide-eyed enthusiasm—like a dog with his head sticking out of a speeding car. It bothered me that he simply couldn't understand the fact that Grace and I were an exclusive item, but a tiny bit of me was flattered by how absolutely taken he was with her. How could I be mad at someone who saw as much great in Grace as I had?

"Listen, Trust," Doran continued. "I was about ready to give up on Grace altogether. Believe it or not, I get discouraged as much as the next guy. And I haven't exactly been getting positive signals from her. But last night I had a dream, or a vision . . . actually it was a dream. But in it I saw Grace in white. She was beautiful, Trust."

"I'm sure she was," I agreed.

"Not just worldly beautiful, but forever pretty," Doran insisted. "I can't just ignore that."

"I'll tell you what," I said. "Let's forget your T-day plan. But I'm fine with you seeing Grace as often as she will let you."

"You mean it?" he wagged.

"Sure. It's up to her."

"I knew talking would help," Doran grinned. "I just knew it. Thanks, Trust."

Doran and I both walked down the hall and entered priesthood late. I took a seat next to Brother Scott McLaughlin, the ward hermit. Brother McLaughlin was a fifty-year-old single man with a huge head. He still came to elders quorum because he didn't like the slow-paced lessons in his high priest group. He was a loner who was best known for the fact that he used White Out to highlight his scriptures. He found it much easier to simply cover up the verses that he didn't understand, or was offended by. I saw him eliminate two before the lesson ended.

I left my meetings that day uplifted.

29

SMEAR

DECEMBER 6TH

Doran had really fouled things up for me by taking my job with Brother Barns away. I strongly disliked looking for work. I had thought about just not working until school started in a month, but I needed something to do. I had volunteered to help my mother out around the house, but she wasn't as enthused about that idea as I was. Brother Victor had come over the night before and informed me of all the possible positions that he was aware of. There weren't many glamorous options at the moment. Two of the better ones were taking part in a three week diabetes test, or cleaning out kennels at the Southdale econo-pound.

Brother Victor had left my house more depressed than I was.

Now it was Monday morning and I had an entire day of job hunting ahead of me. I put on an outfit that didn't look like I was trying too hard while still looking like I'd tried enough. My first stop was the large bookstore that had just gone in about a mile from my house. The store was called Ink Tonic. There was a huge banner hanging outside that said "Four-Day Sale." I wondered which four days, seeing how it had been hanging for months. I walked inside trying to appear assertive. After asking a clerk named Timmy where to apply, I was directed to a woman named Opal. Opal, the manager, led me upstairs and asked me a few questions about myself while I sat on a couch that was so puffy I seemed to get lost in it. Opal sat behind a thin desk that had a fish tank on it.

"Have you worked in the last six months?" she asked without looking at me.

"I've done some work for my father," I answered, sounding a tad more pathetic than I would have preferred.

"And before that?"

"I was serving a mission for my church."

"Oh," she said unenthusiastically. "What are you, some sort of Christian?"

"I guess you could say that."

"Well, as long as you aren't a Mormon."

"Actually that's what I am," I said awkwardly.

"Well what is it? Christian or Mormon?"

"You can be both," I pointed out.

"Not me," she snubbed. "I couldn't stand being just another cookie-cutter sheep."

Opal had the same hairstyle as every other girl downstairs, was wearing exactly the same boots that Timmy the clerk had been wearing, and had so many name brand logos visible on her outfit that it would have taken me a full ten minutes to read them all. She was quite the picture of individualism.

"Express yourself," I joked, hoping she might lighten up just a bit.

"Ha-ha," she said coldly.

"I'm a pretty good worker," I tried.

"Well, we are short-staffed, and my sister said Mormons were reliable despite their restrictive beliefs. Plus, you aren't too hard on the eyes."

This was such a proud moment.

"I can only guarantee the job for the next month. And it will only be about three days a week," she sighed. "After the holidays, things will die down considerably."

"Sounds fair."

Opal looked me up and down.

"Can you be here tomorrow?"

I left Ink Tonic feeling pretty good about myself. I figured that I had to be doing something right to procure a job on the first try. I decided to get something to eat at the small bagel shop next door. While I was eating, Noah Taylor came in and ordered lunch. Once he noticed me, he smiled and asked if he could sit down. With my mouth full I couldn't properly decline.

"So, Trust," Noah said after he had been seated. "What are you up to?"

"I was wondering the same thing about you," I answered back.

"Sorry about nobody believing you." Noah smiled. "It must really hurt to have Grace take my side."

"What's your deal, anyway?" I asked.

"I'd tell you more, but our last conversation left me looking less than perfect."

"I can see that," I said, knowing full well that the effects of my fist were no longer visible.

Noah smirked.

"So are you getting the town all prepared?" I attempted to be civil.

"It's a daunting task," Noah said while smiling at one of the female employees.

"You know, I can't understand how Grace has not discovered what a phony you are. She's usually so perceptive."

"Love can be blinding."

"Don't flatter yourself," I said, taking a bite of my bagel sandwich.

"Why should I when I have Grace around to do it for me?"

"You're nuts," I shook my head.

"You're jealous."

"Am not."

"Are too."

The couple sitting one table over looked at us as if we were a couple of silly grade school kids.

"Oh, Trust," Noah said. "If I wanted to, I could make this so much harder for you than I have. You do know what I mean, don't you?"

"I know what you mean," I said defensively.

I didn't have the faintest idea what he was talking about.

"What do you mean?" I backpedaled.

"I'm certain Grace would jump at the chance to go off

with me when all this is over. Maybe I'll just extend the invitation and see what happens."

"Like I said, you're nuts." I stood and picked up my trash.

"If believing that makes it easier," Noah said, "then you just keep on believing."

I was tempted to hit him again, but I restrained myself, walking out of the restaurant without further altercation.

I had gotten only a few steps out of the bagel shop when all of a sudden a ragged homeless person approached me. I thought it rather odd, seeing how this was the east suburbs, and I had never seen a vagrant or a wino in this area before. I had just begun to think of King Benjamin and his beggar speech when this particular bum addressed me by name.

"Trust," he whispered hoarsely.

"Leonard?"

"Not bad, huh?" he said, referring to his getup. Then he did a little spin so that I could take in the complete ensemble.

"What are you doing now?"

"I was tailing Noah. I wrote down the entire conversation you two had in there."

"You could hear us?"

"No, but I'm not half-bad at reading lips," he said proudly.

"My back was facing the window." I laughed.

"I had to just guess at your dialogue."

"So what were we talking about?" I asked, amused.

Leonard pulled out a pad of yellow legal paper and began to read back my and Noah's conversation.

"You said, 'Have you been to see Leonard Vastly's Bio-Doom?' And he said something about being jealous. You said, 'I can't believe how prepared that Leonard is.' And he said, 'Southdale sure had a long growing season.' I'm not sure why he said that, but I guess it's in reference to planting grain. How'd I do?" Leonard asked.

"Well," I began to say.

Leonard pulled out a glass bottle from his long wrinkled coat and took a big swig. It was obvious the drink was part of his undercover disguise. He wiped his mouth with the back of his sleeve and *ahhhed*.

"What are you drinking?" I questioned.

"I'm glad you asked," Leonard brightened. "This is Fiji prana juice. It's from Fiji."

"That would explain the name." I smiled. "Where'd you get it?"

"I'm selling it now. I ditched the magnet deal. Too many complications."

"Complications?"

"Well, yesterday after I talked to you, I was walking downtown through the swap meet and I unknowingly attracted a few pieces of jewelry to me. Long story short, did you know you can post bail with a credit card?"

"I had no idea."

"Technology is really changing things," Leonard reflected. "Anyhow, I've decided to try selling this juice. You need some of this, Trust. It's from a rare fruit, and it stabilizes your entire body. Only fifty bucks a bottle."

"I can't afford it." I smiled.

"You can't not afford it." Leonard smiled back.

"I'm not buying any of your juice, Leonard."

"Just hear me out," he said, handing me his bottle to look at. "This is the only company that takes the juice in its freshest form, seals it up, and sells it to you. You might have seen Fiji prana pills, but those things are ineffective, processed until all the good is taken out of them. This juice goes straight from the tree to the bottle."

"But it says it's bottled in Provo." I pointed to the bottle.

"Listen, Trust, if you're not interested, just say so."

"I'm not interested."

"See, wasn't that easy? I don't believe in high-pressure sales. If the product is good, people will come to me."

"That's smart."

"Before I go, however, I just want you to take this tape."

"Leonard."

"Listen to it in your spare time. It tells all about the Fiji prana fruit. Fascinating really. If you have any questions just call the 800 number on the cover. If they ask who gave you the tape give them my membership number there on the back."

"753CON?"

"Those letters are assigned randomly," Leonard lamented. "I'm trying to get mine changed."

"Thanks," I said, slipping the tape into my pocket. "I'd better head home."

"You go ahead," he said, giving me permission. "I'll keep an eye on Noah."

"That's not really necessary, Leonard."

"Oh, Trust," he said, shaking his head as if I were a little child and there were still so many things that I didn't understand. "I'm doing this . . . there he goes!" Leonard whispered fiercely, having just spotted Noah coming out of the bagel shop and heading the opposite way.

And with that Leonard was gone.

I went home and told my mother all about my new job. She said, "That's nice" at least twelve times.

It was time for my father to come home.

30

LOVE VIGILANTE

◆

Roger Williams was not in good shape. The motorcycle had pulled him down the Girth River until he got snagged on a rotting tree that was reaching into the water. He was lucky. A few hundred more feet and he would have been thrown over the falls. By the time he was rescued, however, he had been knocked around enough to do his body some harm. The town had carried him back and put him up at Sister Watson's house so that she could be on constant watch. Toby was called for. He brought his Ace bandage and wrapped the worst-looking bump on Roger's head. Then he prescribed lots of rest and maybe some fresh air when he was feeling better. The prescription fell on deaf ears. Roger was out cold. Toby gathered his things and quietly came out of the room.

"Can I see him now?" President Heck asked Toby as he emerged.

"Sure," Toby replied, wondering why he was asking him. "He's just in there."

President Heck walked into Sister Watson's spare bedroom and looked at Roger as he lay there. Sister Watson followed him.

"Does he look a little purple to you?" Ricky Heck asked her.

"That'll pass," she hushed.

"He could have died." President Heck tisked.

"He's lucky to be alive," Sister Watson agreed.

"Should we call someone or something? I mean he might have family that could worry over him." President Heck fretted with concern.

"No one knows who to call." Sister Watson sighed. "He had his bags all packed as if he were planning to leave, but there were no papers with his things. And I think his wallet must have washed downriver."

"You think it's okay if we just leave him here?"

"Sure," Sister Watson said. "The body's an amazing thing. He'll heal, and then he'll tell us what to do."

"I'm glad you're around to know that," President Heck said.

"Why Ricky Heck, did you just pay me a compliment?"

"Sorry," he said softly.

Sister Watson fussed with the blanket lying across Roger.

"You know what would be real nice?" she asked reflectively.

"A big dish of hot pie," President Heck answered without thinking.

"Wouldn't it be though," Sister Watson said distractedly. "But I was also thinking that Roger here might enjoy a nice haircut. Wad's always complaining about how people never sit still. I bet he'd sort of enjoy cutting on a knocked-out person. Plus, when Roger wakes up he'll look better."

"Mavis Watson, you are a genius."

"You're a married man, Ricky Heck." Sister Watson blushed. "Don't go flinging honey in places you can't reach."

Ricky Heck laughed, pretending that he knew what she was hinting at.

"You know, I think he's lost a little weight," Sister Watson observed.

"I think I found it," President Heck joked, patting his round belly.

"With his face a little thinner, he sort of resembles our Elder Williams," Sister Watson pointed out.

"You know, you're right."

"I tell you, the first thing this man is doing when he comes to is his genealogy," Sister Watson snipped. "Who knows, Elder Williams could be his long lost cousin or nephew."

"Or relative," President Heck said sincerely.

"You just never know, do you?" Sister Watson mused.

"Nope, I really don't."

31

DATING MYSELF

DECEMBER 9TH

The idea behind this date auction was this: if a cake auction can bring in a couple hundred dollars, then a people auction should really clean up. It was skewed logic.

The auction was to begin at six. The actual auction being done by seven, everyone besides those who had bid would depart, leaving the participants and bidders to dine in the cultural hall for a very informal group date. It was sort of an exclusive ward activity that only those who contributed could attend.

"You'd better get me." Grace smiled as we got ready to head out. "I don't want to get stuck with anyone else."

"We'll see how the other girls look," I joked.

"I'm serious, Trust."

"You don't have to do this," I informed her.

"I need to support Noah."

I tried not to roll my eyes too loudly.

"What?" Grace smiled, perfectly aware of how I felt about her boss.

218

Grace and I had talked a couple days earlier about what Noah had told me at the bagel shop, and once again Grace had chosen not to believe. It wasn't that Grace thought I was making up lies to turn her against him, she just felt I was misunderstanding what Noah was actually trying to say. I had volunteered to wear a wire and get a conversation with him on tape, but Grace simply told me to be the bigger man. Actually, she begged.

"Noah's just using this town," I said, trying to not sound too heavy.

"Let's not talk about it," Grace said, fixing her hair.

"I didn't mean to spoil your big night," I joked.

Grace looked at me and smiled.

"It's only one date," I added. "And it's a fixed group date in the cultural hall at that. It won't be too bad."

"We'll see," she said. "How do I look?"

"Perfect," I answered, unable to think of a single English word that accurately described how beautiful she was.

"Your opinion's no good," she piffed. "You're in love with me."

"Uh, huh."

Grace leaned up and kissed me.

The last two days had been so nice. Grace and I had gotten along perfectly. We had both worked during the days and spent the evenings talking and being together. The more I found out about Grace, the more enamored I grew. And the more she discovered about me, the more . . . well, we really liked each other. The only unpleasantries we had encountered over the past couple of days were the constant phone calls that Doran was making to Grace, now that he had my permission to pursue her. He was going at it "full guns." I'm not really sure what that meant, but it had been the last line of the latest poem he had written her. The other concern in my life was the emotional deterioration that my family was going through. My father had still not called. Even his partners at work said they didn't know where he was. They added that if he didn't report to work in two weeks, they would have to take disciplinary action. It didn't look good. But Mom refused to call the police to report him missing. That would be going public, according to her, and she had more faith in Roger than that. Besides, she said, she felt strongly that he was okay. Whatever he was doing was important and we just needed to be patient. Abel, Margret, and I prayed for the best and tried not to fear the worst.

The sky was dark by the time Grace and I arrived at the church for the auction. The cultural hall was one happening place. It was trickier getting in than we had anticipated, due to Brother and Sister Phillips protesting the auction outside. The two of them were marching around carrying signs that said, "Going once, going twice, going down the drain," and, "The low bidder isn't the only loser." Apparently, I wasn't the only one bothered by Noah and his ideas. Either that or Brother Phillips didn't want to put out any money to bid on his wife.

Once inside, I hung up our unneeded coats and looked around at the large crowd. Everyone was there, looking and smelling their best. The Scouts stood inside the doorway to welcome people to this, hopefully, once-in-a-lifetime event. The walkway looked sturdy enough, and tables lined the walls filled with covered food and drink. There were hundreds of chairs scattered everywhere, and garlands were looped liberally through the basketball hoops on either end of the room. Grace wandered off to take her place behind the curtain. I took a seat near the middle of the room, right next to Sister Cummings.

I didn't really know Rachel Cummings all that well. She and her husband, Keith, had moved into the ward while I was serving my mission. She was an attractive woman with a mousy disposition. She was one of only a handful of women in the ward who didn't color her hair, letting a touch of gray show through the dark. Keith was in the military and had an amateur magic business on the side. They had five very little kids and lived in a nice house they had fixed up themselves. It was no secret that she was a nervous woman. She was always worried about finding the right thing to say.

She nodded politely at me.

I picked up a program lying on the chair beside me. I looked it over and set it back down.

Sister Cummings suddenly pointed across the room toward my brother. "Abel looks nice in his new Scout uniform."

I looked at Abel. He had come earlier to help set up the chairs. His neckerchief was hanging loosely around his neck, his hair was matted in a hat ring, and his shirt was untucked and wrinkled. Sister Cummings was obviously just being kind.

"Thanks," I replied.

Sister Cummings sighed, happy that her comment had gone over all right.

I think she was about to say more when Noah Taylor strutted out onto the walkway and stood there waiting for everyone's attention to be focused solely on him.

"Brothers and Sisters," he finally began. "I am honored and sobered by your participation tonight."

I started to get sick. Noah was wearing another sweater with khaki pants, and his hair was doing that hair thing. He held the microphone like an Englishman would hold a cup of tea, his pinkie sticking up and out.

"I would like to thank all of those who have helped put this together. Many hands have made light work. I'd list you all by name, but this old mind of mine isn't quite as sharp as it used to be," he said in an attempt at self-deprecating humor.

A few folks chuckled. I noticed, however, that people weren't quite as quick to find everything Noah Taylor said as amusing as I had thought.

"A brief reminder to us all," he continued. "The proceeds from this event will go to help those who cannot afford their own preparedness. We will take this money and stock up all those who are less fortunate." Noah cleared his throat loudly. "Also, we have been busy getting the warehouse on Frost Road ready. I'm happy to say that all of you who have made the monetary commitment are now one hundred percent prepared. Take comfort in knowing that your food storage is up to date and stored in a climate-controlled place where you won't be tripping over it. It's sobering to think how close the seventeenth is, but come heck or high water, we're prepared."

A few people clapped.

"Back to the matter at hand," he chirped. "After the auction, all those who have been lucky enough to get a date will stay here and enjoy a great meal put on by Sister Barns and the Relief Society. Sister Barns, will you please stand so that all of us can recognize you?"

Sister Barns stood and bobbed out a couple of curtseys. She was wearing a bright yellow dress with puffy sleeves that made it hard for me to see her whole face. From the parts I could see, however, it appeared as if Sister Barns had chosen this night to experiment with new makeup. On a normal day, Sister Barns was above average in height, but tonight, with the heels she had chosen to wear, she towered over most people in the room. She smoothed and tucked her dress behind her rear and sat back down.

"Thank you, Sister Barns," Noah said. "Now, our auctioneer tonight will be Brother Clyde Knuckles. So after our opening song and a prayer from Brother McLaughlin, we will begin."

Noah Taylor stepped down from the walkway, and Sister Morris began playing "Count Your Many Blessings" while young Celion Morris directed poorly. After the song, Brother McLaughlin walked to the front and gave a long prayer begging the heavens that even with his limited income he might be able to afford one of the nicer-looking sisters being auctioned for dates tonight.

Brother Knuckles climbed up onto the walkway. Clyde Knuckles was an active Mormon—as long as "active" meant activity. He came out to all the ward plays, the bar-becues, the socials, anything that meant food served up in the cultural hall. He just usually didn't make it to Sunday services. He worked for a big bank in the city. He was a tall, thick-haired guy with a smooth voice. Brother Knuckles was always chosen as MC. If the activity required a vocal tour guide, Clyde Knuckles was the one doing the talking.

"Good evening," Brother Knuckles said. "I hope you're all as excited about this as I am. I know that . . ."

Bishop Leen slipped him a note.

"This just in," Clyde said. "The bishop wants me to say that he hopes this evening will go over in the spirit in which it is intended."

"The spirit of slavery!" Sister Phillips shouted out from the back of the crowd. She had just slipped into the room to cause trouble. Two young Scouts quickly whisked her away.

"All right then," Clyde continued unscathed. "Without further fuss we'll begin. Volunteer number one is Sally Wheatfield."

Sally stepped brashly out from behind the curtains as Noah Taylor handed Clyde a small stack of cards. Sister Morris played soft music on the piano as Brother Knuckles described Sally's attributes.

"Sally is the seventh child from a family of eight. She has just recently received a degree in veterinarian studies and prelaw. Sally describes her age as moderate . . ."

Sally Wheatfield was an attractive young woman. She had big blue eyes and an innocence about her that made it hard for you to believe that she could be interested in prelaw. She was currently dating Michael Fits, a member of the Rockwedge Ward. As she walked down the runway, she smiled and waved to Michael. Michael got out his wallet.

"All right," Brother Knuckles said. "Who will be the first to bid?"

"Two hundred dollars!" Brother McLaughlin yelled, having been suddenly struck with auction anxiety and prematurely bidding everything he had the first chance he got.

"Two hundred dollars?" Clyde asked incredulously.

"Two hundred dollars," Brother McLaughlin tried to say with confidence.

Sally Wheatfield looked worried.

Brother McLaughlin was considerably older than Sally. And even though the winners weren't required to hold hands or do much more than simply eat next to each other, the idea still smacked of inappropriateness. I saw Michael Fits frantically count the bills in his wallet and realize he couldn't match the current bid.

Michael looked at Sally. Sally looked at Clyde. Clyde looked at Noah. Noah looked at his papers and shrugged. Sally buried her face in her hands and ran from the stage crying.

I had a feeling we would see a lot of that tonight. This wasn't such a good idea.

Brother McLaughlin walked up to Noah Taylor and handed him his two hundred dollars. Then he walked back and took his seat.

Noah nodded to Clyde, indicating that he should continue.

Brother Knuckles cleared his throat. "Our next contestant is Daisy Cravitz."

Everyone gasped. No one could believe that Sister Cravitz would willingly submit herself to be auctioned off. Even more than that, no one could imagine anybody bidding for her. Sister Cravitz walked out with confidence. She had on her biggest and shiniest brooch, and her hair was done up like one of those old movie stars that no one but she could possibly remember.

"Daisy Cravitz is the second child of a family of twelve," Clyde read. "She was raised up north in the wholesome environment of Idaho but has spent the last thirty years of her life out here. She is currently retired and addicted to latchhooks, whatever that means . . ." Brother Knuckles added. "She would like for her bidders to know that she is all woman, except for her artificial knees."

Everyone winced silently. I wondered who the marked man was that was supposed to bid on her. The idea behind the auction was that no one would participate unless there were a surefire bid. I didn't have to wait long to find out.

"Who will start the bidding?" Clyde asked.

"Twenty dollars," Brother Victor waved.

Everyone turned to stare. There was obviously something going on with these two older singles that the entire ward had been previously blind to. When no one else offered a bid, Brother Victor yelled out, "Fifty!" topping his own amount.

"Fifty, going once, going—" Clyde began to close.

"Seventy!" Brother Victor hollered.

Everyone looked at him, wondering if he was familiar with how auctions actually worked.

Brother Knuckles rolled his shoulders and continued. "Seventy, going once—"

"One hundred dollars!" Brother Victor yelled, acting as if he had just discovered gold.

Sister Cravitz blushed onstage, happy to be the subject of such attention.

"Is there anybody here besides Brother Victor who would like to bid on Sister Cravitz?" Clyde asked.

I had never seen the ward in such universal agreement.

"Sold to Brother Victor for one hundred dollars."

Clarence Victor gave Noah his money and then sat back down.

Brother Knuckles took a sip of water, licked his lips, and continued.

"Our next contestant is Grace Heck."

Grace walked out from behind the curtain, smiling with embarrassment. The entire room lit up. She was like a golden grain in a sea of common rye. Her red hair and white skin shone under the makeshift stage lights like stars in the night sky. She had on jeans, with a brown shirt tucked into them. Never had brown looked so fetching. Her green eyes flashed out at me, sending hurricane-like winds to every region of my soul.

"Grace Heck is a native of Thelma's Way, Tennessee," Clyde Knuckles described. "She is the oldest of three children and is currently working with Brother Noah Taylor. She lists her age as twenty-three. Grace would like for whoever bids on her to be about six-foot-two, with blue eyes, and have a name that starts and ends with 'T.'"

Everyone turned and looked at me as if I personally had written Grace's card for her.

"Who will start the bidding on the lovely Grace Heck?" Clyde hollered out.

Brother McLaughlin raised his hand. "Will you take jewelry, or does it have to be cash?"

"You already have a date," Clyde pointed out.

"I know," he huffed. "But I think I spent my money too soon."

"I'm sorry," Clyde said. "No refunds, no exchanges."

"But—"

"And no buts," Clyde joked. "So, who will start the bidding on our lovely Tennesseean?"

"Twenty dollars!" seventeen-year-old Leon Treat hollered, his voice cracking as he spoke.

"Thirty," I threw out.

"Thirty-two dollars and . . . sixty-eight cents," Leon bid, looking at some loose change in his hand.

"Fifty," I yelled, actually feeling a little bad about ousting Leon.

"Shoot," Leon complained and looked toward his father in despair.

"One hundred dollars," Noah Taylor jumped in.

"Two hundred," I hollered.

"Three," said Noah.

"Four," I offered, personally vowing that there was no way I would let Noah win.

The crowd inhaled at the bid of four hundred dollars.

"Five." Noah smiled.

"Seven hundred dollars," I said, knowing that I had just over that amount in my checking account.

The audience *ohhhhed*. Sister Laramie fanned herself as Brother Knuckles looked at Noah.

"Too rich for my blood," Noah said.

"Seven hundred dollars going once, going twice—"

"Nine thousand dollars!" a voice boomed from behind me.

The entire room gasped. Necks craned to see who it was. I turned around to see Doran Jorgensen holding the biggest wad of cash I had ever seen in my life. I had forgotten he was going to come out tonight. I was reminded in a big way.

"Nine thousand dollars?" Brother Knuckles asked in disbelief.

"Nine thousand dollars," Doran bragged as he strode to the front of the room waving the money.

Noah's eyes widened to the size of bike tires. Clyde Knuckles looked at Noah as if to say, "what should I do?" Noah was amazingly quick to hiss, "Close the bid."

"Nine thousand going once, going twice, sold to the young man with more money than sense."

Everyone cheered. Everyone except me.

Doran gave the money to Noah Taylor and climbed up on stage to claim his prize. Grace stood there looking wounded. I tried to explain to her with my eyes that I didn't have that kind of money, and that if I had, I still probably wouldn't have tried to outbid Doran, because all she would have to do is put up with one lousy group date and then she and I could go out and spend the nine thousand dollars that I didn't actually have on something far more exciting and worthwhile. Unfortunately, my eyes just weren't that expressive.

This was awful. I just kept thinking that I had let Grace down, and that Doran was an idiot not to have bid lower. Grace would have been his for the taking for a mere seven hundred and fifty. And where had he gotten nine thousand dollars? He must have come from a far wealthier family than I had imagined.

"That tall kid is nuts," a hooded woman sitting on the other side of me said. "More nuts than a squirrel."

"Yeah," I said, staring at her out of the corner of my eye. I turned away from her and then looked quickly back, realizing that there was something oddly familiar about her.

It was Leonard.

He was dressed in a huge muumuu and house slippers. He looked half-Arab, half-frumpy housewife.

"Is that you, Leonard?" I whispered. "What the heck are you doing?"

"Hiding," he whispered back.

"This is ridiculous," I whispered back. "Someone's going to notice that you're not a woman."

"I can't help it," Leonard said urgently. "I've always had big hands."

"It won't be your hands that give it away," I said, looking at the hairy ankles that his disguise didn't quite cover.

"I had to tell you about Noah," he insisted.

"What about Noah?" I asked, trying to not look like I was talking to him.

"The warehouse he's supposedly stocking is empty."

"What do you mean empty?"

"Empty, not full."

"But I thought—"

"Forget what you thought, you were right about him, Trust." Leonard congratulated me.

"Are you sure about this?" I asked.

"I couldn't be more sure."

"Like, halfway empty?" I tried to verify.

"Completely empty," Leonard said squarely. "I knew Noah would be busy with this auction tonight, so I snuck into the warehouse to see if I could find anything on him. I found something all right. Nothing."

"I can't believe this," I mumbled.

"It's true," Leonard insisted. "And now he's got that skinny kid's nine thousand dollars. You have to do something about this, Trust."

"What can I do?" I said, turning to find Leonard gone. I thought maybe he had quickly jumped up so as to get out before he was noticed. Then I spotted him over by one of the serving tables picking at food that was covered and set there to feed the winning bidders later tonight.

I looked up at Noah Taylor on the walkway. He was blabbing about how Doran's nine thousand dollars was going to help a lot of folks get prepared. He was also going on and on about how surprised everyone was going to be when they saw how well he had organized their food storage for them.

I couldn't just sit there. I stood up and tried to say what

I had to in the most tactful and unsensational way possible: "Noah Taylor is a big fat liar, and I can prove it!"

Everyone turned to stare at me in disbelief.

"The warehouse is empty," I said, hoping that someone would believe me.

"Brother Williams," Noah said, looking hurt. "I know that you and I have had our differences, but is this really necessary?"

"The warehouse is empty," was all that I said.

"Is this true?" Bishop Leen asked Noah.

"Of course not," Noah scoffed. "I'm afraid Brother Williams here is just a little sore about losing his date tonight."

A couple of people laughed, but most folks were more willing to hear me out than I had anticipated. Grace looked at me with angry green eyes. She seemed to say, I can't believe that you would bring this up now and in front of all these people since there is no possible way that you could actually know what you are saying because you've never even been inside of Noah's warehouse, so I'm figuring that this is just some last-ditch effort to make Noah look bad.

Her eyes were far more expressive than mine.

"Listen," Bishop Leen said. "I'm not sure that this is the time or place to be making such accusations."

"If I've been paying Noah for nothing," Brother Treat yelled, "then this is the perfect place to make those accusations."

"Someone's been in the warehouse and seen if it's full, haven't they?" Brother O'Shawn asked in a panic.

Nobody responded.

"Grace?" the bishop inquired. "You work there. You've seen all the food and supplies."

"Actually," Grace said, uncomfortable about being put in such a spot. "I work in the front office. I've not been into the warehouse. Noah keeps it locked. But I have seen trucks coming and going."

Everyone began to holler and stamp their feet. Noah Taylor held up his hands.

"Listen, everybody," he yelled. "Your food is all there."

"Prove it!" someone screamed.

"Right now?" Noah asked. "What about the auction?" he whined.

"Right now!" Sally Wheatfield hollered, sensing a chance to get out of sitting next to Brother McLaughlin the rest of the night.

The whole body of Saints began filing out of the building, running swiftly to their cars. I found Grace and pulled her to the side.

"Trust, this is ridiculous," she said above the rush of excited members. "Noah's not a crook."

"We'll see," I replied, happy that everyone had taken me seriously. "Let's go and check if it's empty."

"I thought you knew already?" Grace questioned.

"Not firsthand."

As we were shoving our way out of the cultural hall and into the parking lot, Doran grabbed my arm.

"Trust," he said with great animation. "Could I get a ride with you?"

"Where's your truck?" I asked, slowing just a bit.

"I sold it."

"You—"

"Sold it," he said curtly.

"What for?" I asked, the answer coming to me as I spoke. "For nine thousand dollars!"

Grace was shocked. "You sold your truck to have dinner with me?" she said, sounding more flattered than I felt was necessary.

"Grace, I had this dream, and—" Doran began to say, but before he could get it all out Sister Cravitz knocked him down making a beeline for her car.

"Let's just go," I insisted.

Grace and I got into my car and Doran followed. We followed the stream of vehicles up Frost Road and over to the warehouse. Everyone got out and surrounded the building's entrance. One after another people tried the front door to see if it would open, working themselves into an angry mob.

"Where's Noah?" someone hollered.

"There he is," someone else screamed.

Noah was pulled and pushed through the crowd until he was finally standing in front of the door. He fumbled with his keys, trying to tell everyone to calm down.

It was too late for that.

The moment the door swung open, people crunched and shoved to get inside. The front offices were packed in no time. Once again Noah groped desperately for the right key that would open the door to the warehouse.

"Hurry up!" Brother Lewis demanded.

"Listen," Noah tried. "This is all one big mistake."

"Open the door," everyone yelled.

Noah found the key and unlocked the door. The crowd moved though the small door and into the huge warehouse with one big surge. Someone flipped on a light. We all just stood there staring, slack-jawed, wide-eyed.

I was in big trouble.

The walls were lined with food and supplies. Mountains of cans rolled throughout the warehouse like sand dunes of self-reliance. Boxes of wheat and grain and noodles and vitamins and so on flooded the floor, leaving us neck deep in emergency preparedness. There were little signs labeling what was whose and how much each had purchased. Labels and canisters sparkled under the long fluorescent lights which were blinking as if the glow had just awakened them.

I was dumbfounded—and found to be dumb.

Every eye turned to me. When I said nothing, Noah spoke for me.

"I've kept this room locked off because I wanted this all to be a surprise. I didn't think anyone would challenge my honesty."

I guess I was anyone.

"Trust," Bishop Leen said in his gruffest voice. "What is the meaning of this?"

"I . . ." I looked around at all the angry faces. "Leonard Vastly did it," I said, folding like a spineless jellyfish with a weak threshold for pain. "He said the place was empty."

"Leonard Vastly's locked up in his own house, everybody knows that." The bishop hung his head out of shame for me. "I hope you're happy, Trust."

I wasn't.

"Listen, let's not let this ruin our whole evening," Noah said graciously. "If we hurry back to the church, we may still be able to salvage some of tonight's festivities. People paid, after all. And the food's still there."

Everyone began to walk out past me. If I had any doubts about how people felt, they were quickly dispelled by the comments thrown as they walked by: "What has Noah ever done to you?" "I can't believe you would do this." "Your mother will be ashamed . . ."

I offered weak apologies to each of them, but it did no good. Grace looked at me as if I were someone with an embarrassing tattoo on his forehead.

"Grace, you have to believe me," I tried. "Leonard said it was empty."

Doran stuck out his arm for Grace to take hold. She looked at me. She looked at Doran. She looked over at Noah. She took Doran's arm and the two of them walked off together. Grace looked back and sighed. I guess they were going to find a different ride back.

I was now all alone except for Noah. He glanced around to make sure no one was within listening distance and then said, "Trust, you really are a piece of work."

I held my tongue.

"It's been fun messing with your head, but this time you saved me the trouble." Noah smiled meanly. "I'll almost miss you when I'm gone."

I walked out toward the parking lot, making an effort to ignore him. Most people were already pulling away, heading back over to the church. Noah locked up the building with his keys, got into his shiny little car, and waved sarcastically as he drove off. I got into my car and started it up. I looked in the rearview mirror to back up, and there was Leonard's face, staring back at me.

"Leonard!" I scolded, "you've got to stop sneaking up on me this way!"

"Sorry," he said. "But how'd it go?"

"How'd it go?" I asked incredulously. "How'd it go? The place is loaded with food."

"I was afraid it might be," Leonard said abashedly.

"I thought you said it was empty!"

"I thought Noah's warehouse was the one over on Pine Street. When everyone pulled up here, I realized my mistake."

I banged my head against the steering wheel and moaned.

"What?" he asked innocently.

I looked at him full on in my rearview mirror. He still had on the pink hood and the exaggerated makeup. He looked so stupid in his getup that I suddenly felt pity for him. I decided not to take the discussion any further.

"Do you need a ride home?" I asked dejectedly.

"Sure." Leonard smiled. "But drop me off at that park near my place. I wouldn't want anyone to see me coming and going from the Bio-Doom."

Leonard Vastly was one curious individual.

We passed the church on our way home. I could see shadows in the cultural hall windows mingling about. The steeple was lit and cars were in the parking lot. I felt confident that had I rolled down my window I would be able to hear the sound of laughter coming from the building, but I left my window shut. I was also pretty certain about what they would be laughing over and I didn't want to hear.

"So, do you think the auction's going all right?" Leonard asked, taking off his hood and primping his hair with both hands.

I had enough to think about it.

32

FRIES LIKE US

My night was ruined. After dropping Leonard off I drove back over to the church in hopes that it had caught fire and the group date had been forced to be cut short. I had the worst luck.

The chapel was just fine. In fact, it seemed to be inappropriately dark.

I drove home slowly, thinking about Grace, steaming over Noah, stewing about Doran, and wishing Leonard had not decided to make perfume an integral part of his most recent disguise. I rolled down the car window and stuck out my head in the hope of getting some fresh air. The wind whipped around me, cooling my still-uneven haircut. As I pulled up to my house, I noticed a red car parked at the curb. There was a blond head decorating the front porch. I retracted my noggin and turned off the engine. I stepped out and faced the music.

It was Lucy Fall.

She stood there in a black sweater and faded jeans. Her

blond hair under the porch lights made her look angelic. She was smiling at me. She was laughing. I thought perhaps that she was just really happy to see me. It turns out, however, that she was just reacting to my windblown hair. I smoothed it down and caught myself trying to act cooler than I actually was. Despite all that life had led me through in the last few years, Lucy's effect on me was still just as strong.

"What are you doing here?" I asked as we stood on the porch.

"I just got here," she said, brushing a still-standing piece of my hair down. "I've been trying to call you for a while now, but you're never home."

"Really?" I asked with far too much enthusiasm.

"I was wondering if . . ." Lucy paused as a car drove past. "Do you think we could go somewhere to talk?"

"Margaret's inside," I nodded toward the front door of my house.

"Are you hungry?" Lucy asked.

"A little, why?"

"We could get something to eat," Lucy said seductively.

Okay, it wasn't at all seductive. In fact, she probably used the exact same inflection and flare when asking the price of dish soap at the supermarket. But for some reason the air between Lucy's lips and my ears had always been against me. It was as if her words were warped and manipulated to make my mind go crazy.

"Eat?" I asked, unable to tackle more than one word at a time.

"Just a quick bite."

There she goes again.

"Well . . ." I hesitated.

"I need to ask you something, Trust," she seemed to plead, a sense of nervousness appearing for the first time in our conversation.

Normally, I wouldn't have even entertained the idea. Grace was so much more than Lucy could ever hope to be. Sure Lucy had this effect thing going, but it was all just smoke and mirrors. Grace's hold on my heart was no illusion. But truth be known, I was more than a little sore about Grace not believing me, and then skipping off to spend the evening with someone who threw cash around like it was lawn fertilizer. I mean, if she was on a sort of date, then what harm would it do for me to do the same?

"Okay," I agreed. "Where should we go?"

Lucy took my arm and led me to her car. We drove over to a small diner called Nick's Pit. We sat down at what felt like far too cozy a booth and pretended we were adult enough that this situation didn't faze us. Lucy was far more convincing than I.

I was just beginning to enjoy myself when a beautiful redhead came into the diner, hooked onto the arm of a tall thin-haired guy.

Apparently the intimate ambivalence of a packed cultural hall was not good enough for Doran and Grace. I waited for the rest of the ward to come in after them.

They never did. The two of them were alone!

I would have been completely disgusted if it had not been for the fact that I was sort of in the same spot. Regardless, Grace and Doran had shifted from a group date in an open place to a cozy meal in the most secluded corner of Nick's Pit. And I couldn't decide if I should stamp over to them in self-righteous indignation, or try and sneak out the back door.

Lucy noticed the storm in my eyes.

"What is it?" she asked, unable to see who had come in from where she was sitting.

"Nothing," I said abruptly.

The waiter brought our food. I found myself peering through the bush partitions between tables, over at Grace. I swirled my fork through my meal and tried to fake interest in the things Lucy was saying. I must have been somewhat convincing, judging at least from the fact that Lucy kept on talking.

Images pushed and scattered through my mind like a theater crowd at the cry of fire. Now that I thought about it, Grace had never said straight out that she didn't have feelings for Doran. I mean, it's possible she had just been stringing us both along. Maybe this last little while had simply been a time of sifting for Grace. Sure, Doran wasn't exactly what I would call "dishy," but I suppose in a sort of "I just got done plowing the north fields and I'm looking for a soap strong enough to clean me up" type of way, he was okay. Maybe Grace preferred that. She did hail from a rather small town. That was it. All those years of living in Thelma's Way had made her go for tall gangly guys who chewed on toothpicks and were intimately acquainted with gun racks. She was probably just sort of teetering on the line between choosing Doran or choosing me and the nine thousand dollars had tipped her over.

242

"Trust, are you all right?" Lucy asked again, pulling me back to my meal. I gazed across the diner at Grace. She was sitting closer to Doran than she absolutely had to. In fact, a real gentleman would have asked the waiter to put a chair on the end of the booth so as to eliminate the possibility of accidental footsies.

Lucy's shoe brushed my ankle as she shifted.

"Sorry," she said, blushing.

Need I say more?

I took a bite of my meal and *uh-huhhed* at Lucy's latest remark.

Grace was laughing. Things were worse than I thought. Doran had a speck of sauce on his cheek and Grace brushed it off with her fingers. I couldn't believe it. I remembered Grace comparing Doran to Leo Tip from Thelma's Way. She had said they seemed so similar. But wasn't it Leo that the entire town had thought, although wrongly, Grace was sweet on? Maybe subconsciously she had felt sorry for letting everyone down with Leo, and liking Doran was a way to put things right.

That was it. It all seemed so clear.

Lucy asked if she could have one of my fries.

"Go ahead," I answered, as if nothing now mattered.

I watched Doran slyly spill his water, causing Grace to have to dab his table setting and shirt with her napkin. It was obvious that I had played Doran for a far bigger fool than he actually was. The old spill and dab was a brilliantly devious trick.

Our male waiter came to our table and asked if everything was all right.

"Yes," I lied.

Then he took a long look at Lucy and left.

Lucy kept talking for a minute and then stopped.

"Trust, you haven't been listening to a word I've said, have you?" she asked.

"If that's what you want," I replied, looking past her at Doran who tenderly split a breadstick with Grace and then scooted at least an eighth of an inch closer to her. The nerve of that guy.

"Would you rather just leave?" Lucy asked.

"Isn't it the truth?" I fidgeted.

Suddenly Lucy sounded hurt. "Trust, I thought you would help," she cried. "Here I am pouring my heart out to you and all you can do is keep staring at that bush?!" She reached up and brushed her tears away indignantly.

She was making a scene. People all over the restaurant were starting to notice.

I panicked, not wanting Grace to see me here with Lucy.

I quickly slipped to the other side of the bench and put my arm around her, hoping to quiet her down. But it only seemed to make things worse. She sobbed without holding back. "There, there," I said. "Shhhh . . ."

Out of the corner of my eye, I could see Grace with Doran. It didn't look like they had noticed all the hubbub. Doran was saying something with great animation. He was pulling his wallet out and fishing through it for money. He threw some of it onto the table and the two of them stood up to go.

Lucy pressed her palms against her eyes and continued

to unravel. I leaned my head in close and tried to calm her. At the same time, I tracked Grace with the corner of my eye like a laser beam as she and Doran reached the exit. Doran pulled open the door for her. Somehow, they had not yet noticed me and Lucy. It seemed like the whole rest of the restaurant was staring in our direction. But as Grace started to step out into the night, Lucy wailed. Like a spigot with a busted nozzle, she bubbled forth with force and volume.

Grace paused.

She turned slowly, her green eyes locking onto my blue. She saw me sitting there with my arm around Lucy and my head on her shoulder, looking as if I had just been caught with both my hands deep in some grand cookie jar that the heavens themselves had forbidden me to snack from.

Grace's eyes darkened as if in mourning. I tried to tell her that this wasn't what she thought, but the words didn't come. Doran noticed us too. He shook his head and pulled Grace from the building as if he were a cop removing her from some gruesome crime scene.

The doors swung shut. Grace was gone.

I thought about running after them, but I was worried about leaving my heart on the floor where it was now lying. Plus, Lucy was really in distress. I couldn't just leave her there alone. I weakly smiled at her, trying hard to appear put together.

"I'm sorry," I said. "I know you're going through a lot. I'm sorry I wasn't listening."

She waved it away, embarrassed over everything she had been through.

"I'll be all right," she said bravely. "It's not your fault my life's a wreck."

I asked our waiter for a to-go box, and helped Lucy out to her car. It took some effort, seeing how I wasn't exactly in any wonderful emotional state myself. When we reached my house, Lucy insisted she would be all right, so I got out.

She drove off slowly.

I watched out my window until 1:30 in the morning, but Grace never came home. It was obvious to me that catching me with Lucy had persuaded her to give even more serious consideration to Doran. It seemed like a good time to take up swearing. But since there was no one around to swear to, I resisted the temptation and fell into a restless sleep instead.

33

ASSUME

◇

DECEMBER 10TH

I woke up early the next morning. I wanted to make sure that there was no way I could miss Grace coming out of Wendy's house. Giving little thought to personal appearance, I ran downstairs in my shorts and T-shirt. I went out front and sat on the porch, watching and willing Grace to emerge. My powers were weak. Actually, pathetic was a far better description. Instead of Grace emerging, I conjured up Doran walking down the street. He cut across our December lawn and stepped boldly up to me, claiming that he had something important to ask me. I would have responded with a few questions of my own, but as if it had been previously orchestrated, Grace stepped out of Wendy's front door and walked across the yard to join us. She looked radiant in the morning light, but her eyes were still dark. I wanted to feel for her, but my own insides were rapidly bruising.

"Grace, I . . ." I started to explain.

"Trust," she interrupted, "I need to tell you something

before I go to work." Whatever it was, it was obvious that she wouldn't be comfortable saying it.

"Doran," Grace greeted him.

"Grace," he replied sweetly, "I'm glad you're here, seeing how what I came to say involves you and all."

This was it, and what a way to go. They had both come to break my heart in stereo. Grace took a deep breath as if she were about to dive into a deep pool when Lucy's bright red car distracted us all by pulling into my driveway.

"Is that Lucy?" Grace asked.

"I think so," I replied, as if it could possibly be someone else.

Lucy stepped out of her car and walked up to the three of us.

"Hello, Grace," she offered.

"Lucy," Grace replied back.

"Hello," Doran said, offering his hand to Lucy. "I'm Doran."

"Nice to meet you." She smiled.

"So, now everybody knows each other," I tried to joke. They all just stared at me like I was out of place. It could have been my outfit, seeing how they all were dressed nicely and I looked like someone who had just rolled out of a dirty clothes hamper.

"So what are we all doing here?" I asked.

"Don't you remember?" Lucy sighed. "We sort of had a date."

"A date?" Grace asked.

"Well, not a . . ." Lucy began to explain.

"Actually, Trust," Doran interrupted, "I feel I should speak my piece and get it over with."

I shrugged, not sure if I really wanted to hear what he had to say.

"You see, last night—"

"Maybe I should speak first," Grace interrupted, touching Doran's arm.

Doran consented.

"I can come back later if you want me to," Lucy said, sensing that she might not be welcome.

"That's all right," Grace said with a tinge of jealously. "I don't want to ruin your early-morning date."

"Really, it's not a date, it's—"

"So, you two are seriously dating?" Doran asked Lucy, finally catching on.

"No." Lucy hesitated. "We . . ."

"That makes no difference." Doran stood tall. "I have a couple things to say, and I'd best say them quickly."

"Maybe Lucy should speak first," Grace considered.

"I'm all right," Lucy insisted.

"I'd agree with you there," Doran complimented her.

"Thanks." Lucy blushed as if she meant it.

"I really do need to get to work," Grace pointed out, hoping to speed things along and acting more bothered than I had ever seen her.

"What I aim to say," Doran spoke, "is that Grace and I . . . well . . . as you both know, we spent a little time together last night. And I wanted to let you know—"

"Listen," I said, holding up my hands, not wanting to

hear what was coming. "I think that Grace and I should talk first. Alone."

"Really?" Grace's eyes grew brighter. "What about?"

"Trust," Lucy interjected uncomfortably. "We can meet up later," she said, taking a step back.

"I didn't know you were dating other people," Grace said, ignoring Lucy and focusing in on me.

"I'm not, I . . . what about you and Doran?" I helplessly flared. "I saw you two sitting there last night, laughing—*sharing breadsticks*."

"The electricity went out at the chapel," Grace explained. "Sister Barns snipped the main wire while trying to find a way to dim the lights."

"Still," I defended. "Splitting breadsticks?"

"It was the last one," Doran explained.

"Besides," Grace simmered, "what were you two doing there?"

"Oh, no," I said. "You can't turn this around on me. Lucy lured me there. I can't help it if she wants us to get back together."

"Get back together?" Lucy fumed.

"There's no need pretending," I insisted.

"Who's pretending?" Lucy snipped. "I just wanted a blessing."

"What?" I asked. "What did you say?" Her words sounded so out of context that I almost didn't understand them.

"You told me you would give me a blessing this morning before I went looking for a job," she said in disbelief.

"I did?"

"I knew you weren't listening," Lucy complained, her emotions surfacing again.

Everyone glared at me.

"Well, what about this big marriage news that Doran has?" I tried desperately to change the subject. "Or the fact that you never came home last night, huh? What about that?"

"Me?" Grace asked.

"Yes, you. When I fell asleep at 1:30, you still weren't there."

"I must have gotten back before you did," Grace said in disbelief. "I went to bed early."

"Well," I tried, "that sure is convenient."

"Trust," Grace said kindly, her eyes now open to the reality of what a big misunderstanding this was. She smiled and once again said, "Trust."

"So what's Doran's big news then?" I said, making a last-ditch effort to take the focus off of me.

"I just wanted to apologize," Doran said. "I don't want to marry Grace any longer. We set things straight last night, and I now know that she and I can never be. I was hoping you'd forgive me for everything I've done."

"Uh . . . sure." I tried to be gracious.

It was too little too late.

"I'll be leaving town in a few days," Doran added. "I hope I haven't ruined everything for you guys."

Doran nodded and turned. He had said all he was going to. He walked across our brown lawn and off down the street. I watched him for a moment and couldn't help noticing that without his truck he looked like a fish out of water.

"Maybe I'll talk to you later, Trust," Lucy said, placing great emphasis on the word "maybe." She didn't wait around for me to apologize or say anything else. She got into her car and drove away, leaving Grace and me alone on the porch.

"So I guess I sort of blew it," I sighed.

"Yeah, you could say that."

"You think you'll ever be able to forgive me?"

"I'll work on it," she said. Then she added, "Marry Doran?" trying not to laugh.

"Well," I defended, "you thought I was capable of dating Lucy."

"You used to date her all the time," Grace pointed out.

"Well, Doran looks a little like Leo back in Thelma's Way. And everyone used to think that you liked Leo and all. And I just . . ." I stopped speaking before I said anything else stupid.

Grace smiled, more with her mouth than her eyes. "Trust, we've been through a lot together. How could you even think that there could be someone else for me?"

"I don't know," I said lamely. "You've surprised me before.

"When?" Grace insisted.

"Taking Noah's side."

"Just because I think you don't understand him doesn't mean I care for him any more than as an employer."

"Really?"

"Really."

252

"Sorry," I offered. "About everything," I added.

"I should be really, really mad at you," Grace pointed out. "So are you?"

"Only if it means we get to make up in a spectacular way."

"What you see is what you get," I said, holding my arms out.

"Let me get back to you on that." Grace smiled again, more with her eyes than with her mouth.

Was it any wonder I loved her?

34

ONE WISH

Sister Watson's home was packed. Everyone crammed to get in and get in place. It had been only an hour or so ago that Sister Watson had noticed Roger stirring. News of his possible coming to whipped though the meadow at breakneck speed. Everyone came bearing gifts and bulk food. President Heck occupied the best seat in the house—a folding chair pulled right up to the bed. Everyone else was forced to stand and huddle over. Ricky Heck took Roger's hand in his and stroked it.

"Are you there?" he asked quietly.

Once again Roger stirred, and it looked as if he were making an attempt to open his eyes. It took every ounce of self-mastery that the town was capable of mustering to simply not cheer.

"Roger, it's Ricky," President Heck said. "You're here in Thelma's Way. Do you remember us, Roger?"

A shallow and barely audible "Yes" escaped from his lips like a ghost of good things present.

The entire house emotionally and collectively *hurrahed*. The very foundation that everyone was standing on expanded and contracted in one giant and joyous sigh. No one cared about being on the front of a book at the moment. All anybody felt was happiness over their friend having held on to life.

President Heck held Roger's hand to his face and cried.

It was a great day.

35

I THINK WE'RE FALLING

DECEMBER 13TH

Monday morning I sent Grace flowers and begged her to forgive me for doubting her. I even asked her forgiveness concerning Noah Taylor—for falsely accusing him. She was willing to accept the flowers with the condition that I would not bother him again.

I sort of promised that I wouldn't.

Monday night after work, Grace and I went to hear the tri-ward choir concert being held at the Southdale community amphitheater. All three wards had practiced separately and were now coming together in what would be a beautiful "pre-Christmas, bring your nonmember friends, missionary and goodwill, family home evening program" (at least that's how the flyers had described it).

Unfortunately, before the first note was sung, problems had surfaced. The three wards began squabbling over who would get the center section and who would be stuck singing from the less-prestigious wings. They ended up drawing straws to solve that one. Our ward drew the long straw and won themselves the center spot. Then they all became concerned about who would direct whom. The solution to this was to have one director facing each individual ward choir. Three directors, one voice. Brother Stablin, our ward chorister, took his place in front of the group.

Brother Stablin had been directing our choir since before I could remember. He was a thick man with flowing white hair growing from both his head and his ears. He had flaming blue eyes and a belly that his belt had a hard time confining. Often he would pull his trousers up over his belly, only to have them work their way down until his stomach sprang in release. He taught physics at the university here in Southdale and took the position of choir director very seriously.

Grace and I spread out a blanket on the ground in front of the open-air theater. It wasn't cold enough to warrant jackets, so I just had on a heavy shirt and Grace was wearing a hooded sweatshirt. She looked like a casual Eskimo with her hood pulled up around her face—her hair spilling out like red grass from an Easter basket. We had brought Margaret and Abel with us, but they ran off to be with friends as soon as we arrived. My mother was supposed to be singing with the choir, but she was not in the mood to do anything festive. I worried about leaving her home alone anymore because her depression was getting worse. We had not heard anything from my dad in weeks. I was worried, but for some reason I felt certain he was all right, and would be coming back soon. I hoped it wasn't just that I had seen too many Christmas specials on TV.

Grace scooted up next to me as we watched the three ward choirs bunch up together in preparation for the show to begin. All those singing tonight had been instructed on what to wear. The men were to wear dark green sweaters, and the women were in red. Two notes into the first song, however, I noticed that nobody had given any thought to where certain people would be standing. Thanks to the way everyone had ended up on the risers, the women's red sweaters spelled out a big red minor swear word—a word that could have been used to describe their performances so far. The moment after I noticed the sweater message, Grace did also.

"Do you see what I see?" she asked festively.

"I do," I replied, trying to appear disgusted by it.

The expletive looked huge, and perfectly arranged. It could not have been clearer if they had tried.

"Should we say something to someone?" Grace asked, giggling.

"And ruin the performance?" I scoffed.

Margaret came up to Grace and me with a couple of her friends.

"Trust, can we borrow some money?" she asked. "We want to get something to drink at the concession stand."

"I'm broke," I told her, stretching my legs out on the blanket.

"I've got a few dollars," Grace volunteered. "Mind if I come along?"

Margaret gave the fifteen-year-old "yes" nod. Grace

stood up, leaving me alone. I listened to the music for a few minutes, closing my eyes to get a stronger effect, and to block out the hidden message of their wardrobes.

"Nice night, isn't it?" a voice said from above me.

I looked up to see Leonard's big head eclipsing the moon.

"Should I be concerned that you always know where I am?" I asked.

"I think 'comforted' is a better word."

I thought so too, but unfortunately that's not how I felt. Leonard had on a long-sleeved shirt and ball cap. And for some reason both his hands were tucked into a muff that was strapped around his neck and hanging at waist level. He saw me look crookedly at his muff.

"If you're going to make fun of the muff, I'm leaving," Leonard said as if he had already experienced his fill of muff jokes tonight.

"I didn't know they still made them" was all I said.

"They don't." Leonard sat. "I made this myself out of big and tall socks and a bungee cord."

"Impressive."

"Keeps the hands warm," he explained. "Plus, it's a lot cooler than those goofy-looking fanny packs."

That was an issue for debate.

"So, what are you doing here anyway?" I asked.

"I came to see the show."

"Can you read the message they wrote out for you on their sweaters?"

Leonard squinted. "Crab?" he said. "I bet the final number has something to do with the ocean," he reasoned.

"That's a *p*," I pointed out.

"Oh," Leonard realized, "it seems mighty unChristmas-like." Then he sat down and lay back on our blanket.

"You know, Grace will be here in a moment. She'll see you're not in your dome."

"All right," Leonard whined, sitting up. "I'm leaving. Before I go, however, I was wondering if you drove here tonight?"

"I did," I answered. "Do you need a ride?"

"Actually," he smiled, pulling a small bottle of something out of his muff. "I had a product I wanted to show you."

"Leonard."

"It cleans your car without any water," he said excitedly. "You just smear some of this all over your vehicle and then brush it off."

"I appreciate it, Leonard, but I'm going to pass."

"It's your future."

"I'm glad you see it that way."

"I'll tell you what, though," Leonard tried again. "I'm walking in on the ground floor of this one. Do you want to know how much money I deposited yesterday just from selling this product?"

"I don't suppose I can stop you from telling me."

Leonard ignored me, pulling a pen and a piece of paper out of his muff.

"I'm going to write down a figure here," he said, biting his tongue as he did so. He then handed me the paper.

"Fifteen hundred dollars?" I read.

Leonard just smiled.

"You made fifteen hundred dollars on this stuff?"

"Well, not actually, but if I sign you and four other people up before January, I'll be eligible to win a two-day cruise to Alaska."

"So you didn't make fifteen hundred."

"That's just an example, Trust."

"An example of what?"

"I didn't come here to be made fun of," Leonard said, adjusting his muff.

"Sorry, Leonard," I said, laughing.

"So I guess things are going all right with you and Grace?"

"I think so."

"I hear your father's still gone," Leonard said casually.

"He is."

"I know I'm not exactly the first person people turn to for help," he said, blushing shyly, "but if I can do anything for you . . ."

"Thanks," I replied, surprised by the offer.

"You guys got enough food?"

"We're fine."

"Well, let me know."

Before I could say "thanks" again Leonard was gone and Grace was approaching. She sat down in front of me so that I could wrap my arms around her. I pulled her hood down around her neck so as to let loose her red hair. I kissed her on the ear and whispered something about liking her.

I could hear her smile.

The choir began singing some somber, reverent song

that I didn't recognize. A few bars into it, however, the three directors fell out of sync. By the time the song was really going it was as if they were singing it in a round. It was like a sacred "Row, Row, Row Your Boat." The pianist was desperately trying to keep up with one of the directors, but eventually the task became impossible and she stopped playing altogether. The choir continued to sing three rounds of what was supposed to be a very somber and peaceful piece.

I noticed Sister Johnson from the ward sitting six blankets in front of us. She seemed to be enjoying the music until her bad eyes focused in on the word that the choir's sweaters spelled out. She frantically tried to cover her kids' peepers. Then I watched as she instructed her husband to do something about it. He argued with her a little and then got up and wandered down to the stage. I saw him whisper something to a woman standing on the side with a clipboard. The woman stepped back a few steps and read for herself. She gasped and then in a frenzy tried to sneak on stage to rearrange the sweaters. The choir members were already confused by the round they were singing, and now this woman was tugging madly on selected members and making them move to different spots.

The lady with the clipboard quickly finished shifting them. They now spelled "crud." Brother Johnson returned to his wife. She nodded over a job well done, taking her hands off of her children's eyes.

Grace bent her head back and kissed me on the underside of my chin—the only spot she could get to from her position.

"What was that for?" I asked.

"I was just making sure you were still there."

"Wouldn't dream of leaving," I said, sounding sappy. I pulled Grace closer as the choir began to sing "Jingle Bells."

"You know, Christmas is only thirteen days away."

"I thought there'd be no Christmas," I joked. "Seeing how the world will end on the seventeenth."

"Noah's not saying it will end, just be disrupted."

"And do you believe him?" I asked.

"No." Grace smiled.

I pushed Grace's hair to the side and kissed her on the nape of the neck. I could feel her respond warmly. I lifted my head to see her amazing profile. Her eyes were softly closed, as if she were soaking in everything that was transpiring around her. I kissed her ear and whispered something about it being such a nice night.

"Mmmmhuumm" was her only response.

The choir finished "Jingle Bells" and tore into "Here We Come a-Caroling." Halfway through the song, however, it became obvious that the choir was now facing a new dilemma. With the reshuffling of members to correct the sweaters, somehow all of the heavier singers had ended up on the back row of the risers. Now whenever those in the front row would lean back, the entire set of bleachers would tilt, lifting a couple of inches off the ground. The singers didn't quite understand what was going on, thinking that it was simply their beautiful voices making the earth move. Unfortunately, the next song was a fast-paced, get-into-it number. The singers all smiled and swayed.

Then in one fluid motion, the whole group leaned back. The risers rose. The entire choir flew backwards, men and women falling on top of and over each other.

The congregation went wild.

Well, as wild as a choir congregation could. The concert was temporarily postponed while cuts and bruises were attended to. The singers also took this time to remove their sweaters, seeing how it wasn't cold enough for them anyway.

By the time they began singing again, Grace and I were long gone.

36

GRAINY DAYS AND TUESDAYS ALWAYS GET ME DOWN

DECEMBER 14TH

Tuesday evening Grace went with my mother and Wendy to homemaking meeting at the chapel. I made myself some dinner and waited impatiently out on the porch swing for them to return. It was a nice night. High above me the sky was clear, and the pinpoint bodies of a million stars were pulsating in the hard black.

But by 9:00 Grace still had not returned home. I found myself counting headlights as they passed, teasing me with their flashy beams. At 9:30 I went in and lay on my bed. The mattress was soft and warm, and I wondered why I hadn't been waiting there all along.

I let my mind wander over the things in my life. Not the least of which was that I was contemplating asking Grace to marry me. We both knew it was coming, and I couldn't think of a single reason to make it later instead of sooner. I felt very sure of who, and how wonderful, she was. Part of me wanted to wait until she had some schooling. But another part of me thought getting hitched before the semester began was a better idea. My mind buzzed as I considered the possibilities. But I grew sleepy and dozed off before Grace had returned.

Sometime a little while later I felt hands brush against my face.

"Mmmmm," I said, imagining that it was her.

My imagination could not have been more off.

"Save it for Grace, Trust," Leonard said, slapping a piece of duct tape over my mouth just as I opened my eyes. I tried pulling away, but my wrists and legs were taped together. "Sorry about this," Leonard apologized. "But believe me, it's for your own good."

Leonard tried to lift me out of my bed, but I was too big for him. He pulled a piece of rope from his bag and tied it around my ankles. Then he yanked me off the bed and dragged me out of my room and down the hallway. For a man that was so much smaller than I was, he was amazingly strong. I struggled to break loose.

"Maaaaaaahhhhhhh!" I tried hollering.

"Shhhhh," Leonard whispered. "You'll wake your family."

I couldn't help thinking that was the idea, but it didn't work.

Leonard kept dragging. He approached the steps leading down and didn't slow his pace one bit. With big strides, he hurried me down the steps, the back of my head whacking against each corner. By the time we reached the wood floor at the bottom, I was seeing stars. Leonard noticed Abel's skateboard. He rolled me up onto it and pulled me out the front door and over to his car, my head dragging against the sidewalk. With a huge heave he shoved me into the back seat of his car and slammed the door. He got in and we drove away. I struggled like mad, willing him to stop and remove the tape from my mouth. I had a few words I wanted to say to him. Eventually he pulled over and turned around to face me. He reached back and yanked the tape off my mouth.

I wouldn't need to shave again for a year.

"What's going on?" I demanded, rubbing my cheeks.

"I needed to talk to you," he said importantly.

"You could have just called, or rang the doorbell, or thrown pebbles against my window," I said out of frustration. "I think those stairs gave me another concussion."

"I did throw a rock at your window," Leonard insisted. "But I guess I was tossing it at the wrong room."

"What room?"

"A room in the wrong house," he added.

"Leonard," I said, shaking my head.

"I didn't know glass could shatter into so many pieces," he contemplated, pulling a pocketknife out of his glove box and cutting the tape around my wrists.

"So, what's so important?" I asked, wondering if he had yanked me out of bed simply to pitch another product to me.

"I got something on Noah."

"Oh, no," I waved him back. "I'm done messing with

Noah. I've learned my lesson. I'm not making another fool of myself."

"This is different," Leonard insisted. "You remember Sam the cop who was married to my sister Tina?"

"Yes," I replied.

"Well, I had him run a background check on Noah Taylor. And guess what he found?"

"I have no idea."

"Well, he didn't find anything exactly, but he discovered a Noah Talmage that had prepared a town in Maine for a coming hurricane he had predicted."

"Noah Talmage?"

"No, do you?"

"Leonard."

"What?"

"Anyhow," I prompted.

"Anyhow, this Noah got everyone prepared and then the warehouse burned down. It appeared to be an accident, but after Noah collected the insurance money, he disappeared. The case is still open in Maine."

"And you think that Noah is our Noah?"

"Could be."

"What did Sam say?" I asked.

"He told me I was watching far too many mystery shows, and to please not bother him at work. So what are we going to do?" Leonard asked.

"Nothing," I said adamantly, unwrapping the duct tape from my ankles.

"Nothing?"

"There is no way that anyone would listen to a word I

said," I reminded him. "My credibility is pretty pathetic at the moment."

"I'd listen to you, Trust," Leonard said seriously, reaching over the back seat and putting his hand on my shoulder.

"Thanks," I joked. "But the only way I'm going to believe any of this is if I wake up one morning and the warehouse on Frost is burned to the ground."

"All right," Leonard tisked. "I just feel so sorry for Scott."

"What do you mean?"

"I just feel real bad about Brother McLaughlin," Leonard said.

"All right, Leonard," I bit. "What are you talking about?"

"Well," he said with new excitement, "at this warehouse fire in Maine, the security guard got hurt real bad."

"How?"

"Seems the electricity was off, and the guard lit one of those hundred-hour candles to find the fuse box and *kabamo*. All the gas that was stored in there with the food and supplies went up in flames. The guard was wounded, and blamed for it all."

"That's awful," I said.

"Yeah," Leonard replied coolly. "But I guess there's nothing we can do."

"What do you have in mind?" I asked in defeat, beginning to wonder if there really might be some connection between our Noah and this fire in Maine.

"I say we arm ourselves with weapons and hold the warehouse hostage until Noah clears out of town."

"Any real suggestions?"

"We could knock out a couple of the city's power grids," Leonard schemed. "Then, in the dead of night, steal everyone's car keys so that no one will be able to drive. Once that is accomplished. . . ."

I shook my head.

"Too complicated?" Leonard asked.

"Just a little."

"I'm tapped as far as ideas," Leonard said, as if I'd be disappointed in him.

"I thought you had already run a check on Noah?" I asked, remembering a past conversation with Leonard. "You said he was clean."

"I had spelled Noah wrong when doing my search on the Internet," Leonard said, embarrassed. "Turns out I was getting personal information on some other guy."

I sighed in defeat.

"I'll tell you what," I offered. "Let's just drive over to Noah's place and tell him what we know. If it's true, he's sure to get spooked and leave town. If it's not, well then, he'll throw us out, and we can go home and get some sleep. Does that sound okay?"

"You realize it's 12:30?" Leonard pointed out.

"So *he* loses a little sleep for a change," I said callously. "If what you say is true, we need to know now."

We drove over to the edge of town and back into the Dintmore Hills. I knew Noah was renting a farmhouse in the hills, but I had no idea where it was. Luckily, Leonard had a small hand-drawn map that he had sketched out a few days ago after secretly following Noah home. When we were close enough, we flipped off our headlights and crept over the small crest in front of Noah's temporary house in the dark. At about two hundred feet away, Leonard stopped the car and shut it off. In the clear night I could easily see the outline of the house and barn next to it. It was a nice-sized home, with a huge square barn sitting no more that fifty feet away. Next to the barn were what looked to be a couple of old grain silos. They stood next to each other, one significantly taller than the other, looking like giant batteries with their weathered tops eroding and gone. A tiny porch light was on at the house. It was a small light, little more than a decoration, but in the moonlight, I could see Noah's tiny white car parked out front. He was home. With any luck he would still be up.

I hesitated, both mentally and physically.

I knew that Noah was capable of lying and deception. But insurance fraud and arson really didn't suit his sweater-wearing charms. The last thing I wanted to do was walk in there and accuse him again, only to have him blab to Grace about what a complete idiot she had for a boyfriend, or ex-boyfriend if he chose to put it that way.

"Go on," Leonard prompted.

"I don't know," I stalled. "Besides, aren't you coming with me?"

"And blow my whole dome thing?" Leonard asked incredulously. "Besides, from what you've told me, Noah seems to talk a whole lot different when it's just you and him."

"I need a witness, though."

Leonard looked hard at the house in front of us.

"I'll tell you what," he whispered, forgetting that there wasn't another hearing ear within two hundred feet of us. "I'll slip into that barn and hide. You see if you can talk Noah into having your conversation in there."

"How am I going to do that?"

"That's up to you," Leonard said. "But if you can get him to talk in there, I can witness everything that's said. Plus if he goes ballistic on you, I can let the cops know what happened afterward."

"Thanks for the comfort," I said.

Leonard quietly got out of the car and crept across the field and up to the barn. The barn was old enough that getting in presented no problem. After a few moments, I said a quick prayer and drove the rest of the way up to the doorstep. I got out and looked down at my wrinkled clothes. I was thankful that I fallen asleep dressed.

I walked to the front door, the dry ground shifting under my feet like sheets of paper. I could hear a TV or radio on inside. I readied myself and knocked.

Thirty seconds later I was staring into the uncertain face of Noah.

"Trust," he said uneasily. "What are you doing here this late?"

"I wanted to talk to you," I said.

"Well, I do have a phone," he snipped. "Why don't you just run on home and call me in the morning?"

"Actually, it's about Maine," I threw out, wondering if he would bite.

He flinched ever so slightly. My heart began beating faster.

"What about Maine?" Noah feigned disinterest, looking over my shoulder to see if anyone else was around.

"We're alone," I said.

"You came out here by yourself?"

"Do I have reason to be afraid?" I asked him.

"No, of course not."

"Well then, could we just talk a moment?"

"Maybe we should," Noah conceded. "Why don't you come inside."

"Actually, I was hoping we could talk out here."

"And why is that?"

"Well . . ." I had no idea what to say. My mind whipped wildly as my thoughts fought to align themselves. The best I could come up with was, "My grandmother died in a farmhouse like this one."

"Really?"

"Yeah," I said, knowing I had no choice but to complete the lie. "It was awful," I mournfully explained. "Somehow one of the old walls collapsed, and, well . . . well, she and I were really close."

"What's going on here, Trust?" Noah asked, obviously not buying my story.

"Nothing," I insisted. "I'd just rather talk out here."

"It's so windy," Noah said, informing me of something I already knew quite well and falling right into the conversational trap that I had so brilliantly been weaving.

I looked around and acted as if I was just noticing the barn for the first time. "We could go in there," I suggested.

"You're okay with barns?" he questioned.

"Sure," I shrugged. "My grandmother loved barns."

"I don't exactly know what you're trying to pull, Trust, but I'll play along for fun," Noah said snidely. "Just let me grab a sweater."

"Of course." I smiled.

A few moments later Noah stepped outside. We walked over to the barn, both of us keeping our distance from each other. We went in the same door I had seen Leonard go through moments before. Once inside, the sound of wind died down and the night seemed to become even emptier around us. My forehead hit against a small hanging object. I pulled on it and light flooded the room. I hoped Leonard was well-hidden.

"So is this all right now?" Noah asked.

"This is fine."

"Well then, speak your piece and get on with it," he demanded.

"Listen," I said, trying to start the discussion on a good note. "I know you and I have not exactly gotten along, but I didn't come here to make any more trouble than I have to."

"I'm not afraid of you, Trust," he snipped. "Say what's on your mind."

"All right," I sighed. "Have you ever done one of these emergency preparation operations in Maine?"

"And what if I have?" He grimaced.

"Well, does the name Noah Talmage sound familiar?"

I had asked the question in a nice enough way. But I guess Noah felt differently. He pulled a gun out from under his sweater and motioned with it for me to put my hands up.

"What are you doing?" I asked in alarm.

"You're a real thorn, Trust," he said. "I took you for smarter than this. And let's just say, I knew you were no genius."

"So that *was* you in Maine?" I said, amazed.

"I'm not going to answer a single one of your stupid questions."

"Listen, Noah, I don't care what you did in Maine, really. Just don't do it here."

"You act as if you have some control over the situation."

"This can be worked out," I reasoned.

"Actually, I'm doubting it can," Noah sneered. "You know, I've never shot anyone before. Then again, I suppose you've never been shot before. Huh . . . I guess there's a first time for everything."

I was just about to make a break for it when I noticed Leonard up on one of the haylofts behind Noah's back. He crept into position as if to jump down on top of him.

I tried to stall. "Really, Noah? I'd guess a guy like you had killed dozens of people."

"You think you've got me all figured out, don't you?" Noah asked. "Well, you're wrong. You've been wrong from the start. And anyway, it doesn't matter now. You know, Trust? Maybe after you turn up missing, I'll go over and comfort Grace. She really is a nice girl. You were right about that." The words were like grease dripping from his lips. "I know I was shooting my mouth off about the babes in Tahiti, but there's just something about that Grace."

Noah licked his lips and smiled.

"I'll have to make sure and spend a little time with her before I leave town."

"Don't make me sick," I spat.

"I'll make you more than sick," Noah laughed. "I'll make you dead . . ."

From the top of my eye I saw Leonard leap off from his perch. He seemed to hover in the air for a moment before plummeting down. I guess he was planning to land on Noah, but unfortunately he missed completely. He smacked against the dirt floor two feet away. But the commotion was enough to distract Noah, and in that split second, I threw myself into him, pushing up his arm. The gun fired into the barn ceiling as the two of us fell backwards into a mound of moldy hay.

Leonard grabbed a loose board lying on the ground and swung it wildly toward Noah's head. It would have been helpful had he hit Noah instead of me. The already bruised and swollen back of my head throbbed with pain. I rolled off of Noah and into Leonard's legs. My momentum threw Leonard off balance, flipping him forward into Noah. I blinked my eyes, trying to remain conscious. When my double vision finally became one again, I saw Leonard struggling with Noah on the ground, the gun lying in the dirt about three feet beyond them both. I started crawling for the gun. Noah kicked Leonard free, sending him flying into a large wood beam that was supporting the upper loft.

Leonard's eyes almost burst from the impact of it. He slid to the ground in a lifeless lump.

"Leonard," I yelled, taking my eyes off the gun.

Noah began scrambling for it, pulling my focus back. Both of us got to the gun at the same time. I reached out and Noah bit my arm. Then he tried to scratch my eyes. I was not at all surprised he fought like a little girl. I fell onto him again and we rolled about, trying to gain possession of the gun. Finally I got a good enough hold on it to be able to toss it up into the air and away from the two of us. It flew into the hayloft.

Noah dug his knee into my chest and pushed my face down as he fought to get up. I let him, only to grab his ankle as he jumped onto the ladder leading up to the loft. He kicked like a mule on fire, the back of his shoe clipping me in the face. I stumbled backwards as he made it the rest of the way up the ladder. I felt the blood on my face. With new resolve, I jumped to the middle of the ladder and pulled myself onto the loft. I stood up and realized that we were higher up than I had expected. Noah was digging through the hay like a madman. But it was no use—the gun was gone. I walked up behind him.

"You'll never find it," I said, wiping my bloody mouth with the back of my hand.

Then he did what I considered to be a rather thoughtful thing. He turned toward me just enough so that I was able to connect a strong punch to his jaw. He stumbled back, trying to catch himself. As he got his bearings, he looked around in a panic for some sort of exit. There was none. The ladder leading down was behind me, and I was blocking him from the edge of the loft. He glanced over at what looked to be a grain chute on the wall behind him.

"Give it up, Noah," I said, exhausted.

"I never should have spoken to you," he said hatefully. "This is my fault. I knew you were a moron, so I thought I'd have a little fun with you."

"You mean this isn't fun?" I joked.

"You really are a piece of work," Noah said. "Grace talks about you like you're something great. She's just as dumb as you are."

"Excuse me?"

"She's as stupid and deluded as you are, Trust," he said childishly.

Silly me, I had thought I was through hitting Noah—I ran to him and slammed him against the wall. He rolled out of my grasp. The entire barn seemed to moan and wobble. He grabbed the edge of the grain chute and pulled himself down into it. I could hear him banging around as he slid his way down. I should have just let him be, but I didn't want to risk him getting away. I took a big breath as if I were diving underwater and jumped in after him.

The grain chute was about ten feet long and connected to one of the silos I had seen earlier. It was rusted and weathered, but I still fell through it at a pretty good speed. I flew out the end of it and down into the empty silo. My hands hit first as I rolled into the ground and up against the inside wall. I felt around for anything broken. I seemed to still be latched together. I quickly glanced around the silo floor for any sign of Noah. The moon outside was just bright enough that I could see. Noah wasn't there. I pulled myself up and tried to open the door leading out. It was sealed shut. I thought for a moment that Noah had made it out and locked me in. I felt panic flush through me until I looked up and saw his dark form hanging upside down from a rope near the opening of the chute. It appeared his leg had gotten caught in it as he flew out. He was wiggling around trying to disengage himself. I followed the rope with my eyes up from Noah's leg to where it was hooked to a little door high up on the silo wall. I could see through the eroded roof that the little door fronted a chute from the other, taller silo next door.

"Help me down," Noah pleaded.

"How?" I asked. "I can't reach you."

Noah flipped and turned as he dangled up above me. The rope slipped a notch, becoming completely taut and tugging hard against the little trapdoor.

"Maybe you shouldn't be moving around so much," I hollered. "There could be something behind that little door."

"So what?" Noah yelled. "Get me down!"

I tried the latch on the lower door again, knowing it was no use. Noah swung his upper body up to grab hold of his ankle. It was that move that did us in. The rope jerked, pulling the door above us open. Grain doused us like a weighty waterfall, the pressure of it knocking Noah out of the rope and pushing him down to the floor by me. I fought desperately to keep the stuff off of me. It was no use. In a matter of moments we were waist-deep in wheat.

I frantically began to bail, scooping grain away from me with my hands as more rained down. It was a lesson in futility. There was no place else for the grain to go. The flow of wheat surged, suddenly burying us up to our shoulders. I thought about trying to get my arms up before it was too late.

It was too late.

The wheat packed around us, binding my arms to my side so tightly I could scarcely wiggle my fingers. We were strapped in for the long haul. I tried to move my legs but the weight of the wheat was crushing. I prepared myself for suffocation, certain we were going to die. Wheat flew around my head like bursting fireworks. It was in my hair, in my ears, and rising over my shoulders and up my neck. I kept my mouth shut, desperate not to breathe in the dirty grain. The wheat was inching up right below my nose when suddenly the flow from above miraculously stopped. I wiggled my head and tried to pull my arms out. I couldn't do it. Wind dipped down into the open-topped silo and seemed to suck the dust from the old grain up into the night. I opened my eyes expecting to see long-dead relatives waiting to greet me. There was no one there except for the top half of Noah's head. I assumed I was still alive, though just barely.

Noah was a couple inches shorter than I but I must have been standing lower in the silo because the level of our heads above the grain was just about equal. He spat out wheat and tried blowing it away from his mouth. I did the same, experiencing similarly weak results.

"Can you breathe?" I finally coughed, wishing away the dark.

"A little," he answered.

"Can you move?"

"I don't think so."

"Save your strength," I huffed. "Leonard will find us."

I don't think either one of us felt comforted. The wind kept reaching down into the open-capped silo and whipping around in our hair. I pushed my head back as far as I could and opened my mouth wide to breathe. I noticed a few stars through the rotted roof. I cast my eyes over at Noah and almost started to laugh. The sight of his half-head sticking above the wheat seemed so absurd and brought me a small amount of joy. I said a prayer begging God to please not let me die this way. Then I willed Leonard to find us.

A number of hours later, I felt pretty confident that neither God nor Leonard had been listening. It was almost impossible to stay awake any longer. Noah had knocked off a while earlier. I panicked for a bit, not knowing what the consequences of falling asleep like this might be. I remembered learning that if you dozed off in the freezing cold, you would never wake up. I just couldn't recall ever having discussed what to do when you were buried in wheat. So I kept myself awake by reciting anything I had ever memorized. Songs, poems, ads, the Boy Scout Oath, anything. I drifted in and out, dozing off a couple of times, but the pressure of the grain pushing up against my lungs made it impossible to breathe at moments and helped to keep me awake. The sun eventually rose on the two of us planted there like tulips. And sometime near its zenith, Noah began to stir and started sobbing.

"We're going to die in here," he moaned. The small bit of his head that was visible looked like a hairy anthill.

"Well, it's not my fault," I huffed.

"Where's Leonard?" he cried. "You said Leonard would find us."

"He hit that pole pretty hard," I reminded him. "He's probably in worse shape than we are."

"I don't think that's possible," Noah complained.

"Just hang on," I encouraged. "Someone will find us and dig us out."

"Who knew you were coming here?" Noah asked. "Anyone?"

"Just Leonard."

"We're going to die."

"Can you get your arms above the wheat?" I asked him.

"I can't even move my hands," he snapped.

I tried again myself, but with no luck. The grain had a suction-like hold on my whole body.

"This is it," Noah lamented. "Killed by food storage. How befitting."

I couldn't help chuckling. He was right.

"This could have been avoided," I sputtered, spitting wheat all the while.

"Thanks for pointing that out," Noah yapped.

"I only—"

"Just shut up," Noah said sharply. "We're going to die."

I was just about to agree with him when I heard something outside the silo. A couple of seconds later, I could distinctly feel the grain being pulled down and away from my body.

Someone had opened the lower silo door.

The wheat continued to slide out until we could see our waists again. As it lowered I saw two teenage boys standing there in the doorway. One of them had a pack of cigarettes, and they both were looking surprised. I think they were hoping to find a little solitude, not a few tons of wheat with a couple of dirty-looking bodies in it. The moment they realized we were still alive, they backed away and took off running.

"Stop!" I tried to holler. But being teenagers like they were, they didn't listen to a word I said.

I put my hands under my right knee and pulled my foot out of the grain. It came up shoeless. My body was so exhausted I could hardly stand. Noah was leaning on his hands, slowly extracting his legs as well. There was dirt and wheat clinging to almost every part of his body. I thought about tackling him so he wouldn't get away, but I was too spent. Instead, I crawled through the waist-high wheat and fell out the door onto the ground. I looked across the field and noticed that Leonard's car was gone. I just lay there for a moment, thinking how curious that was, when I drifted off into sleep.

37

TALL DRINK OF WATER

Lucy couldn't believe how nervous she was as she answered the door. Even though her father and mother would be back from their long European vacation in a little more than two weeks, Lucy had decided to call the full-time missionaries and finally get the blessing she had so desperately sought. She figured they were the perfect people to ask. They wouldn't judge her. And even if they did, they would be transferred out of Southdale before long. At this point, she didn't really care what anyone thought anyway. She only wanted some comfort for the pain and confusion she was still wading through.

Lucy opened the door and Elder Nicks and Elder Minert entered, followed by Doran Jorgensen in a denim shirt and tie.

"Three of you?" Lucy observed out loud.

"Brother Jorgensen is driving us around," Elder Minert

explained. "We were just over at the Williams house giving Sister Williams a blessing. I guess she's not feeling too well."

"Was Trust there?" Lucy asked without thinking, still bothered by how he had reacted a few days back.

"No," Elder Nicks said, fielding the question. "Actually, they don't know where Trust is."

"I hope that you don't mind me coming along?" Doran said shyly. "I thought, since we'd already met and all . . ."

Such sincerity.

"Not a problem," Lucy replied, looking Doran up and down and recognizing something comforting and strong in the way he held himself. "I'm just thankful that you came," she replied.

"Me too," Doran said softly.

"Who would you like to give the blessing?" Elder Minert asked.

"It doesn't really matter," Lucy said, while sort of hoping it would be Doran.

The choice was made.

The blessing was given.

Lucy was comforted.

38

CONFINED

Roger Williams yawned, causing the checkerboard that was lying across his lap to jiggle. He had been confined to his bed for some time now. And even though it was not what he would choose to be doing, the locals had done a rather nice job of keeping him entertained. Narlette put on a puppet show with some of Digby's old socks. Pete Kennedy gave him a personal gun safety course, and Leo Tip read to him from some of his favorite comic books. And now here was President Heck taking time out of his not-necessarily-busy schedule to play a game of checkers.

"I can see that," Ricky Heck joked as the board jiggled again.

"See what?"

"The old tilt and cheat," he said. "You think Roswell's never tried that on me before?"

"Have you played a lot of checkers with Roswell in bed?" Roger laughed, the color rising in his face as he did so.

"Well, not lately." Ricky scratched his head. Then he jumped Roger's playing pieces until he was victorious. He smiled wide.

"Happy?" Roger asked.

"I suppose I am," he answered. He glanced at the clock on the wall. "I better get along. Wad needed me to help him paint his shack. Can I get you anything before I go?"

"You've already done too much," Roger said.

"You sure now?"

Roger paused as if remembering something. "You know, I would like to make a phone call. Do you think you could help me over to the boardinghouse to make one sometime?"

"I'd be honored to." Ricky sort of bowed. "But the phone doesn't work. Lupert accidentally chopped down one of the phone poles thinking it would make good firewood. The phone company hasn't been able to make it out here to fix it."

"I don't suppose anyone here has a cellular phone I could use?" Roger asked.

"Is that the fancy kind without the round dial?"

"No, actually it's the one that you can carry with you and use from anywhere," Roger smiled.

"Nope, none of those. Although I bet the stake president in Virgil's Find has one. He's real progressive," Ricky stated. "I can try and get it for you if you'd like."

"I'd really appreciate it," Roger said.

"Consider it almost done." President Heck stood. "Anything else?"

"Actually, there is," Roger remembered. "You know, it

287

won't be too much longer until I can go home. And, well, I was hoping to do a little fishing on the Girth before I leave."

"You get your legs back, and you're on." President Heck clapped. Then he left Roger alone in the spare bedroom of Sister Watson's home.

Roger sat himself up and sighed. His strength was coming back slowly. He looked over at the small nightstand and saw the blue paperback Book of Mormon that Toby had given him. He picked it up and thumbed through it. Toby had mentioned that he had highlighted a few of his favorite passages. Roger could find only two markings in the whole book. The first one was First Nephi, chapter 13, verse 22.

And I said unto him: I know not.

Roger wondered for a couple of minutes about what had possessed Toby to mark that certain scripture. He finally concluded that it must be some sort of personal motto. The second and only other marked verse was Helaman, chapter 4, verse 15.

And it came to pass that they did repent, and inasmuch as they did repent they did begin to prosper.

Roger touched the word prosper upon the page. He smiled, thinking about how wise Toby Carver really was.

39

A NORMAL BLOOD FLOW

DECEMBER 15TH

By the time I woke up, the sky was turning dusky and my body was stiff. I pulled myself up and looked around for Noah. I couldn't see him right off, and his car appeared to be gone. I walked to the farmhouse and tried the door—it was locked. I picked up a huge rock lying near the mat and heaved it through the front window. The sound of falling glass almost made me feel as if I were having fun. I knocked out the remaining shards and stepped through.

No Noah.

I looked around for his phone, but couldn't find it. His whole house appeared in disarray. Drawers were pulled open and papers were thrown about as if Noah had been in a hurry to leave. I figured he must have packed up and gotten out while he still could. Most likely he had taken his phone as well. I decided that instead of just waiting around and taking the chance that someone would come find me, I should start hiking home. I noticed a crumpled piece of clothing that had been crammed back behind the couch and left behind. I picked it up and shook it out.

It was a sweater.

I slipped it on and found a towel to tape around my shoeless foot. Once improperly prepared, I set off. By the time I walked out of the Dintmore Hills, it was pitch dark. I thought back to when Grace and I had done this same thing just a couple weeks back. I longed to have her with me. I was just not the high-caliber company that she was. I called my home from the same gas station that Grace and I had used before. My mother answered and sounded so relieved to hear my voice that I was suddenly glad to have been lost for a while. She promised to get Grace and hurry over to pick me up.

When they arrived, both of them fawned and fussed over me like I was a two-thousand-dollar hairdo after an afternoon in the wind. My mother had discovered me missing shortly after Leonard had dragged me out of my house. She called the police, but it wasn't their policy to get involved until more time had elapsed. So, my mother and Grace had done nothing but sit around and worry for the last twenty hours. Mom had even become so over-whelmed by everything that she had asked Doran and the elders to give her a blessing.

I filled them in on everything that had happened as we drove home. Both of them were absolutely blown away by how wrong they had been about Noah. Grace apologized repeatedly. She couldn't believe that her instincts had failed her. I watched her eyes gloss over as she realized how wrong she had been. It was a moving moment. She kissed me on the hand, promising there would be more once I cleaned up.

It was nice to be alive.

40

SETTING THINGS RIGHT

DECEMBER 16TH

The day before the end of the world was a day like any other. The sky hovered, clear and open, the ground was dry, and the sun shone like a mother's face at a child's first recital.

At around noon I called Scott McLaughlin and warned him about lighting any candles over at the warehouse. He asked me why, so I told him the entire story. He was speechless. I made him promise to stay away from the warehouse until the police could have a look at it. He thanked me, still a little unsure of what to think. Then I called the police and recited the story again. I thought that they would congratulate me for making it out, for stopping Noah and revealing him to be what he really was. Instead, they insisted I come down to the station immediately so that they could question me in person.

When I got there, they asked me every possible

question about Noah. I looked at pictures, filled out forms, and gave descriptions.

"About yay high and wearing a sweater," I said.

On the way home, I decided to drive over to Leonard's to make sure he was still okay and find out what had happened to him.

I pulled up to the front of the Bio-Doom and parked. He had his bay window curtain open and was inside doing exercises. I got out of my car and stepped up to the window. The second he recognized me, he became extremely animated, waving me to the side of the single-wide as if I were a winning horse coming down the final stretch. I slipped around back and crawled under the skirting and up into his kitchen. Leonard was waiting.

"Where have you been?" he said with excitement.

"That's what I was wondering about you," I responded. "The last time I saw you, you were knocked out against a pole."

"That's right," Leonard gleamed, acting as if we had both just recalled a thrilling memory. "Boy, what a night, huh?"

"So, where did you go?" I asked, frustrated.

"Well, when I came to, you weren't there. So I went down to the mall to finish up my Christmas shopping."

"You went shopping?" I asked in disbelief. "You're serious?"

"They're having some great sales." Leonard clapped his hands. "Look at this," he said, pulling a pair of snowshoes out from behind a pile of canned olives. "Got these babies at forty percent off. And how about this," he beamed, walking up to the wall and pointing to a small framed plaque. It was one of those common biblical parchments with your name and its meaning written out in calligraphy. It had the name "Leonard" written in big letters and the definition below it read: "Reorder."

"I think knowing what your name means really builds the old self-esteem, you know? Mine's not bad, is it?" He elbowed me. "Reorder. I'm sure it has something to do with the reordering of the Melchizedek Priesthood."

I didn't have the heart to tell him.

"So you didn't even wonder what had happened to Noah and me?" I asked, bringing him back to the conversation at hand.

"I figured you would work things out."

"The last you saw he was pointing a gun at me," I huffed.

"So, is he all right?" Leonard asked.

"The gun was pointing at *me*."

"Trust, you're repeating yourself," Leonard said, acting like a second grade teacher.

"We both almost died," I argued.

"I guess we've got a lot to be thankful for."

"You could have at least called the police and sent them out to find us."

"And jeopardize my dome life?"

"This is amazing."

"So where's Noah?" he asked.

"Who knows?" I blurted out. "He took off when I slipped into a state of exhaustion. The police are looking for him now."

Leonard looked at me with renewed interest. "I should have signed him up for pre-billed legal while I had the chance. Could have saved him a bundle in law fees."

"You're selling law consultations?" I asked. "What happened to the waterless car soap?"

"Turns out people enjoy using water," Leonard said sadly. "But that's in the past. Now I'm part of a huge team of important lawyers."

I didn't want to know any more. I went back down through the hole in the linoleum and outside, leaving Leonard to sell to himself.

Late that afternoon, Grace and I snuck off together and headed down toward Southdale River. We climbed up under one of the covered bridges and spread out a blanket on the steep slope beneath it. We pulled out the few items we had brought along to eat.

"You know, this could be our last day on earth," I said coyly.

"Well, I guess that makes it no different than any other day," she replied.

I lay down on the blanket and listened to the river rushing below. Water flopped down its course like a clumsy adolescent snake. I looked up at the bridge above us as a car rolled across.

"So, I guess I was right about Noah," I said, not confident that I had yet milked it for all it was worth.

"Let's not talk about him," Grace replied, her green eyes deep and dark in the light of the afternoon.

"All right," I agreed. "Let's talk about tomorrow."

"What about it?" Grace asked.

"Well, it's the seventeenth," I reminded her.

"Did you bring me here to this secluded spot to talk about unimportant things like the end of the world?" Grace smiled. "Or was there something more pressing on your mind?"

"Well, now that you mention it."

"I didn't realize I had mentioned anything." Grace shifted in her cross-legged position, bringing her knees up next to the side of my chest. She leaned over so that her long hair dangled above my face. I could smell the ends of it teasing me. Her lovely mouth smiled in delight over the feelings she knew she was inducing.

"Do you still love me?" she asked.

"More than ever," I whispered.

Grace bent over farther and softly touched her pink lips to mine. My toes exploded like a string of firecrackers, each one setting off the next. And my fingers all detached and rolled helplessly down the river bank. I was in awe of what was happening. Visions of my childhood and every day I had lived since seemed to be rushing toward me like some great wind.

It was a hard feeling to describe, but similar to when I was seven years old and our family owned a huge Labrador retriever. I used to go out into the backyard and call for her, not knowing exactly where she was. The moment I hollered her name, she would appear, running as fast as she could and hurling her weight toward me. It used to scare me, and yet thrill me too, to see her heading straight toward me. Each time I had to steel myself against the urge to run, standing my ground and waiting for the inevitable.

The fear would build until the moment when she would bowl me over, covering me with her paws and licking my face.

That was the feeling I had now. Every part of my life was speeding toward me at breakneck speed. I looked myself straight in the eye as it approached, falling on me like hail, stinging me all over, and reminding me I was alive.

I opened my eyes to see Grace looking down at me. She pulled back her hair with her left hand while touching my face with her right.

"Will you marry me?" I asked.

"Of course," she replied.

I moved up onto my elbows and kissed her. I could feel her warm breath and cool skin as she kissed me back. Her hair surrounded me like light. She pushed me nearer to the ground and then stopped to smile a knowing smile at me.

"I thought you'd never ask."

41

OH BUOY

DECEMBER 17TH

By the time I got out of bed in the morning, it had already been raining for four straight hours. I looked through the kitchen window at the now-flooded streets and sidewalks. I wondered if I shouldn't start shoveling sand bags. The rain was thick and heavy, drops slapping against the window like overripe plums.

"Can you believe it?" Margaret asked me as she came down for breakfast.

"Amazing," I smiled.

"Noah Taylor should have built us an ark," Abel joked.

"Noah Taylor should never have come," Margaret added.

"So, Trust," Abel asked with a mouth full of cereal. "When are you and Grace going to get hitched?"

I had come home the day before and told my family the good news. Everyone was excited. Even my mother seemed mildly pleased. Mom was doing better. The blessing the elders had given her a few days back had seemed to lift her spirits. She still worried night and day about my dad and touched base with the police regularly, but we all seemed to sense that whatever happened would be for the best.

"We're thinking of this spring," I answered Abel.

"I think spring is the best time to get married," Margaret said, pulling out a cereal bowl from the cabinet and taking a seat at the table.

My mother came into the kitchen looking like she had just seen a naked ghost. Her hair was a mess, and she appeared emotionally disoriented. It looked like she had had another bad night. She walked over to the table and sat down.

"Are you all right, Mom?" Abel asked.

"Your father," she said. "He called."

"Daddy called?" Margaret asked with excitement. "What did he say? When is he coming home?" My sister gushed, barely able to contain herself.

"He sounded so different," was all my mother said.

"Good different, or bad different?" I asked nervously.

"He couldn't talk long." She shook her head and started to cry. "He said he'd be home soon . . . and that he loved me."

Margaret burst out bawling, tears dropping into the bowl of cereal she had just poured—her shredded wheat getting soggy before any milk even touched it. Abel wiped his mouth with his sleeve. From my seat it looked like he had just rubbed on the world's biggest smile.

I called Grace and told her the news. She ran over as fast as she could. When she came into the kitchen, my mother hugged her even though she was now wet.

My father was coming home.

My mother was hugging Grace!

We all ate breakfast talking like we had just received free tickets to the celestial kingdom in the mail. My mom went over and over the few words my father had said to her. He said he had been hurt, and that he was fine. He told her he couldn't talk long because it wasn't his phone, but that he would be coming home as soon as he possibly could. And then he told her that he loved her more than anything in the whole world.

I had never seen my mother so happy. It made me more proud of my father than I had ever been.

I think we would have all stayed indoors, basking in our state of bliss, if it had not been for the fact that shortly after eleven o'clock, water began building up against our house and leaking through the door. Mom called over to Wendy's to see if she was doing okay with all the rain. As soon as my mother got the question out, the phones went dead. Two minutes later, Wendy was knocking on our door, begging to come in. Abel opened the door and water rushed in like loose mercury, sloshing across the floor and into every corner of the front room. I expected it to be cold on my feet, but the high temperatures had kept the rain warm. It took both Abel and me to get the door closed after Wendy came in.

"What should we do?" Wendy asked, wearing a white silk pajama top and fishing waders. "Should we make some of those sandbag things or something?"

I would have answered her, but the electricity suddenly went out, distracting us all from her question. I could see the flood level rising against our large front window as rain continued to dump down. It was too late for sandbags. Everyone ran around the house collecting things and moving them up to higher ground where they'd be safer. We all made some lame jokes about how it looked like Noah Taylor was right about the end of the world after all. But by twelve o'clock no one was laughing. Our front window gave out first, shattering inward, allowing a huge deluge of water to push into our home. Luckily, Mom had had the foresight to gather us together far from the windows before it got to that point. We climbed up on the kitchen table and chairs.

By 12:30 Margaret was genuinely scared, and Abel was asking my mom things like, "If someone stole a baseball mitt from a friend, and he didn't get a chance to return it before he died, would he go to heaven?"

Mom would have answered with a stern lecture, except I think she was too busy worrying about what to do next. She was a determined woman—determined to still be around when my father came home. He had said that he loved her.

We all moved up into the second story as the water climbed the steps at an amazing rate. Grace and I sat on the top step watching it rise toward our feet as everyone else huddled in the master bedroom looking out the window for some sign of relief.

"Can you believe this?" I said, more in awe than in anger. "I keep thinking that we should do something besides just sit here."

"I've never seen so much water," Grace replied. "What happens if it doesn't stop?"

"I suppose we get really wet," I answered, trying to keep things light.

"Your house is ruined," Grace said sorrowfully.

"I'm sure my parents have flood insurance." I *wheewed*, thinking about how nice it sounded to say "my parents" with such confidence for a change.

The water was six steps away from us.

"Should we move up?" Grace asked.

I would have replied, but it was suddenly silent. I was a little spooked by the quiet until I realized it meant the pounding rain had stopped, at least for now.

"There's some blue sky rolling in," my mother hollered, fit to burst.

Instantly the fear fled, and hope eased its way back into the room. I could hear Abel begging my mother to let him swim around the living room, and Margaret asking if we still had the air mattresses up in the attic. Suddenly everyone was all right. Our poor house was ruined, but we were thankful to be alive.

An hour later the skies were clear, and the water was at about half the level it once had been, allowing us to walk around the bottom floor of the house. I stepped outside and surveyed our street. It was like a mighty river slowly draining away. As I turned to go inside I heard someone holler from off in the distance. I looked to see Bishop Leen and his wife paddling toward us in a rowboat. They paddled up to me and he jumped out of the boat, fastening it to a tree nearby. Bishop Leen was wearing a long yellow coat and had a shortwave radio strapped to his belt.

"Are you all okay?" he asked.

"Just fine," I answered. "Can you believe this?"

"God can do some mighty works," the bishop declared. "There'll be some lush lawns this summer."

The Lewis family across the street came out of their house and waded over to us. I could also see the Phillips children two houses down beginning to swim over as well. Grace and Margaret came out, followed by Wendy and my mother. A couple of seconds later, I spotted Abel paddling up to us on an air mattress. I could tell this was a day he would never forget. It wasn't long before we were surrounded by a nice-sized portion of our ward and neighbors.

"I've never seen anything like this," I said, baffled. I put my arm around Grace. "It came on so fast. Those drops were huge."

"The ground was pretty dry," Bishop Leen suggested. "Water stacks up quick when it can't be absorbed."

"I'll say," Sister Lewis chirped. "We've got a watermark as high as our second floor."

Everybody nodded, anxious to let each other know that they too had high marks.

"So was Noah right?" Brother Lewis asked the bishop. "Is this the end of the world?"

"We're still here, aren't we?" a wet Sister Phillips pointed out. "This has nothing to do with Noah."

"Not only that," Bishop Leen spoke up. "But I just got a radio call a few minutes ago from an employee of mine who lives near the warehouse. I guess Noah hadn't made sure that old warehouse was secure after all. All this water pushed down the walls. My employee wasn't sure, but she figures that almost everything that was in there is ruined."

"You're kidding?" I asked in astonishment.

"I'm not," he said.

"He's not," Sister Leen confirmed.

I wanted to laugh out loud at how dumb we all had been.

"We trusted in the wrong person," the bishop said sadly.

I felt "I told you so's" were in order, but I held my tongue. Grace squeezed my hand, indicating that she was well aware of my restraint.

"Trust was right?" Sister Lewis asked skeptically.

"Dead on," Bishop Leen replied.

People began slapping my back, and apologizing profusely.

"What do we do now?" Wendy asked.

"Luckily this water should be gone soon, and at least it's not too cold," the bishop continued. "We'll have a muddy mess, but we should be able to operate somewhat close to normal. I guess God's going to give us a chance to do it right."

Some final clouds passed and sunlight lit down across the receding waters, lighting the surface like an electric globe. I was just about to comment on the astonishing beauty of it, when I noticed a number of small objects floating toward us all. As they got closer, I realized that they were Ziploc bags full of red licorice.

"These are Leonard Vastly's." I laughed, looking up to

see hundreds of other bags drifting down the street. I couldn't imagine what might have happened to have caused Leonard's life supply of food storage to now be flooding our street. Fortunately I didn't have to wonder long.

As the entire neighborhood began harvesting the bobbing manna, a noisy engine sounded in the distance. It grew louder and louder until it was on our street heading toward us. The source of the sound was a small truck with huge wheels racing through the knee-deep water, creating waves that were at least ten feet tall. The truck slowed as it drove by those people collecting food in their front yards. Eventually, it stopped in front of our house. A number of people from the ward piled out of the back of it. Sister Cravitz, Brother Victor, the Morrises and Brother Clyde Knuckles, who obviously viewed this as enough of an activity to attend. Doran stuck his head out of the driver's side window.

"Everyone okay here?" he asked.

"We're fine," the bishop answered.

"So what do you think?" Doran asked me.

"About the rain?"

"No, about the truck."

"Very nice."

"I know my father warned me about getting into debt," Doran said. "But I figure he never set his eyes on this beauty."

Leonard Vastly climbed down out of the passenger side. The moment people realized it was Leonard and that this was his food floating about, everybody stood silently wondering what he was going to do. The truth was, a lot of the people in this neighborhood needed this food. Most kitchens had been soaked, ruining any immediate supplies anyone had had on hand. Plus, it would take a while for the stores to clean out and get running again after this water. Leonard looked at everyone.

He held up his hands, silencing an already silent crowd.

"Just so you know," he spoke loudly, "all the food you see has already been prayed over. But I don't suppose God would complain if you thanked Him again before you ate it."

Everyone cheered! Then they continued to grab anything floating their way. Cans of food and sealed bags of dried fruit were everywhere, dotting the surface like oil spots on the surface of cold soup. I reached down and pulled up a bag of beef jerky.

Leonard was about to feed our entire neighborhood.

Everybody gathered what they could and began trading for what they wanted. Eventually we all figured it would just be easier to all eat together. So as the water lowered to a manageable level we sat anywhere we could find, feasting on not half-bad food.

Bishop Leen labeled it our "doomsday buffet," compliments of Leonard Vastly.

Leonard explained what had happened as we ate. His mobile home had been washed over by the flood, splitting an entire wall and sending all his hard-earned supplies everywhere. He said that he had fought to remain in his dome, but that nature had finally washed him out. He also claimed that because of the flood's course, Varney Street, one block over, had received all his best food and above-ground pool.

The water continued to recede and people began to help one another clean up. Men lifted wet couches through doors and out of houses while children scraped mud from out of living rooms with shovels and buckets. Leonard used his newfound popularity to try and sell tea tree oil to anyone who would listen. It didn't take long for him to realienate himself from everybody. My mother let those who would be interested know about my father's phone call and even bragged a bit about my engagement to Grace.

After helping Sister Lewis drag a huge muddy area rug from her family room I stood outside surveying all that was before me. The end of the world had knocked, but then it just walked away. Some major damage had been done, but I felt like more had been repaired.

It would be a cold wet night.

No one seemed to be complaining.

42

ONE LAST FLING

Roger Williams cast his line and watched it wiggle through the cold air and snap just above the moving water. He reeled it back in, glancing over at President Heck who was trying to extract yet another fishing fly from his right hand.

"You got it?" Roger asked.

President Heck tugged one last time on the bait. It came loose with a minimal amount of blood. "Not a bad day," he observed, ignoring his small wound.

"Not at all," Roger replied. "A little cold, but who's complaining."

Roger stepped across the snow and close to the river. He was packed and ready to leave Thelma's Way. He was simply taking a couple of hours to fish with a friend. He had recovered nicely from his entanglement with the motorcycle and river. The entire town had helped nurse him back to health. And not since the day he had woken back up had a single person besides Roswell even mentioned the book that he had lied about planning to write.

People just helped him because they cared.

Roger had forgotten that that was an option in life.

"I'll sure miss this place," he said.

"We'll miss you," President Heck replied, tightening the homemade scarf around his neck. "That's the nice thing about Thelma's Way, though. We'll always be right here. You can go away, change, get married, lose a loved one, but we'll still be sitting here. All you got to do is wander back for a spell. Wad will still be cutting hair, and Toby will still be mending breaks."

"You're a lucky man," Roger said, amazed that those words were coming out of his mouth.

"We're all lucky," President Heck said. "God fills our lungs with air, then lets us wander around till we're stupid enough to step in front of a bus or eat something that will kill us."

"Well, God seems to keep a pretty good eye on you here," Roger sighed, flinging his line back out across the Girth. "I wouldn't be at all surprised to see Him step out from behind the boardinghouse, or rise from the snow in the meadow."

"Wheeew," President Heck whistled. "That would scare the tack out of me. Not that I would mind it, but I just don't think I would know what to do with such an experience."

"Think of how strong your faith would be afterward," Roger reeled.

"I s'pose. But you know an angel could come skippin'

down the Girth tossing out gold coins and I wouldn't be any more impressed or sure about God," Ricky stated soberly. "People are always looking for stuff to touch, or see. Like Toby after he heard Pete could do that unsettling thing with his ears. I told him, Mavis told him, and Frank told him. But he didn't believe us until he saw it for himself. Now he won't stop whining 'bout how he can't get the image out of his head."

"I guess you're right," Roger said.

"I am?" Ricky said, surprised.

"My life is one giant bag of signs and markers illustrating clearly that I'm being watched over. I had to come here to remember that."

"The world loves to help you forget," President Heck said. "That's for sure."

Roger Williams thought about what was just said. It was almost unbelievable, the amount he had changed within the last month. He couldn't wait to get home so that he could begin mending everything he had once forgotten about.

"Had enough?" President Heck asked.

Roger smiled, patting his friend on the shoulder. "For now," he replied.

Six hours later he was at the airport in Knoxville waiting for his flight home.

43

DING

◇

DECEMBER 22ND

We had all just sat down to dinner in our water-worn dining room when the doorbell rang. Thanks to the flood our ringer no longer ding-donged, it just went "Diinggggrrr-rrrrrr-rrrrrr-rrrrrrr," until someone pounded the box on the wall by the stairs. Abel got up from the table and ran to do the pounding. A couple seconds later we could all think straight again.

We had been expecting Wendy to come over, so there was little thought given to who might be at the door. Grace passed me the pepper and Margaret began to pick the tomatoes out of her salad. After a bite of food I began to wonder what was taking Abel so long to let Wendy in.

"I think Abel must have gotten lost," Margaret said, apparently thinking the same thing.

I took another bite and stood up to quench my curiosity. I walked into the living room and spotted the back of Abel as my father held on to him as if he were life itself.

"Dad's home," I hollered.

I was practically bowled over by my mother and Margaret as they came bolting out of the dining room. Dad hugged us all as Grace looked on. This was a different man than the one who had left us so many weeks ago. His face was hollow and bearded, and his hair was short and light. He was dressed in casual clothes that reminded me of someone. I just couldn't place who.

As we were smothering him, my father noticed Grace standing off a ways. He stood tall and walked over to her. Without saying a word or explaining why, he wrapped his arms around her. She responded in-kind.

The four of us stared at the two of them. I looked at my mother as she cried, my sister as she beamed, and my brother as he sighed.

Dad was back.

44

WHEN ALL IS OVER-DONE

DECEMBER 24TH

Abel tugged on the plush purple bath towel that he had pinned around his head. He crouched down in front of Grace and me as we hovered over an elongated punch bowl with a small, blanket-wrapped fire extinguisher lying in it. I watched Grace as she knelt beside me. She had a faded quilt draped over her head, looking every bit like Mary of old. Me? I was Joseph.

My father read from Luke as Abel, the head shepherd, waved his cronies in closer. Mom and Wendy approached the manger.

"And the angel said . . ."

Margaret raised her arm as if she were an angel addressing the world. She had on a large white garbage bag with arm- and neck-holes torn out of it. The whole scene was rather authentic looking.

We had not reenacted the nativity on Christmas Eve

for years. It was a family tradition that had been dropped a long time ago. Well, things were changing around the Williams house.

After my family's production, Grace and I slipped out into the backyard to be alone for a few minutes. We walked over to the long flat bench that sat behind the big leafless elm tree. Grace sat pretzel-style as I straddled the seat facing her, our knees touching. The wood bench was cold as we sat down, but it soon warmed under the presence of Grace and me. The motion sensor light that we had triggered by stepping out the back door flicked off, no longer able to detect our movement. The clear sky burned black, the lights from the city giving it a glowing base and tinting the canvas of God.

"I love you, Grace Heck."

"I love you back," she smiled.

"We're engaged," I pointed out.

"I'm aware of that," she replied.

"That means marriage, and . . ."

I would have finished my rambling statement if it had not been for the presence of Grace upon my lips.

Once again my life flashed before my eyes, the past speeding up to run headlong into the present. As the ever-alluring now grew nearer, my mind slowed, replaying the events of the last week.

I had spent days shoveling mud out of all the houses on our street. In all of Southdale only the lower areas and the warehouse district near the river had suffered much damage. Our entire neighborhood had become one in purpose—putting things back together as much as possible before Christmas. Well, tomorrow was Christmas, and even though there were still watermarks and warped walls to contend with, everyone had a home to celebrate in. For the first time in my memory the Thicktwig Ward had banded together and grown. We had collectively discovered that we could not only be wrong, but we could be watered. The flood had been a soggy wakeup call to bring us all to our spiritual senses.

I had needed to take time off from work to help set things right, but Opal at Ink Tonic refused to make allowance for my cleanup schedule. So I had been forced to quit. Actually, it wasn't as if I left Opal hanging, seeing how I offered her Leonard to take my place. Amazingly, she agreed. Leonard was loving having steady employment again, and Opal saw him as some sort of odd nonconformist that gave her store character.

Luckily Leonard's ruined mobile home had flood insurance. Just yesterday I had gone down to "The Real American" mobile home and RV center and helped him order a brand-new double-wide trailer. We had matched carpets with appliances and paint colors with moldings. I felt so domestic. His new home wouldn't be here for about six weeks. He had already made arrangements to stay at Scott McLaughlin's apartment until it arrived. I could only imagine the conversations those two would have.

The ward had come together to mourn the loss of their food storage. The water disaster had completely destroyed the entire warehouse. Unfortunately, Noah had not taken out any flood insurance. Plenty of fire, but no flood.

The good news was that Noah had not gotten away. He

had been apprehended by the law. He was caught making a phone call at a rest area just over the state line. He had on a fake beard and sunglasses. He would probably have been overlooked, but the arresting officer said the sweater gave him away.

Justice was sweet.

It was nice to know that he was behind bars. The state of Maine was already making motions to get him back and try him. I felt confident that he wouldn't bother my city again.

One nice thing had come out of all this. Thanks to the auction Noah had put together, Brother Victor and Sister Cravitz were seeing one another in the open. Tiny Brother Victor had been taken with the assertive and opinionated Sister Cravitz for quite some time. It had been the auction that had finally given them courage enough to be openly adoring. I would have said that they made a cute couple, but a few days ago I had seen her pick him up and carry him over a big puddle, and, well, that sort of ruined it for me.

Grace still talked about how foolish she felt about believing in Noah. I would always brush it off, insisting she needn't worry, and then ask her to tell me more, after which she would go on and on about how cute she just remembered he was. It didn't bother me—Noah was one competitor I need not worry about. I suppose I could also say the same for Doran. Doran Jorgensen and Lucy Fall appeared to be an item. The blessing he had given her seemed to have made a long-lasting impression.

I was amazed to the point of disbelief.

Unbeknownst to any of us Doran had gone back the day after he gave her the blessing to confess his love to Lucy. He claimed that the only reason the heavens had told him to pursue Grace was so that he would be around to find Lucy. He had seen her every day since. I just couldn't believe how much Lucy had changed. The girl I had dated all those years ago would have been too busy listing Doran's faults to ever take him seriously—not to mention the remarks she would have made about his truck. But now she seemed to hang onto him, amazed by his devotion to her, and she was so relaxed about life that her entire being seemed almost unrecognizable. Mixed with my amazement was a huge pile of honest happiness for the two of them. It was also nice not to have him hanging around Grace anymore.

Young Leon Treat probably would still have had his mind set on Grace if it hadn't been for the accident that had occurred during the flood. I guess Leon had gotten his natural disasters mixed up, mistaking a flood for a fire. When his mother started panicking over the heavy rain he ran up to the attic and jumped out of the window, landing on top of his father's old van. He had broken one leg and one wrist. While recovering in the hospital he developed a crush on a candy striper named Nicole. She was ten years his senior, but the way she dispensed magazines and pillows made age seem so trivial.

The elders had finished their lessons with Grace, and in doing so had really hooked Wendy. Wendy had sat in on most of them, and had begun to see some things that just might fit in her lifestyle. She had already asked them if they would teach her again, promising that this time she wouldn't keep saying things like, "What kind of fool could swallow that." The elders agreed, seeing how they both had just received word that they were going to be transferred out of Southdale next week. They would leave Wendy to whomever replaced them.

So with everyone out of the picture only I was left to fumble over Grace. Unless of course you were to count my father's newfound fatherly interest in her. He still had not told us where he had been, claiming the experience was too personal to talk about just yet. He promised, however, that in time he would fill us all in. Whatever the story was, it had caused him to see Grace in a completely different light than he once had. He asked her constantly about her hometown, and about each and every person there. He was most interested in her father and all he had been through in his life. I was rather impressed with how fast my dad memorized everyone's names, and how respectfully he spoke of them. He had even suggested that we take a trip back there someday.

I was all for that.

I missed Thelma's Way horribly. I was glad that Grace had come here, but deep down I hoped that she would beg me to take her home soon. I missed the meadow, the mountains, the people, and the problems. I thought of the two Christmases I had spent there, and how I had ached to be back in Southdale. I can't believe I could have ever been so naïve.

My mind moved to the present.

"What are you thinking about?" Grace whispered, her lips next to my ear.

"Home," I replied, kissing her on the eye and then the cheek and then the mouth.

I put my hands on her back and pulled Grace toward me. I could hear her breathe and felt her eyes close. My fingers became tangled in her long red hair as she moved to get even closer.

I was just about to confess my love again when I noticed Leonard crouched down about six inches away. He was staring right at us. We both jumped.

"Looks like things are good for you two," he commented, raising his bushy eyebrows.

"Leonard," I protested.

"Don't let me bother you," he insisted. "I just had a little something I wanted to drop off for the both of you."

"Leonard, you didn't have to," Grace said kindly.

"I know," he replied. "That's why I gave it to Opal. I hope you don't mind."

Grace smiled before I could. My father pushed open the back porch door and called us in for cake and cider.

"Want to join us, Leonard?" I asked.

"Well I did need to . . . sure," he said with excitement.

We walked inside, passing the Christmas tree in the living room on the way to where my family was gathered. Leonard broke away, leaving Grace and me alone again. We looked down and noticed that there wasn't a single present under the tree.

I could think of nothing that bothered me less.

My family broke out in song in the other room, their

voices mixing with the smell of the Christmas tree. I felt Grace shudder under the weight of how perfect this was. It didn't matter that our carpets were still damp, or that no presents had been purchased. God had stocked us up with more than we could ever possibly rotate. Once again He had moved me around until I stood where I was supposed to. I lifted my face to the ceiling, almost expecting Him to be there.

"What are you thinking about?" Grace whispered.

There were no words to properly describe it.

Acknowledgments

I like to thank people. It's easy. "Hey, thanks," is all it usually takes. Of course, there are moments when words so simple not only don't cut it, but they're insulting. I'm sure that Superman would have been quite unsatisfied if the citizens of the world had just thrown out a casual, "Appreciate ya," after he had saved them from complete destruction. I forgot where I'm going with this. Oh, yes, the importance of proportionate gratitude. I am hugely thankful to, and for, everyone at Deseret Book. This series would never have taken root without the help of so many amazing people: Richard Peterson, Kent Ware, Bronwyn Evans, Sheri Dew, Ron Millett, my longtime friend Richard Erickson, and, of course, Emily Watts. Roger Toone, who has been more of a support and help than he could possibly know. Timothy Robinson, who has cheered and challenged me across lines I was previously comfortably ignoring. And to all the people who have sold and bought my books with such enthusiasm and kindness—

this would have been impossible without you. So, these few words may be simple, but they couldn't be more sincere. Thank you all! Finally, I would like to publicly declare (to those of you who didn't tune out sentences ago) that my life would be completely two-dimensional and tiny without the strength and love of my father, Farrell Smith. Dad, you're the best. Thanks for giving your children such spectacular vision.

About the Author

Robert Farrell Smith lives in Albuquerque, New Mexico, with his wife, Krista, his daughters, Kindred Anne and Phoebe Hope, and his son, Bennett Williams. He is the owner of Sunrise Bookstore in Albuquerque. Robert is a man with few hobbies. He played the drums for one and a half weeks when he was ten and took two tennis lessons back in 1996. Fortunately, or unfortunately, depending on whom you ask, writing is the one thing he stuck with. As a result, Robert is the author of several funny books, including *All Is Swell: Trust in Thelma's Way*, book one of the Trust Williams Trilogy.

If for any reason you wish to scold, criticize, compliment, or bother Robert, please do so by writing to:

>Robert Farrell Smith
>P.O. Box 37050
>Albuquerque, New Mexico 87176

Or on the web at:
>www.robertfarrellsmith.com